NOT EXACTLY WHAT I HAD IN MIND

Kate Brook has a PhD in French Literature and Visual Art from King's College London, and a Masters in European Literature and Culture from the University of Cambridge. Her short-form writing has been published in The Fiction Pool and The Real Story. She lives in London, and *Not Exactly What I Had in Mind* is her first novel.

NOT EXACTLY WHAT I HAD IN MIND

KATE BROOK

CORVUS

Published in hardback in Great Britain in 2022 by Corvus,
an imprint of Atlantic Books Ltd.

10 9 8 7 6 5 4 3 2 1

A CIP catalogue record for this book is available from the British Library.

Hardback ISBN: 978 1 83895 500 7
Trade paperback ISBN: 978 1 83895 501 4
E-book ISBN: 978 1 83895 502 1

Printed in Great Britain

Corvus
An imprint of Atlantic Books Ltd
Ormond House
26–27 Boswell Street
London
WC1N 3JZ

www.corvus-books.co.uk

MIX
Paper from
responsible sources
FSC
www.fsc.org   FSC® C171272

For my friends

Part I

1

HAZEL DIDN'T KNOW much about Alfie except that he
was tall and couldn't grow a full beard, and that he wore
socks and sandals around the flat but somehow that was
okay; also that he was a primary school teacher, and was
half Jamaican but didn't seem to ever eat Jamaican food,
instead surviving on pasta and pesto and that bagged salad
from Sainsbury's with the grated beetroot mixed in. She
knew that he had lived in two London flats before this one,
that he liked *Black Mirror* and Louis Theroux, that his
most cherished pipe dream was to hike across Europe from
Sweden to Sicily, and that his top three fears were fascism,
climate change and terminal disease. She also knew he had
an electric toothbrush, and a one-person cafetière that he
never washed up except when he was about to make coffee
in it; and she knew he'd had sex last week, because the
woman had been so noisy that the whole procedure had
been audible from her own room across the hall. Now she
herself was kneeling naked on Alfie's mattress, forehead on
forearm, various parts of her pressed against the textured
wallpaper. He was thrusting from the back and fingering

from the front, his spare hand on her breast. His coordination was virtuosic. The bed was squeaking and she was moaning as loudly as that other woman, probably louder, and then louder still until the moans became ecstatic sobs. In the next room Tony was playing World of Warcraft, raising the volume in tandem with her, so that by the time she came the soundtrack was blasting self-righteously through the wall.

Afterwards they lay on their backs and stared at the swirling Artex above. Hazel wondered how ill-advised it had been on a scale of one to ten, where one meant they would fall in love and ten meant such extreme discomfort in each other's company that one of them would have to move house. Almost certainly over five; possibly an eight, maybe even higher. But it had also been inspired. The afterglow was warm and potent. Even if it was a ten it might still have been worth it.

'Can we make a pact that this won't be awkward?' said Alfie. What was meant by this was that awkwardness was a likely outcome, far more so than love, and Hazel, for all that she knew this was true, felt a stab of something like disappointment.

'I think that's a very good idea,' she replied. She turned onto her side to face him, and they shook hands.

'It's probably time for bed,' she said after that, and Alfie reached for his phone and said, 'It's one thirty.' Hazel swore, pushed back the covers and sat up.

'You can sleep here, you know,' said Alfie. 'I mean, if you want to.'

'I feel like that'd make it harder for us to stick to the pact? Might make it sort of ... complicated?'

4

'Oh, yeah,' said Alfie with a slow nod. 'You could be right. Whatever you think.'

She got up to gather her clothes from the floor. 'Night, then.'

'Are you going out there in the buff?'

'I think I can make a dash for it.' She grinned and reached for the door handle, then hesitated and turned to look at him. She was tempted to lean over and kiss him on the cheek, but on leaving the bed she had crossed over into separate territory, and it did not now seem right to go back. 'Thanks, by the way,' she said instead. 'That was awesome. A-plus-plus.'

'Agreed,' he said, smiling.

She opened the door a fraction and looked out. The hall was empty and Tony was still shut up in his bedroom. 'Got to run,' she said, and in two paces she was in her own room with the door shut behind her.

Alfie was a bad idea, she thought in the morning as she got dressed for work. It was far too early to be up on a Saturday, especially a rainy Saturday. Every day had been rainy lately. The July heatwave had been washed decisively away and the cracked earthenware parks now stood lush and swampy and empty. If it carried on there might be floods. It felt wrong. It was pre-apocalyptic, a micro-sample of the psychotic weather that was coming for them, only no one liked to say so.

Alfie was a bad idea, she thought as she brushed her teeth and blinked down onto a mascara wand. He was a slut, quite possibly very unscrupulous. He was affable in a way that she had taken to be natural but now suspected of being calculated. She would not be surprised if all his behavioural decisions were made with the end goal of sex in mind. He was evidently a man who followed his cock.

Because Alfie was such a bad idea, she did not respond when he texted her saying: *Great time last night. Still thinking about it. X*

It sounded like he might want to repeat the experience, which was flattering, but she would not allow herself to be drawn in. The stakes were too high. She couldn't move house; she couldn't afford it. The landlord had only put her rent up once in the three years she had been there, which meant everywhere else would be more expensive by now, and anyway, she didn't have enough in her bank account to cover the costs of moving. If she was going to have to listen to him driving women wild every weekend it was best she try to forget that she had once been one of those women herself.

To avoid the temptation of messaging him back, she left her phone in her bag, hanging by the staff toilet at the café, and for several hours made a concerted effort not to think about it. On her lunch break she didn't go near it, instead picking up a crime novel from the bookshelf by the sofa, which hooked her for the entire hour. You were supposed to leave a book if you wanted to take one, but since they only paid her minimum wage she reasoned that a second-hand paperback was the least she deserved. When she put it in her bag her hand hovered over her phone, but with a monumental effort of willpower she resisted, and went back out to the coffee machine.

It wasn't until three o'clock that she allowed herself to break the embargo. As her hand closed around the phone she felt a rush of excitement and relief. Then she saw that she had twenty-four WhatsApp messages, five missed calls and two voicemails. Every single one of them was from her older sister, words to the effect of 'where are you?' and 'have we got the date wrong?' and 'are you okay?'

She remembered now: Emily and Daria were supposed to be visiting this weekend. She'd forgotten about it because she'd written it down on a scrap of paper instead of in her calendar, and then when someone asked to swap a shift with her she had looked at the calendar and seen nothing there. She called her sister back.

'Oh my God,' she began as soon as there was an answer. 'I'm really sorry, I'm so useless, were you waiting in the rain? What are you up to? Did you find a café or something?'

There were voices in the background.

'It's fine!' said Emily, laughing at something. 'Your flat-mate let us in.'

'Oh? Which one?'

'Er,' said Emily, pausing, and then quieter, as if she'd moved the phone away from her mouth: 'I'm so sorry, remind me what your name is?'

'Alfie,' came Alfie's voice.

'Alfie!' said Emily, full volume again. 'We're just having a beer. When are you getting back?'

2

ALFIE HAD RETURNED home that afternoon to find two women standing at the entrance to his building. He held the door open for them, assuming they were waiting to be buzzed up, and they walked behind him up the stairs to the second floor, then followed him along the corridor that led to number twelve.

'Oh!' one of them had said when he put his key in the door. 'Do you live in this flat?'

'Y-yes?' said Alfie, suddenly wondering whether he did or not.

'Then you know Hazel?'

Alfie felt his face warm up. 'I know Hazel, yeah. Are you …?'

'Her sister,' said the woman, holding out her hand, which he shook. 'Emily.' Her hair was the same dark blondish colour as Hazel's, only it was cut just above her shoulders and she had a fringe. 'This is my wife Daria,' she said.

'Nice to meet you both,' he replied. 'I'm Alfie. Come in.'

'So where is she, do you know?' said Emily as they piled in through the door.

'At work, I think. Were you expecting her to be here?'

Emily sighed and exchanged glances with Daria, who laughed and said, 'Oh my God.'

'She *knew* we were coming!' cried Emily. 'We discussed it! She said she was free! I'm so sorry, turning up on your doorstep like this. We were supposed to be staying here for a couple of days. Hazel, honestly.'

'She never mentioned it,' said Alfie, in surprise. He considered himself fairly easygoing, as a rule, but he wouldn't have *minded* a little advance notice. 'I guess she forgot.'

'Is it inconvenient?' said Daria, looking worried. 'We could probably find a Travelodge or something?'

'Oh, no!' cried Alfie. 'Don't be silly.' He smiled broadly, for good measure. He couldn't honestly say it was convenient, when he'd had hopes of being the sole or at least the main object of Hazel's attention that evening, but they seemed nice enough, and he didn't want them to feel unwelcome. 'It shouldn't be too long before she gets back,' he said. 'Would you like a cup of tea? Coffee? Or a beer?'

They requested beer, and sat sipping it at the kitchen table while he gathered up all the dirty dishes and stacked them next to the sink. 'Sorry,' he muttered, leaning across them to wipe the crumbs off the table, and they sat back a little to give him more space. They talked all the while, unfazed, telling him about Australia, where they'd been living for two years while Daria did a post-doc at the University of Melbourne. They'd been back a fortnight. Daria had been offered a permanent job at the University of East Anglia, Emily told him proudly, putting a hand on Daria's shoulder.

Daria smiled, looking slightly embarrassed. 'Which means we need to find a place to live in Norwich,' she said hurriedly, 'which is why we're here. We've got some house viewings on Monday. You're only a couple of stops from Liverpool Street so you're saving us a good two hours' travelling time.' They were staying with Emily's parents in rural Kent, they explained, which had no direct transport links to any of the places they needed to go, and no decent coffee either, and certainly no decent vegan food.

At the first break in the conversation Alfie excused himself and hurried to the bathroom, ostensibly to use it, but really to make it halfway presentable before either of them went in there. A deep scowl settled on his face as he removed Hazel's hair from the shower and Tony's shaving scum from the sink. He couldn't remember whose turn it was to clean that week, but it certainly wasn't his. When it looked less like an undergraduate hovel he returned to the kitchen and opened a beer. Emily and Daria launched into an interrogation, asking him how long he'd been in London (eight years) and how long he'd been in the flat (four months). What had possessed him to move into a shithole like this, Emily asked ('Em!' cried Daria), and he wondered if he should have bothered cleaning the bathroom after all. He told them he wasn't long out of a relationship and this was just an interim measure.

'Oh man, sorry,' said Daria, and he said it was fine, which it was, sort of, only he wasn't sure they believed him. They were quiet for a while, and then Emily pointed at an empty Yazoo bottle in the recycling bin and said, 'You can tell Hazel lives here.'

At the mention of Hazel, whose fondness for choco- late milk was juvenile and very charming, Alfie's cheeks warmed again. What was it like living with her, Emily wanted to know, and he replied that it was good, fine, great. He would have stopped there but they were looking at him expectantly, so he said he wouldn't object to her taking the cleaning rota a little more seriously, and they laughed, satisfied.

'So are you an academic too?' he asked Emily, keen to change the subject.

'Oh God, no. I'm a software engineer.'

Alfie said that was cool; he wished he was a bit more techy. The world was your oyster when you were techy. Emily asked what he did, and he told them about primary teaching and the school where he worked.

'I've got a uni friend who's just left teaching,' said Emily. 'She was written off for three months. Stress. Then she just said fuck it.'

'I'm not surprised,' said Alfie. 'We've had one or two at our school. I've thought about quitting so many times. I just can't really see myself being any good at anything else.'

From there began a discussion about education policy, during which Alfie talked in great depth about SATs and phonics and academisation, and Emily and Daria groaned in all the right places, and frowned, and asked him lots of very pertinent questions that required time-consuming answers. Then they talked about governments, British and Australian and American, and then about where they were the night Donald Trump got elected. Alfie had had a beautiful dream about Hillary winning, he recounted, then woken up at four a.m. with a jolt of nervous dread.

They were on to Brexit when Hazel rang. After that they talked about climate change and the many ways in which they were all fucked, and they must have kept this up for quite a while because suddenly the door banged and Hazel was there, looking at them all with bemusement.

'Fancy seeing you here,' said Emily.

'I'm really sorry,' Hazel replied, pulling out a chair. She had a stud in her nose and her hair was done in a complicated sort of plait. A few strands were coming loose about her face. She was smiling apologetically, which brought out her dimples. Or maybe it was just the one dimple, Alfie couldn't quite remember. She was sitting side-on, so that he couldn't see the other cheek.

'You should have messaged me yesterday,' Hazel continued.

'Don't victim blame!' said Emily. 'You're just a flake!' She reached over and squeezed Hazel's face until her lips were folded up and bulging. 'What are you?'

'A flake,' said Hazel through her squashed-up mouth.

Emily released Hazel's face and ruffled her hair instead, until she was crowned by a nest of tangles and electricity. The complicated plait was ruined.

'Fucking hell!' Hazel cried. 'Are you satisfied?' She flopped back in her chair and started undoing the plait, combing through her hair with her fingers.

'Give the woman a beer,' said Daria, and Alfie did so. Hazel sighed and muttered her thanks.

'I don't know about the rest of you,' Daria went on, 'but I'm getting hungry.'

'Shall we get a takeaway?' said Alfie. 'I could eat a dirty pizza.'

'Oh,' said Hazel, shaking out her hair and tying it back in a messy knot, 'have you not been made aware? These guys are *vegans*.' She rolled her eyes.

'Shit! I forgot. I'm so sorry.'

Emily and Daria told him not to be silly. 'You don't have to worry about offending us,' said Emily. She turned and looked pointedly at her sister. 'But Hazel does, because she's a *dick*.'

Hazel laughed, and choked on her beer. Daria reached over and thumped her on the back, explaining as she did so that Hazel had once done a hatchet job on veganism in an article for her university paper, and Emily had never forgiven her.

'I didn't know she was vegan when I wrote it,' said Hazel, when she'd recovered.

'She always says that!' cried Emily. 'As if that makes it better!'

'What's your problem with vegans?' said Alfie, like he didn't have three cans of foie gras in the cupboard, left over from the trip to Paris he and Rachel had made in a last-ditch attempt to save their relationship.

'I don't have a problem *now*,' said Hazel. She launched into a story about a vegan potluck she'd attended once with a friend who was dabbling, where everyone had been very unfriendly and a woman ('a real *vegan*, like *profoundly* vegan, you know?') had insulted her chickpea salad.

'So you wrote an article as revenge?' said Alfie, thinking how creative it was to respond in such a way.

'A terrible article,' she replied.

'Worse than terrible,' said Emily. 'It was hate speech.'

'It was ten years ago!' Hazel protested. 'It was a different time!' Emily simply shook her head.

'Can I read it?' said Alfie.

'Absolutely not,' said Hazel. Their eyes met, and something squeezed beneath his ribcage.

Then Daria pointed out that they still hadn't decided what kind of takeaway they were having, and Hazel went to fetch her laptop so they could look at Deliveroo. Alfie sat back and sipped his beer and thought, Now this is a family.

EMILY AND DARIA found a little house in Norwich, fifteen minutes from the city centre, with a back garden and period features and a park opposite. The estate agent gave them a form to sign and told them they would receive the final documents once the landlords had given their approval. At the station they bought a bottle of prosecco in the M&S while they waited for their train.

On the way back to London they listed all the virtues and drawbacks of their new house, and then listed them all again using slightly different words. Then they settled into their usual argument about Emily's future commute, which was going to be very long because she was applying for jobs in Cambridge, where all the tech companies were. She thought two hours on a train each way was doable; Daria disagreed, and had made much of her willingness to live somewhere between the two cities.

'I'm just saying, it's not too late,' she said now.

But it was clear to Emily that Daria, a gay Middle Eastern vegan, would be ill suited to life in a leave-voting town in the arse-end of nowhere. 'You need your scenes, babe,' she said. 'You need a music scene and a gay scene and a vegan scene, just as much as I do.'

'I just can't stop thinking about you being all pregnant and exhausted,' said Daria, and Emily smiled.

'I know,' she said. She stroked her stomach, which was flat. 'You might be right. Let's just give it a year, okay? Then we'll see where we are.'

'I would do it, you know. I'd move to the arse-end of nowhere, if it made your life easier.'

'I know you would,' said Emily, putting her head on Daria's shoulder and taking her hand. 'Because you're sweet and selfless and I love you.' Daria put her arm around Emily, and they sat like this for a while. Then Emily said, 'Alfie's nice, isn't he?'

'Oh my God, so nice!' said Daria, and Emily could hear that she was smiling.

'Can we steal him away? Take him to Norwich with us?'

Daria laughed. 'I think Hazel would have something to say about that. Do you think there's something going on there?'

'I wish,' said Emily. 'But I won't get my hopes up. Hazel has terrible taste in men.'

When they broke the news about the house Hazel whooped so loudly that Alfie put his head out of his bedroom door in curiosity.

'What's going on?' he said.

'We found a house!' said Emily. 'Come and have some prosecco!'

When the cork had popped Hazel asked how much the rent was, and when they told her she snorted and said, 'Are you serious? That's literally only a hundred quid more than I pay for that cupboard.' She gestured in the direction of her room, which was big enough for a single bed and not very much else. She muttered that London took the piss, she would have to start thinking about moving.

'Don't do that!' cried Emily. 'Where will we stay when we visit?'

Hazel looked at her witheringly and opened the fridge to inspect the contents. She took out a packet of tofu and an array of vegetables. 'I'm doing a stir-fry,' she said to Alfie. 'Do you want some?'

Alfie did want some, partly because he'd noticed that his own section of the fridge was empty except for a shrivelled yellow pepper and a jar of tartare sauce, and partly because he'd ended up enjoying their company so much on Saturday night that he had entirely forgotten he was supposed to be going to someone's house party instead.

'Well. Maybe. I don't know,' he said, because he also didn't want to intrude, or seem too keen. 'Will there be enough?'

Hazel said there would be plenty, and Alfie vacillated until she said, 'For God's sake, I'm going to make you some anyway, okay?' He thanked her, and donated his pepper.

Over dinner Emily asked Hazel about work and Hazel wrinkled her nose. She'd had a few freelance illustration gigs this year and her webcomic had a growing following, but none of it was enough for her to quit working in the café. She was having trouble imagining that it ever would be. But then, she said, she might not quit even if she could. She complained about it, but she did like it. It was a world away from working in an office, for which she would forever be grateful. It was tiring, but nothing like the mental drudgery of staring at spreadsheets all day. The regulars liked her, and she them, and two of her colleagues were genuine kindred spirits. It was just that the pay was so bad.

'Yes, but if you're happy,' said Emily, through a mouthful of stir-fry.

'Yeah,' said Hazel uncertainly. 'I'm happi*er*, definitely. What about you? Have you got a job yet?'

'No,' said Emily. 'But I've got my feelers out.'

'You can get in trouble for that, you know,' said Hazel, and Daria tittered. Emily sighed and looked at Alfie.

'So juvenile,' he said, shaking his head, as if saddened.

After dinner Daria stretched out her arms and said, 'So are any of you losers going to take me on at Scrabble?'

They'd finished the prosecco but there was still beer in the fridge, so they took it into the living room with them and settled themselves on the floor around the coffee table. Hazel extracted the Scrabble set from a heap of clutter on the bookshelf, and the letters were mixed and distributed. A concentrated silence descended on the room, broken every so often by oohs and dammits, sighs of satisfaction and tuts of regret, and on one occasion by the entrance of Tony, who shuffled into the room to get his phone and then out again without saying anything, leaving behind him a lingering scent of unwashed polyester.

For most of the game, Daria and Hazel were neck and neck, overtaking each other with every turn. But then Alfie put down *EXPECTING*, enclosing the P of Daria's *STEEP* and the N of Emily's *LAWN*. The X was on a double letter score, the T on a triple word score, and he'd used all his letters at once, which gave him a fifty-point bonus.

'Ugh,' said Daria. 'Fuck it.'

'You jammy bastard,' said Hazel, as Alfie added up his score.

'A hundred and thirty-seven!' he crowed.

Emily said nothing. Her heart was thumping drunkenly in her chest. Of all the words! Obviously she didn't believe in signs from the universe, but say such things existed. They didn't, but say they did. If you gave your imagination a free rein, there could be no doubt that this was a pretty fucking good one.

4

HAZEL AND ALFIE had not been alone together since It happened, because she had been at work all weekend, and on Monday he had been off somewhere or other that couldn't have been work, because it was the school holidays. There had therefore been no opportunity to acknowledge It, much less to discuss It, or even skirt awkwardly around It. Hazel was glad of this, in a way. Better a clean break, she thought. Never mind that her belly swooped downwards when the front door banged; never mind that her cheeks burned when he smiled in her direction. Feelings like these tended to lead her into situations from which she would sooner or later want to extricate herself, and as such were best ignored. To assist her in ignoring them she arranged to go on a date, and made sure Alfie knew about it.

From the outset, it did not go to plan. She was late, and then there were delays on the tube, which made her later. By the time she arrived her date was two pints in.

'Excuse me? Brandon?' she said, and he looked up from his phone.

'Yes! Hazel, hi!' he said, standing to kiss her on the cheek. 'I'm so sorry,' she said gravely. 'The fucking Central Line.'

'Oh God, I know,' he said, shaking his head. 'It's hell, and I mean that literally. Let me get you a drink. What d'you fancy?'

She asked for a glass of white wine, and settled herself at the table while he went to the bar. She was too warm, but she kept her jacket on to hide her sweat patches.

Brandon came back with her wine, and an additional pint for himself. The wine was vinegary, and Brandon, though not yet drunk, was loud. There was something oddly familiar about him, she thought as they talked. Nothing prominent enough to have shown up on his profile picture, but something in the manner, and the voice. Had they met before? She learned that he was an engineer for a property developer and liked cars, Swiss watches and playing squash. He didn't tell her he liked football, but he gave himself away by letting his eyes wander, at regular intervals, to the QPR–Chelsea game on the giant TV behind her. They might have friends in common, she supposed, but it was starting to seem unlikely.

She bought a second round of drinks, wondering if they would have enough conversation to see them through it. Eventually, stuck for a question, she said, 'I'm sorry, but I really feel like I've met you before.'

'Oh yeah?'

'Is it just me?'

He narrowed his eyes and looked at her, his head slightly tilted. 'Maybe there is something familiar about you, now you mention it,' he said, obviously unconvinced. 'Were you at Exeter?'

'No.'

'King Ed's?'

She shook her head.

'D'you work round here?'

'Nope.' At a loss, they took contemplative sips from their glasses. Then Hazel remembered.

'Oh my God!' she exclaimed. 'Do you have a sister called Hannah?'

'Y-yes …?'

'Hannah Fox?'

'That's her. Do you know her, then?'

Hazel smiled. She'd always had a soft spot for Hannah Fox. 'Do you remember Emily Phillips?' she said. 'Hannah's girlfriend at UCL – ten, twelve years ago now?'

His eyes widened. 'Emily Phillips? Now that takes me back!' He nodded excitedly, not even trying to temper his enthusiasm. 'How d'you know her?'

'She's my sister,' said Hazel.

Brandon almost choked on his pint. 'Your *sister*? What, actually?'

'Yep.'

'So we've met before?'

'Do you remember when Emily and Hannah graduated, and Emily got absolutely paralytic and had to be carried home?'

'Oh yeah! God, that was mental! She was a *mess*. I don't remember a sister, though.'

Hazel sighed internally. 'Well, I was there,' she said. 'In fact, you wouldn't have made it home if it wasn't for me. I persuaded the taxi driver to take us. He didn't want to. He made me swear on his Bible that Emily wouldn't throw up.'

Brandon laughed uproariously. 'No shit!' he said. 'Classic! Yeah, I'm starting to remember you now. To tell you the truth, Hazel, my memory of that night's a bit hazy. I was pretty far gone myself.' He chuckled and shook his head, and took another swig from his glass. His laughter died out slowly. Then he looked up, still smiling.

'Did you … I thought you … Did you say girlfriend?'

'What? Oh. Yeah.'

'Your sister was my sister's girlfriend? Girlfriend as in *girlfriend*?'

'Er, yes?'

'What?' he cried. 'Fuck! No! They were *together*?'

'Oh, wow. You missed that memo, then.'

Brandon had his hand on his forehead. 'Oh my God! I never even suspected! Hannah wasn't out then. They never … I thought … I assumed—'

'They weren't just close friends, Brandon,' said Hazel. She was starting to feel very tired.

'Are you *sure*?' said Brandon wildly. 'Yeah, you're sure. Fuck!'

'Why is this such a big deal? Did you think Emily fancied you?'

Brandon laughed so loudly and for so long at this suggestion that Hazel knew she was right. 'Of course I didn't,' he said.

Hazel drained her glass and reached into her bag for her phone. Discreetly she typed 'SOS' into a WhatsApp message and sent it to her friend Nish. Thirty seconds later her phone rang.

'Hi, babe,' said Nish when she picked up. 'I think you should come over. I've fallen down the stairs. I might have broken my arm, actually, so I'll be needing someone to feed me my noodle soup before it gets cold. You'd better come quick, I'll be dead soon.'

It took discipline not to laugh. She got up and walked away from the table, as if called away by something serious and private, then returned to Brandon with her features arranged into an expression of grave concern.

'I'm so sorry,' she said, 'but I'm going to have to go. A friend of mine just got some really shitty news.'

Brandon raised his eyebrows very slightly.

'Thanks for a lovely evening,' she said, pulling on her coat.

'You too,' said Brandon. He knew, she could tell, but he didn't dare say so. She stooped to kiss him on the cheek, and then started towards the door.

'Hey,' came Brandon's voice a second later, and she turned back. He grinned sheepishly, as if he'd decided to be spontaneous and wasn't sure it was a good idea. 'This isn't very gallant of me,' he said. 'Maybe it's not ... I mean ... Ah, what the hell. Can I just ask what your sister's up to these days?'

Hazel pursed her lips. 'She's a software engineer.'

'That's cool. Is she, er ...?'

'She's married.'

'Oh really? Okay. Great. Good for her. So she's not ... you know.'

'She's married to a woman.'

'Oh, right. Cool. Nice.' He nodded interminably. 'Well, thanks again, Hazel. Tell Emily I said hi.'

Hazel went straight to the flat in Bow in which Nish lived with her other friend Roisin. Both of them worked with

Hazel in the café and, like her, aspired to loftier things. Hazel had her illustration; Nish wrote music on his computer; Roisin had a Masters in Fine Art and a bedroom filled with chicken wire and plaster of Paris.

When she arrived she collapsed onto Roisin's bed and recounted the whole story. 'What the fuck was *that*?' she exclaimed in conclusion. 'Why did I match with *him*?'

'It was just algorithms,' Nish soothed. 'Your sister's probably still friends with his sister on Facebook.'

'Is that why? That's *creepy*! Fuck this!'

'Look, it's always going to be a bit hit-and-miss, Hazel. We all have our fair share of duffers. You mustn't let it put you off. You've got to get back on the horse.'

'And you can always put this in a cartoon,' added Roisin from the doorway. She disappeared, returning five minutes later with three cups of tea.

'Are you working tomorrow?' said Nish to Hazel, blowing into his mug.

'Yeah.'

'Us too. Stay over, we'll all go together. You can sleep in my bed.'

'I don't want to sleep in your gross bed,' said Hazel.

Roisin agreed that this would be unimaginably disgusting. Hazel could have the inflatable mattress instead. This belonged to Roisin but could not be set up in her room because of all the chicken wire, so they squeezed it into the narrow space on Nish's floor. A pillow, a sleeping bag and an old T-shirt were provided. Roisin assured Hazel that the sleeping bag, while not freshly laundered, had been recently aired, and that no one had been having sex in or on it, which was more than could be said for Nish's bed.

A good half-hour was then given over to discussing Nish's latest sexual escapades, most of which were facilitated by Grindr, and required a level of spontaneity and audaciousness that Hazel could not in her wildest dreams have sustained.

'What about you guys?' said Nish when he'd run out of stories. 'I can't be the only person having sex.'

'Nothing to report,' said Roisin, lounging across the airbed. 'I'm having some great wanks, though.'

Hazel didn't say anything, which immediately alerted their suspicions. She let them tease her for a while, and then she said, 'So you know Alfie?' She recounted their conversations at the kitchen table about music and documentaries and webcomics. Then there had been the evening with the gin and the back-to-back episodes of *Black Mirror*, following which they had speculated tipsily about the cyber-dystopia towards which humanity was sleepwalking. Then they'd had sex. Alfie was very good at sex. Suspiciously good. Practised.

'You're saying that like it's a bad thing,' said Nish.

Hazel explained about the cries of pleasure she had heard emanating from Alfie's room the weekend before, but he was unmoved.

'What's your point?' he said.

'I just feel like he's probably the kind of guy who sleeps with someone new every week. Not that there's anything wrong with that,' she added hurriedly, 'but I have to live with him. I should probably just ... not get involved.'

'Right,' said Roisin. 'Recipe for disaster.'

'Have you actually heard him having sex every week?' demanded Nish.

'Well, two weeks ago. And then a week later, with me.'

'And he's lived with you how long?'

'I mean, four months, but ...'

Nish was looking at her with his eyebrows raised. 'So he's had sex twice in the last four months.'

'In our flat, yeah. But who knows what he's been getting up to when he's not at home?'

'Hazel,' said Nish, 'you're inventing problems where no problems exist.'

Roisin asked to see a picture, so Hazel brought up Alfie's Instagram on her phone and they leaned in to peer at it.

'Nice,' said Roisin.

'Sweet lord,' said Nish. 'Hazel, in what world are you not into this guy?'

'I didn't say I wasn't, I just—'

'So you are?'

'A bit, maybe, but—'

'And he's into you.'

'You don't know that. He was into some other girl two weeks ago.'

'Pfff.'

'He texted you saying he couldn't stop thinking about you,' put in Roisin, going over to the other side.

'About *it*. About the sex.'

'Same difference.'

'No it isn't!'

'Hazel, just be grateful to the universe when it gives you good stuff,' said Nish. 'Why are you going on dates with city-boy wankers when you've got *that* at home?'

'Because! I need to move on! Okay?'

'This is too much,' said Nish. He put down his tea and

turned towards her, taking both her hands. 'Repeat after me. *When I get home tomorrow.*'

Hazel eyed him suspiciously, but obeyed. 'When I get home tomorrow.'

'*I am going.*'

'I am going.'

'*To have sex with Alfie for ever and ever amen.*'

Hazel clipped him round the head and he yelped. 'You want me to get screwed over!'

'Yeah, and under! And backwards! And upside down!' he cried, curling up in a ball to protect himself from a volley of tiny blows. Roisin rolled onto her back, laughing.

'When I come to you crying,' said Hazel, 'because my heart's broken and it's too awkward for me to live in my own home—'

'I will wipe your tears away and I will kick out that fucker Julian so you can move in with us,' said Nish.

'Shh,' said Roisin. 'He'll hear you.'

'I swear to you I will,' whispered Nish. 'He picks his nose and flicks it.'

Hazel tensed her mouth so as not to grin. 'This is all going to end badly,' she said. 'I'll regret I ever listened to you.'

'Deal with that when it happens, Hazel!' he cried. 'Carpe fucking diem!'

5

ALFIE HAD SPENT the evening in an intimidating Swedish bar, drinking beer and eating smoked fish on dark bread with his friend Clara. Technically Clara was his ex-girl-friend, but this fact barely registered with him any more because the relationship had been so fleeting and incon-sequential. He couldn't remember what she looked like naked, and assumed the reverse was also true. Even so, he had suggested the meeting shortly after learning that Hazel was going on a date, so that if she asked about his own plans he could say, 'Oh, I'm meeting up with a friend. My ex, actually,' and follow this with a casual grimace, the precise meaning of which would be unclear to her. So far, however, she hadn't asked him anything at all.

Alfie and Clara had been overdue their annual catch-up, so Clara did not suspect an ulterior motive. As usual she had scouted out a new and overpriced location for the purpose; as usual a large portion of the evening was devoted to complaining about work. Clara raged about her manager, who took her for granted, and Alfie raged about a clique of female teachers and classroom assistants who had treated him as a pariah ever since the end of his relationship with Rachel. He and Rachel had been colleagues at the same school for several years, but Rachel, apparently judging this to be untenable post-break-up, had left at the end of last term. The prevailing belief among her cheerleaders was that she had martyred herself, giving up a job she loved so that harmony might be restored in the staffroom, but the irony of this was that any disharmony had been entirely of her own making. Alfie had never been *anything* but civil, had taken *great* pains to keep the fall-out contained, and yet now he was perceived to have driven her away, and resented for not having left himself. He might very well give them what they wanted, he said. He would start checking the job ads in September. Fuck *them*.

He hadn't really thought about any of this since the beginning of the holidays, and was a little taken aback by the strength of his own anger. Clara was pleasingly outraged, but as the conversation moved on she grew quieter, until her voice was small and sad.

'Clar?' said Alfie. 'What's the matter?'

'So much breaking up this year,' she said wearily. 'I've joined the club, actually.'

'Oh. Wait, what? You mean ...?'

Yes, she replied, she was single as of two weeks ago, and miserable about it. She had broken up with a man named Hill (real name), whom Alfie had never met, but whose SoundCloud profile he had listened to with horrified fascination, every last wretched song. It had so appalled him that for a brief moment he questioned the viability of his friendship with Clara, who thought Hill was 'creative' and 'not like other guys (no offence, Alfie)'.

Clara missed Hill, but also didn't miss him, and was also angry with herself for sticking around so long, trying to make it work, when she'd only really been wasting time. Now here she was, back at square one, and turning thirty next birthday.

'Turning thirty's no big deal,' said Alfie, who was the same age and thoroughly okay with it. His hairline was not yet receding, not even a little bit.

Clara raised one eyebrow and reminded him sharply that turning thirty was one thing when you were a man and quite another when you were woman, specifically a newly single woman hoping to have kids in the next five years.

'I didn't know you wanted kids,' he said guiltily.

She sighed and said yes, she wanted *lots*. Three at least. She couldn't help it, she was old-fashioned. She sighed again, more heavily.

Alfie wanted to reassure her that there was still plenty of time, that she would find someone, but given his own romantic history, he suspected it might come out sounding like a hollow platitude.

Instead he said: 'I think I'd like to have kids. I'd obviously be an awesome dad.'

Clara laughed. 'Yeah, you probably would. Fortunately for you, there's no deadline.'

'I don't know. Seventy's a bit old, I think.'

She gave him a gentle shove and said she was going to get another drink. While she was gone Alfie ruminated on what he had just said. Generally speaking parenthood was not something to which he gave much thought, but he hadn't entirely been joking about being an awesome dad. He spent his working week suffering the consequences of other people's parenting choices, which he felt ought to give him a head start.

Clara came back and put a pint of pale ale down on the table in front of him. 'So,' she said brightly, 'who are you going to be making all these babies with?'

'No idea,' he replied, not meeting her eye.

'What, at all? No one you're flirting with? No one at school catching your eye?' He gave her a look. 'Sorry,' she said. 'But seriously, nothing? You disappoint me.'

'Well ...'

'That's more like it!'

'Yeah, don't get excited. It's a big old mess. I slept with someone.' Clara rubbed her hands together with glee, and Alfie smiled a little, at the memory. 'It was ... Well, it was great,' he said. 'But she's my flatmate.'

'Oh!' said Clara. 'Okay. Complicated. Is it making things awkward?'

'I wouldn't say that exactly,' said Alfie. He told her about the appearance of Emily and Daria, and how little time there had been for awkwardness.

'Do you think anything will come of it?' asked Clara, and Alfie shrugged. 'Do you want it to?'

'Wouldn't mind.'

'Do you like her, then?' she said, and when Alfie did not immediately answer: 'You do! You like her! Oh my God, Alfie!' She made her voice go high and put on an American accent. 'Do you *love* her?'

'Fuck off.'

'Flatmates can make good couples, you know. Hey!'

She hit the table with her palm. 'I went to a wedding last month. How do you think they met? Flatshare!'

Alfie shook his head. 'She's not interested, Clara. It was just a one-night thing.'

'Oh,' said Clara, deflated. 'So she used you for sex.'

'Looks like it. The first moment we had just the two of us, she told me she was going on a date this week with some guy.'

'She might be trying to make you jealous?' said Clara hopefully, but Alfie shook his head.

'I don't think she'd go in for that kind of strategy.'

'Oh. Fuck. Well, that's a bummer. I'm sorry.' Clara raised her glass. 'Here's to being a pair of losers,' she said, with unmistakable relish, and Alfie clinked his glass against hers.

On the bus home Alfie's eye started twitching, as it had been doing, sporadically, for several weeks. It was irritating, and made him uneasy. He'd sworn to himself he wouldn't google it, but he felt a strange compulsion to do so all of a sudden. He took out his phone and typed in 'twitching eye'. Lack of sleep, the articles all suggested. Or stress, although this was unlikely in the school holidays. Otherwise too much caffeine – but he'd tried giving up coffee and it had made no difference. Then he got to the end of one article and read that in rare cases a twitching eye could be a symptom of degenerative neurological disease.

In a horrified sort of trance, he followed the link to the article on one such disease and read the list of symptoms. It seemed he had several of them. He held his hand in front of his face and saw that it was shaking. He moved his fingers into different positions, trying to keep them still, but he found that they wouldn't keep still. Then he pushed his hair forward so that if he looked up he could see it in front of his eyes. The strands jumped and pulsated, and he wondered if this was an early signal of 'uncontrollable movement of the head', which, he now knew, was always a serious matter that merited immediate medical attention.

He stumbled into the flat in a daze. He was going to die – soon, and horribly. He thought of making an appointment with his GP, but a wave of nausea hit him when he imagined the sleepless nights leading up to it, then the heavy trudge to the surgery, then the anxious wait to go in. And the grave look, if it was something serious, the gentle tones, the referral for further tests.

He sat down at the kitchen table, at a loss. He could hear the sound of video games emanating from beneath Tony's bedroom door, and for a moment he considered knocking and asking him if he fancied a beer. But that would be an extreme response to any situation. What he really wanted was to talk to Hazel – not about what had happened between them, but about anything and everything else, as they'd done once or twice, long into the night. A cup of tea with her would have distracted him from the possibility of his imminent diagnosis and death. He might tell her about his symptoms and find they seemed entirely inconsequential, once spoken aloud. He might tell her that there were bad genes in his family, that his mother and grandmother had both died of breast cancer before their time, and that he probably shouldn't have kids himself if he was only going to die and leave them. She would laugh at him, most likely, and say something reassuring (if untrue) like, 'You're literally the healthiest person I know' or 'I've had a twitch in my eye since last year'. Or actually, no – she wouldn't laugh at him, she would say something unshakeably logical, like: 'Wow, that's terrible, I can see why you'd worry about cancer, but motor neurone disease? Really?' It was the sort of thing that might have made him feel better if she had actually been there to say it, but in his own head it only reminded him that there was cancer to fret about too. He got up and went into his bedroom, pulled down his jeans and underwear, and felt his testicles for lumps. There weren't any, that he could detect. That was something.

He wondered where Hazel was. Presumably her absence meant her date had been a success. Perhaps he should message her, check all was well. But he didn't know at what point prudence became prying, or if by sleeping with her last week he had given up any right to appear concerned, because concern could too easily be mistaken for jealousy. He typed out a message, edited it to appear more casual, and then deleted it anyway.

He felt like there was something going on with his fingers, though not anything he could describe. Tiredness perhaps. Muscle fatigue. Or maybe numbness. Was it numbness? Had his fingers gone numb? He could feel the panic rising again, the claustrophobia, like he was trapped in a burning building. He looked around for something sharp and found a biro. He pressed the pointed end into his fingers at random, leaving a scattering of little black dots. He could feel the biro, yes. But was he feeling a normal amount of pressure, or had his sensation dulled? He couldn't be sure.

He lay back against the pillows and tried to reason with himself, but he was hyper-aware of his fingers and his hands, heavy and clammy, possibly working properly, possibly not. He was buzzing with an uncomfortable sort of energy, a strange tension.

His phone vibrated and he jumped. It was Jasmine, the woman he'd spent the night with the other week. They'd met at someone's thirtieth and hooked up twice since then. She was the first person he'd done it with since the end of his relationship with Rachel, and it was all very shallow and uncomplicated. She'd made a lot of noise, which was gratifying, but also embarrassing. He hadn't particularly wanted them to announce themselves so stridently. She had a wide-eyed innocence about her that belied her ferocious libido.

Now she was saying she'd just finished having drinks on Broadway Market and if he was up for it she could pop round. He wasn't up for it. He wasn't sure he could perform in this state of fretfulness. He replied that he was 'out with some mates', then got into bed with a box of tissues and masturbated half-heartedly instead.

6

'ANYONE FOR ANOTHER glass of wine?' said Emily's mother after dinner, holding the bottle aloft.

'If you insist,' said Emily's father, raising his glass towards it. Emily sat back and allowed her own glass to be filled. Daria put a preventative hand up and said, 'No, thanks.'

'Are you sure, lovey?' said Diane, perplexed. The bottle hovered in anticipation of her changing her mind. 'Do you want something else, then? I've got whisky? Port? Amaretto?'

'I'm honestly fine,' said Daria. 'I've got to go upstairs now anyway. Skype call. Apparently my brother's got some news.'

''Ello 'ello,' said Jim, settling himself on the sofa with a loud exhale of contentment. 'D'you think he's making an honest woman of that girlfriend of his?'

'Quite possibly,' said Daria.

'Or maybe she's pregnant,' said Emily flatly.

'Oooh! That'd be exciting!' cried Diane, pouring Daria's share of the wine into her own glass.

'Wish him luck from me, either way,' said Jim, winking

at her. Diane tutted and launched into a good-humoured scolding. Daria closed the door on them, and went upstairs to call her own parents.

A faltering image of them appeared on her laptop screen and they all greeted each other in Farsi, waving and smiling. Kamran hadn't yet logged in, so Daria moved her laptop around to show them the room she and Emily were staying in, and described the house they would soon be moving to in as much detail as she could. They talked in a mixture of languages, regularly supplementing Farsi words with their English equivalents.

'Would you look at these cats?' said her mother, when there was still no sign of Kamran. She turned her screen shakily so that Daria caught a pixelated glimpse of Mary Shelley on one of the kitchen chairs and Mary Wollstonecraft on the fridge behind her. The latter was the progeny of the former, which undergraduate Daria had thought very clever until she realised that in real life it had been the other way around. Not that it mattered; Mary Wollstonecraft went by Wally, as a rule.

They began speculating about Kamran's news. 'It won't be anything bad, will it?' said Leila, and Daria and Ramin said no, of course not, he wouldn't announce bad news in advance like that, leaving them to wait and wonder. It would be something to do with Lily. Marriage, almost certainly.

Eventually the symbol next to Kamran's name turned green, and Daria invited him to join the call.

'Hi, guys,' said Kamran. 'How's everyone?'

'We're all fine, darling,' said Leila, 'but hurry up and tell us your news. We've been waiting.'

'Sorry to leave you in suspense,' said Kamran, and paused, as if deciding how best to put the news into words.

'Well?' said Leila.

Kamran bit his lip and took a deep breath. 'Okay,' he said on the exhale. 'Two bits of news, really. The first one is that me and Lily—' He stopped again. The tension was almost audible. 'You're not going to like this. Me and Lily have decided to call it a day.'

There was a collective sigh of disappointment. 'Ah, crap,' said Daria.

'Oh, son,' said Ramin.

'Darling!' cried Leila. 'Has she *left* you? Has she *left* my baby boy?'

'No, no one's left anyone. It was a mutual decision. If anything it's more my fault than hers.'

'Oh, poor Lily!' said Leila, instantly switching allegiance. 'What did you do?'

'I didn't *do* anything. I haven't met anyone else, if that's what you're trying to suggest. Things just haven't been right for a while.'

'And you can't work through it? Relationships are always difficult! You can't just up sticks at the first sign of trouble!'

'No, Mum,' said Kamran, a trace of irritation creeping into his voice. 'I know that. It's not the first sign of trouble. We can't work through it, we've tried. This is the best thing for us both. We're agreed.'

'Is it your job?' said Ramin. 'Those long hours?'

'That hasn't helped,' Kamran sighed. 'It hasn't been easy to discuss things. She works mad hours too. There've been some weeks where we've barely seen each other at all.'

'Perhaps you should think about getting a new job, then,' said Leila. 'I know you don't like the thought of the private sector, but if things are that bad—'

'I'm not doing private work, Mum.'

'I know you have principles, darling, and we're proud of you, but—'

'It's not just principles. I've got a new job already. That's my second bit of news.'

Leila hesitated, her eyebrows raised. 'Oh,' she said. 'I see.'

'It's a bit different,' Kamran went on. 'Still as a doctor. But with Médecins Sans Frontières.'

Daria realised the significance of this before anyone else did. 'Shit, really?' she said.

'Médecins Sans Frontières?' said Leila guardedly. 'What's that again?'

'Doctors Without Borders. You know, they send doctors out to places where … where there are … well, where they don't have proper medical infrastructure.'

'War zones,' said Ramin.

'Not necessarily,' said Kamran quickly.

'War zones?' echoed Leila. 'Oh, Kamran!'

'I'm not going to a war zone, Mum. I'm going to Bangladesh.'

'*Bangladesh?*'

'There are big camps of displaced Rohingya there. I'm going to be based in a clinic on the border with Myanmar. For six months, initially. But with a view to staying longer, depending on how things go.'

There was silence. Leila's mouth hung open. Ramin looked grave, but he was nodding slowly.

'That's amazing, Kam,' said Daria. 'Good for you.'

'And these camps,' said Leila, ignoring her, 'they'll be unsanitary, won't they? Disease-ridden.'

'I'll have a full round of vaccines before I go. They're very careful. They do everything they can to protect the doctors from risk.'

'Yes, everything they *can*,' said Leila. 'Which might not be very much, might it?'

Ramin put his arm around her and pulled her in close. 'I'm very proud of you, Kamran,' he said. 'Your social conscience does us credit. Your mother's proud of you too. She's just worried.'

'Good job one of us has a social conscience, eh, Kam?' said Daria. She felt unexpectedly moved, and a little inadequate.

'Do Médecins Sans Frontières work in Iran?' Leila blurted out.

'I think so,' said Kamran. 'They have done, anyway. I'm not sure if they're there at the moment.'

'So they might send you there.'

'I doubt it. It'd be more dangerous for me.'

'Well, yes. Look at that poor woman who got thrown into jail for no good reason. She was dual nationality, like you.'

'So, if it's more dangerous for me, MSF will be much less likely to send me there. You see? Simple.'

'Oh, Kamran!' cried Leila, close to tears. 'You wouldn't be so blasé about it if you knew what it was *like* there!'

Kamran said nothing; Daria could tell he was working hard to compose himself.

'Mum,' she said gently, 'he isn't going to Iran. Not now, probably never.'

'Promise me you'll never go!' said Leila. 'If they want to send you there, you say no. You quit if you have to. Please, Kamran. Will you promise?'

She extracted a begrudging promise from Kamran, then left the conversation, muttering that she had things to do. Ramin watched her go, and then turned back to the screen and shrugged.

'That went well,' said Kamran.

'It's just a shock,' said Ramin. 'She was expecting a different sort of announcement. I'd better go and talk to her. She'll come round.'

When Ramin had disconnected, Kamran and Daria carried on the conversation in English. It wasn't a spontaneous decision, he told her. He'd always planned to apply to Médecins Sans Frontières when he had enough experience. It had been an underlying source of tension with Lily, a midwife, who thought there were plenty of ways to do good in the world without putting your own life in danger. He'd tried to persuade her to come with him, but she had categorically refused. The arguments were long and bitter. What about starting a family? she kept saying. Did he want them to start a family in fucking *Aleppo*? Eventually they had admitted that the lives they envisaged for themselves were too different to be reconciled.

Daria listened sadly. 'I'm so sorry,' she said when he had finished. 'Really. I don't know what to say.'

'What is there to say?' said Kamran. 'It sucks.'

'When are you leaving?'

'End of September. I've got a week of training in London first. Then I'm off.'

'That's really soon.'

'Yup,' said Kamran, and laughed, as if it was all ridiculous. 'And I've got so much shit to sort out first.'

'Well?' said Diane when Daria went back downstairs. Jim and Emily looked up at her expectantly. Immediately Daria regretted having gone into the living room before she'd had a chance to take Emily to one side and tell her on her own. She wished she had texted from the spare room and told her to come upstairs.

'It wasn't quite what we were expecting,' she said.

'Oh?'

'No wedding, no babies. They've split up.' The room erupted in a chorus of sympathy and dismay. 'And that's not all. He's leaving the country. He's got a job with Médecins Sans Frontières. They're sending him to Bangladesh.'

'Good Lord,' said Jim.

'Bangladesh?' said Diane. 'Why on earth does he want to go there?'

'To help the Rohingya.'

'The who?'

'Refugees,' said Daria, too distracted to explain further.

'Gosh,' said Diane, looking back down at the *Radio Times*. 'Very adventurous.'

'How long's he going for?' said Emily.

'Six months, initially,' said Daria, meeting Emily's eye. 'Maybe longer.' There was a change in Emily's expression, too subtle for anyone else to detect. Daria stayed standing, fielding Jim's questions until a gap in the conversation gave her the opportunity to leave.

'I'm going to bed,' she said, and turned to Emily. 'Coming?'

Upstairs Emily flopped onto the bed and groaned. 'Did you have any idea about this?' she said.

'None whatsoever. I'd have mentioned it otherwise.'

'What did your parents say?'

'Dad was shocked at first, but proud. Mum was getting herself in a tizzy. Dad's going to talk to her.'

'Poor mama,' said Emily. 'Will she be okay, do you think?'

'Eventually, probably. Maybe. She can't understand why he wants to put himself in danger. And she's worried he'll end up in Iran and get put in prison.'

'Oh, shit. That's not likely, though, is it?'

'Well, no. MSF are hardly going to send a dual national to Iran when imprisoning dual nationals is, like, a major part of Iranian foreign policy.'

Emily nodded, saying nothing.

'Hopefully she'll chill out a bit,' continued Daria. 'It's not like he's joining the army. But you can see where she's coming from. One minute she's expecting him to make her a grandmother, the next he's fucking off to Bangladesh.'

'*We* were expecting him to make her a grandmother,' said Emily, tracing the pattern on the sheets with her finger.

Daria sighed. She lay down and put an arm across Emily's waist. 'I know,' she said. 'It's a bit of a spanner in the works, isn't it?'

'Little bit. What are we going to do?'

'Dunno,' said Daria, rolling onto her back and staring at the ceiling. 'Go to a clinic instead, I suppose. Stupid idiot. Why does he have to be such a good person?'

Emily propped herself up on her elbow. 'When did you say he was leaving?'

'End of September.'

'So what, four weeks? That's enough time.'

'Enough time for what?'

'For us to have one go.' Daria looked at her. Emily sat up, suddenly animated. She reached for her phone and tapped at it furiously with her thumbs. 'My period ended on Wednesday. Next one due late September. I'll probably be ovulating around the end of next week. Yeah, look!' She held up her phone so that Daria could see her fertility app. 'Ovulating Friday-ish to Sunday-ish. Saturday's probably the safest bet. That's handy.'

Daria sat up and leaned back against the pillows. 'Are you suggesting we ask him to be our donor in the midst of all this chaos? And then ask him to do a donation *next week*?'

'It's not ideal, obviously, but what else can we do? You know I don't want to use a sperm bank if we can avoid it.'

'We'll probably have to use a sperm bank regardless. It probably won't work the first time.'

'But it might!'

'Well, of course it might, but—'

'Then isn't it worth a try, Dar?'

'I thought we wanted to wait until we'd settled in. We've got to move house. You've got to find a job.'

'Circumstances change, though, don't they?' Emily was speaking quickly, flushed and wide-eyed. 'Obviously, he's your brother,' she continued, more soberly, and Daria wondered if it was her own expression that had extinguished the excitement. 'I know it's weird. We don't have to ask him if you really don't feel comfortable with it.'

Daria said nothing, but wrinkled her nose. She took Emily's hand and squeezed it. 'I've got to get past the weirdness, though, haven't I?' she said. 'Okay. I'll ask. I'll give him a ring tomorrow.'

In bed that night Daria was afraid. Not for any sensible reason – not for Kamran, who might actually be about to endanger himself, but for Emily, who was planning to undergo something that Daria knew to be ordinary but felt to be barbaric. For herself too, because she would have to bear witness to this everyday barbarism, possibly from as early as next week.

She reminded herself that pregnancy happened all the time, and was a reason for joy. For *joy*, Daria, she scolded herself, and if not joy, acceptance, because it's just what has to happen if you want a baby, *which you do*. She even wanted babies, plural. Her desire for a family had not announced itself suddenly or stridently like Emily's had; nevertheless, when she imagined the future there were always children in it. The problem was that nature had devised such a bloodthirsty method of getting them into the world that it made her stomach churn and her heart race and her breath come fast to think of it. And her most precious person, her beloved, whom she had sworn to look after, actively *wanted* to undergo such violence, wanted *nothing* so much as to be maimed and mutilated and ripped open in the name of continuing the species.

Though desperate to swoop in and save Emily from herself, Daria had kept quiet. She hadn't lied, exactly, but she had played everything down, pretending she found childbirth grimace inducing as opposed to panic-attack inducing, and that the most extreme manifestation of her distaste was her unwillingness to ever be pregnant herself. She had disguised her true feelings so successfully that Emily still hoped she might be talked into carrying their second child. Emily herself had bought into the idea of pregnancy as a process both beautiful and benign, lovingly overseen by Mother Nature. It was curious, Daria thought, the way people liked to characterise Nature as a benevolent matriarch rather than as a violent misogynist who ought to be in jail.

She had made subtle attempts at steering Emily towards adoption, framing it as a moral crusade for innocent children in need of loving homes. But this was entirely futile because Emily was now at the behest of an impulse that left no room for negotiation. I'm sorry but I just really want to be pregnant, Daria, she said, with finality. It's not rational, it's instinctive.

It was Emily who had suggested they ask Kamran to be their sperm donor. Daria was less than delighted by the thought of administering semen produced by her own brother, but she did like the idea of being related to the baby. Secretly she expected Kamran to agree, because he had also suggested it himself, tipsily but with sincerity, over a shared cigarette at Leila's sixtieth birthday party. She had never revealed this information to Emily, because Emily would have wanted to act on it immediately, when what Daria needed was time. She had diagnosed herself with primary tokophobia, or a pathological fear of pregnancy and childbirth in women who had never experienced either, and she planned to get over it. She would work hard, she would talk to a stranger about her childhood, she would take any and all drugs prescribed – whatever was necessary to stop herself running away at the crucial moment, leaving Emily scared and alone and in pain.

But it was all moving faster than she'd expected. How was she to give a pregnancy the welcome it deserved when she hadn't had a chance to have any therapy? And how was she to find a therapist when they were about to move house? She lay awake for hours that night, doing mindfulness and lying-down yoga sequences to no avail. She couldn't escape the knowledge that what she wanted most was for Emily to get her period next month, and the thought made her heavy with guilt.

7

HAZEL'S FAVOURITE CUSTOMER clasped her hands to her ample bosom and cried, 'Oh, Hazel! I meant to tell you, I so enjoyed the cartoon today!'

'Really? Thanks, Irma!' said Hazel, who had been furtively checking her Instagram for likes all morning.

'*Very* apt,' continued Irma. 'I was *cringing*. Really just so—' She made a noise to indicate inarticulable horror. 'And of course you don't use the actual word, do you? I had to look it up.' She leaned in closer, lowering her voice. '*Queefing*! What a fantastic word! *Queef*! In German it's very boring. *Scheidenwind*. There's no poetry. Oh, gosh,' she exclaimed, as the customer behind her cleared his throat. 'Almond milk latte, please. Two shots.'

Hazel made the latte and Irma picked up her cup and saucer with both hands, scanning the room for a table.

'Irma,' said Nish, when the man behind her had been served, and Irma turned back. Nish put his elbows on the counter, rested his chin in his hands and said, 'Have you ever actually …? You know.'

Irma took a second to comprehend, and then she roared with laughter. 'What an impertinent question! Is he always like this?' Hazel nodded; Irma tutted. 'How about I tell you I've had three babies, and leave it at that?'

'What's all this?' said Roisin, appearing with a tray of almond croissants and unloading them into a wooden crate by the till.

'We're talking about queefing in yoga,' said Nish. 'And Irma's experience thereof.'

Roisin looked up, astonished. 'Is that a thing?'

'It sounds to me like you haven't read your friend's cartoon,' said Irma gravely. 'Otherwise you'd know.'

Roisin turned to Hazel. 'So it's a thing?'

Hazel cleared her throat. 'Can be a thing, yeah.'

'Wow.' Roisin was the sort of person whose body always behaved exactly as she told it to. Probably she had never done a rancid fart, or a drooling sneeze, or made a panicked attempt to smell her own breath.

'How does it even happen?' said Nish. 'Educate me.'

'Basically,' said Hazel, 'when you turn upside down in yoga—'

'Or Pilates,' said Irma.

'—or Pilates, yeah – all your organs sort of flump towards your head. It creates a little vacuum around your ...' She hesitated, mindful of customers.

'Cunt?' suggested Roisin.

'Right, so anyway, the air rushes in, and then you turn up the right way and it gets squeezed out again. Makes a farting noise. Which everyone can hear.'

'My God,' said Nish. 'So it's kind of like a vaginal *breath*? There's something quite earthy and spiritual about that, isn't there?'

'Oh my, yes!' cried Irma, who hadn't even flinched at

Roisin's profanity. 'Now that's an interesting idea. Gosh. That gives me lots to reflect on.' She stared pensively into the middle distance, then turned away and moved slowly across the café, trying not to spill her coffee.

'Good work,' said Hazel to Nish. 'That'll be on the blog next week.' Irma's blog was a compendium of spiritual musings, medical conspiracy theories and warnings against unproven carcinogens, to which Hazel felt obliged to sub-scribe because Irma followed her webcomic so religiously.

Roisin returned her tray to the kitchen and came back looking down at her phone. 'Fucking hell,' she said, laugh-ing. 'Has this actually happened to you?'

Hazel peered at the phone and saw her own cartoon filling the screen. 'I embellished it a bit, obviously. But essentially, yes. What?' she cried, looking at Roisin's bemused face. 'Don't tell me you've never queefed before.'

'I suppose I must have done,' said Roisin. 'But somehow never in public.'

'Well, la-di-da,' said Hazel.

'Ro's made of porcelain, aren't you, babe?' said Nish, hugging Roisin from behind. 'She doesn't poo either,' he whispered.

Hazel laughed loudly; Roisin swatted him away, and a round of noisy verbal jousting ensued until someone said: 'Excuse me? Guys? Hello?'

Hazel looked around. It was Brandon Fox.

'Oh,' was all she said. She thought back rapidly through the conversation of the night before, trying to remember telling him where she worked. She might have told him the name of the café; he must have googled the rest.

'Yeah, hi, Hazel,' said Brandon. 'How's the friend?'

'Sorry?'

'The friend who got the shitty news.'

She sensed Nish behind her, trying to make himself inconspicuous. 'Oh, right,' she said. 'So-so. Thanks for asking.'

'I'll keep this brief,' he said. From the pocket of his jeans he pulled out a small white envelope, so crumpled that a hole had started to rip in the corner, and slid it over the counter towards her.

'I wonder if you'd mind passing that on,' he said, and registering her puzzlement, added: 'To your sister.'

'My sister?' She picked up the envelope; nothing was written on it, back or front.

'She left it at my parents' house,' Brandon explained. 'Years ago, now. I've been keeping it safe, just in case. I thought she might like it back one day.'

'Right,' said Hazel. 'Sure. Okay.'

'I'd also like a skinny flat white to go.' He looked at his watch and sucked in air through his teeth. 'Ooh, quick as poss, actually. I'm running a bit behind.'

Hazel made his coffee as slowly as she could. When he'd gone Roisin and Nish gathered around while she investigated the envelope. It was sealed, but she could feel a small, hard object inside, which probably explained the tear in the paper. She slid her finger into the hole to make it bigger, and tilted the envelope so that the object moved towards it. It was a ring: an opaque green stone set in a silver band. Behind it, on a scrap of lined paper, was a collection of digits belonging to what she could only imagine was Brandon's phone number.

*

'A *what*?' said Emily into her phone, thinking she'd misheard.

'A ring,' came Hazel's voice. 'Can I open the envelope?'

'Of course!' said Emily impatiently, and there was a sound of paper ripping at the other end of the line.

'Yep,' said Hazel. 'Silver band, green stone.'

'And it's mine, is it?'

'Apparently you left it at his parents' house years ago.'

'Right, well, I haven't exactly missed it. I can't believe he kept it all this time. What a weirdo.'

'It gets better,' said Hazel. 'There's a note here. "Hope this isn't too bold, but give me a buzz if you ever fancy a coffee." And his number.'

Emily screeched in astonishment. 'Are you serious? No. You're joking, aren't you? Hazel?'

'I'm deadly serious,' replied Hazel, beginning to laugh. 'I swear.'

Emily made a spluttering noise. 'Unbelievable!' she cried. 'Right after he went on a date with you!'

'I know, rude! And I told him you were married!'

'Oh, *well*,' cackled Emily. 'It's only a *lesbian* marriage, isn't it? I bet he thinks I'm gagging for some cock. Send me a picture, I want to see which ring it is.'

The photo was badly lit and the ring was half obscured by the folds of Hazel's duvet cover, but Emily recognised it. At the sight of it she laughed out loud, and then drew in her breath, feeling suddenly like crying. Of course it was *that* ring. How quickly and surely the years must have passed, that she hadn't guessed it herself.

She got up from the bed and went down to the kitchen, where something was bubbling in a pot on the stove. Diane was at the sink, washing the chopping board.

'Hello, love,' she said. 'I'm making a vegan bolognese with that whatnot mince you showed me. Will that do you?'

'It sounds delicious, Mum,' said Emily. The arrival of two vegan houseguests had been a source of anxiety for her mother, who had always considered meatless cooking a practice too arcane to be attempted, but who was equally incapable of allowing her visitors to cook for themselves. To Emily's relief, she had risen to the challenge: last week a recipe for vegan chocolate cake had been left open on the family computer, and she had even been prevailed upon to fry some tofu. At the dinner table, however, she and Jim always made their meals more palatable by sprinkling some form of animalia over the top. A block of cheese and a packet of shredded ham hock sat on the countertop, ready to adorn the bolognese.

'Mum,' said Emily, 'would you mind if I had a quick look in the loft?'

'Dinner'll be ready in a minute.'

'Actually a minute?'

'Well, fifteen,' Diane conceded. 'What do you want up there, though, love? It's all in a muddle.'

'I just wanted something out of one of my boxes.' The boxes were full of non-essential items that had been stowed there before the move to Australia. 'I know which box it is. I labelled them all.'

'Well, I suppose,' said her mother. 'Ask your dad to help you with that ladder, though.'

The box was taped shut, with her name and the word 'accessories' scrawled on it in marker pen. Inside was a mess of clutch bags, belts and pairs of knotted tights; another, smaller box was nestled amongst some silk scarves. She

54

took it out and opened it. This was where she kept all the jewellery she never wore but couldn't bear to throw away: a pair of amber earrings belonging to her great-aunt; the cheap gold chain she'd worn with her bridesmaid's dress in the mid-nineties; a collection of beloved beads that she intended, one day, to re-thread. And a ring.

It had a light green stone set in a silver band, exactly like the one in the photo. The only difference, she remembered as she looked at it, was that this one had a grain of paler green that cut across the stone. The ring Brandon wanted her to have was not hers at all, then, but the near-identical one that belonged to his sister. Trust him, she thought, to have noticed the ring on her hand but not its twin, on Hannah's.

She and Hannah had bought the rings on a day trip to Brighton when they were nineteen, perhaps twenty. Hannah had picked hers out from a jewellery stand on the Lanes. Emily had envied it; Hannah had suggested she get one too.

'Then we'll have a souvenir from today,' she said, and this was meaningful because Emily had said 'I love you' for the first time that morning, and Hannah had said it back. After that they wore their rings religiously. Emily only took hers off two summers later, when the relationship came to a tearful end over Skype. Hannah must have assumed hers was lost, if she'd ever thought of it at all.

After dinner, Emily lay on the larger of her parents' two sofas and looked Hannah up on social media. Her parents were on the other sofa, watching reruns of *Blue Planet*. Daria was upstairs working, and possibly also phoning Kamran, although she hadn't said so.

In her Facebook profile photo Hannah held a baby over her head and stared up at it, laughing. It wasn't clear whether or not it was her baby, although the volume of likes suggested that it probably was. A stud glinted in her nose and a single silver earring dangled almost to her shoulder; a sweep of short messy hair, peppered with grey, fell across her forehead. Her cover photo was of a line of people standing behind an Extinction Rebellion banner. According to the *About* tab, she lived in London and worked somewhere called Heron Studios.

After Facebook Emily looked on Twitter, but all she learned was that Hannah rarely tweeted, and when she did she only retweeted, mostly graphs and articles about climate change. Then she tried Instagram: here Hannah was much more active. There were pictures of her and another woman in matching white trouser suits, a friend reading at a spoken word evening, some graffiti in Lisbon, a view of South London from a rooftop bar.

It occurred to her then that Alfie might be on Instagram too. She found his profile easily, but his contributions were minimal and generic: a few of friends, a couple of barbecue-in-the-park shots, the Thames seen from Waterloo Bridge. There was also a back-catalogue of selfies with a red-haired woman, but these had stopped abruptly about six months earlier. Facebook revealed him to be the sort of person who shared articles about child poverty and petitions to ban superfluous plastic. He rarely wrote anything to accompany these posts, the most recent exception being an articulate, angry paragraph about Grenfell Tower. Hazel, she concluded, putting her phone down on her stomach, could do an awful lot worse.

She felt her eyes growing heavy and thought about getting up and going to bed. But she was low on willpower, and she didn't want to disturb Daria, who might be in the middle of a sensitive conversation. She picked her phone up again and rapidly found herself back on Hannah's Facebook profile. She swiped through the photos, which went back further than the ones on Instagram – ten years, even longer. She swiped and swiped.

Eventually she started seeing photos of herself. There were dozens of them, all unflattering, all pre-dating filters. There she was with Hannah, white-faced and red-eyed at a Harry Potter student union night; here they were with Hannah's housemates in a brightly lit kitchen, and now just the two of them – a selfie in the winter sun, Brighton pier in the background, their broad grins just visible over their scarves.

The soundtrack to *Blue Planet* had been ominous for some time; now it built to a climactic frenzy. A predator was closing in on its prey. Emily turned to watch, and as she adjusted her position she loosened her grip on her phone – not enough for it to fall, but enough for her fingers to brush against the screen. When she looked at it again, the prey having died a brutal death, she saw that she had accidentally tapped the 'like' icon on one of the photos.

'Fuck,' she whispered. She tapped it again to undo it, but the damage was done. Hannah would be notified that Emily Phillips had liked her photo, and she would look to see which photo it was, and when she saw which photo it was, and that the like was no longer there, she would know that Emily Phillips had Facebook-stalked her back to 2006, and that she had liked the photo by accident, and then tried to cover her tracks.

Emily got up, thrust her phone into her pocket and trudged upstairs. Nothing good ever came of wasting time on social media. She knew that, and she'd done it anyway.

She met Daria on the landing, heading the other way. 'I was just coming to find you,' Daria said urgently, drawing Emily into the bedroom.

'Oh?'

'I asked him,' said Daria, and Emily forgot about Hannah in an instant. 'He's up for it, in principle. The thing is, he doesn't think it's possible to get the full set of sexual heath tests in time.'

'Really? I thought there was a way to do it quickly.'

'Some of them, yeah. Not all of them. Some of them take a couple of weeks.'

'Oh,' said Emily, trying not to let her disappointment show.

'He says he could get whatever tests he can,' Daria admitted, knowing precisely how disappointed Emily was. 'Then if anything comes back positive after we've done it, he'll let us know and you can go to the doctor. It's up to you whether you want to take the risk.'

Emily considered this. 'He and Lily were monogamous, right?'

'To the best of his knowledge.'

'I can't imagine Lily would have cheated on him.'

'Doesn't seem likely. But you never know.'

'Do you think it's a risk worth taking, then?' said Emily.

'I don't know. Do you?' said Daria, hoping, rather than believing, that Emily might be deterred. Emily frowned, looking thoughtful, then met Daria's eye, a smile wavering at the corner of her mouth.

'I think the odds are probably in our favour, don't you?'

'Maybe. I guess.'

'Fuck it, Daria, let's just do it. Shall we do it?'

Daria looked at Emily, now wide-eyed and childlike with excitement. There was really only one possible answer.

'Okay,' she said.

8

'SO I HAD a message from my sister,' said Hazel to Alfie. 'She was wondering if you might be interested in helping her and Daria move house.' They were in the kitchen, cooking pasta in two separate pans. Two separate jars of sauce stood open and waiting on the counter. 'I'm helping too,' Hazel went on. 'She's selling it as a fun activity for us all to do together, which is obviously bullshit. She says they'll pay you and buy you dinner. Don't feel like you have to say yes.'

Alfie was surprised, but flattered to have been asked. 'I don't know, could be fun,' he said. 'When?' Hazel told him the date and he consulted the calendar on his phone. 'I haven't got plans for that weekend. Sure, why not?'

'Okay,' said Hazel, as if she didn't quite believe him. 'You know, if you don't want to, you can just say. We can think of an excuse to tell Emily.'

'Why, do you not want me to?'

'It's not that I don't want you to per se, I just don't want you to if you'd rather not.'

'Well, I don't want to do it if *you'd* rather I didn't.'

Hazel paused to contemplate the knot into which they had tied themselves. 'I don't *not* want you to,' she said, hoping to clarify things, but only pulling it tighter. Alfie turned around to look at her. She avoided eye contact, pointlessly stirring the pasta as it boiled.

'Do you want me to, yes or no?' said Alfie, feeling as though there was a great deal at stake in this question.

'I don't want you to say yes out of politeness,' said Hazel, still stirring. 'I don't want you to feel pressured into it. I don't want you to feel you have to and then resent it.'

'And if I don't feel any of those things?'

'Well, then that's great.'

Alfie sighed internally and opened the cupboard to look for the colander. It wasn't there; nothing in this kitchen got put away in the same place twice. 'So,' he said, opening another cupboard and then another, making an effort to sound nonchalant, 'you wouldn't mind me coming?'

'Why would I mind?'

'Don't know.' He let the real answer hang unspoken in the air. 'For fuck's sake, it's here,' he exclaimed, finding the colander in the sink, soaking in greasy water.

'Must have been Tony,' said Hazel. She was chopping tomatoes now.

It had actually been Alfie himself; he remembered now, and felt embarrassed. He washed the colander under the tap and said nothing.

'So with the moving thing,' said Hazel, as he dried it. 'Emily and Daria are buying a car. The plan is that one of them will drive it and the other one will drive the van. They've got most of their stuff in a big storage unit somewhere in Bromley. So we can meet them there, help them load up, drive to Norwich, unload, and get the train back in the morning.'

'So one of us goes with Daria and the other goes with Emily?'

'Yeah.'

'Right.' Alfie put the clean colander on the worktop and turned the heat off under his pasta, hoping his disappointment didn't show.

Hazel watched him out of the corner of her eye, filling in the details she could not clearly see. He was wearing a blue T-shirt and a pair of tracksuit bottoms. He had his glasses on, big rectangular ones with red frames. His stomach curved outwards, but only very slightly. His arm stretched more directly into her line of vision, the fine bones in his hands flexing as he lifted the saucepan. Carpe fucking diem, she thought, and blurted out his name.

'Yes?' he said.

'I didn't answer your question properly before. I meant to say yes. I want you to come. I'd like you to be there. I wouldn't have mentioned it if I didn't.'

Alfie grinned. 'Good,' he said. 'Because I want to come too.' She looked around at him, the first time that evening she'd made eye contact. He guessed that if he leaned in to kiss her she would reciprocate. Perhaps he should do it. The moment was now – only it was passing, probably it was already gone. It was the kitchen, was the thing, *their* kitchen, and unlike last time, neither of them were drunk.

'You'd better drain your pasta,' said Hazel.

'Shit, yeah.' The sink made a clunking noise under the weight of the water. Steam rose and dampened his forehead.

'Hey,' he said, setting the pan down on the countertop, 'check this out.' He leaned over to pluck two cherry tomatoes from the plant on the kitchen windowsill and held them up triumphantly, one between each thumb and forefinger.

'Look at that!' cried Hazel, applauding. 'Good job!' The tomatoes had taken a full two weeks to ripen; their siblings on the vine remained determinedly green and hard.

'One for you,' said Alfie, putting the larger of the two on the side of Hazel's plate, 'and one for me.' He popped his own into his mouth; Hazel did likewise, with hers.

'Oh,' said Alfie. 'Oh, no.'

'It's good!' protested Hazel. 'Just a tiny bit – what's that word? Mealy?'

Alfie grimaced. 'I think the only thing really missing,' he said, 'is flavour. Otherwise, no complaints.'

Their eyes met, and they burst into peals of laughter. Alfie stirred in his pesto and sat down at the table, opposite Hazel.

'A valiant attempt, though, honestly,' she said. 'And look at that plant! It really improves the place, aesthetically speaking.'

'One day I'll have a garden,' he said. 'Then I'll do it properly.'

'Of course you will,' said Hazel. 'You'll do it *brilliantly*.' She had no doubt that this was true, and the thought depressed her a little. Alfie was only passing through on his way to better things. A lot would have to change before *she* could contemplate moving somewhere with a garden. She was likely to remain in this flat indefinitely, in fact, unless she accepted defeat and went back to working in an office. Where was the boundary between aspiring illustrator and failed illustrator? she wondered. How would she know when she had crossed it?

'You okay?' said Alfie.

She blinked, and looked at him. 'Fine!'

'Yours looks better than mine,' he said, nodding at her plate.

'Well, it's got more stuff in. You've got a nicer sauce, though.' He shrugged his assent. He had called by Waitrose on his way back from meeting Clara.

'Oh, by the way,' he said, his thoughts returning to that evening, 'how was your date?'

Hazel groaned. 'Terrible,' she said through a mouthful of pasta. 'A mistake.' She did not tell him about Brandon Fox's enduring crush on her sister. She was disinclined to dwell on it. She was no longer sure why she had been on a date at all.

Alfie was waiting for her to elaborate. But when she had finished her mouthful she loaded her fork and took another one, leaving him to draw his own conclusions. He wondered if 'terrible' referred to the date itself or the sex that had followed. She hadn't come home that night, so probably the latter. A 'mistake' – that as good as confirmed it. 'Mistake' was a loaded word. He did not take much comfort from her unfavourable verdict; what struck him was her willingness to do it in the first place, when he had been thinking of no one but her.

'What about you?' said Hazel. 'Have you been up to anything exciting lately?' She winced at her own inanity, her obvious desperation.

'Not much,' said Alfie. 'I've been planning for next term, and then just frittering away my free time, really. I met up with a friend the other night. Well, my ex, technically.'

'Oh,' said Hazel, wondering what she was supposed to do with this information.

'Yeah,' said Alfie, wondering why he had offered it. In his head it had sounded mysterious and intriguing; out loud it sounded smug, a pointless boast.

'Did you have a nice time?' said Hazel.

'Yeah, quite nice. We just went for a drink, had a catch-up, you know.' Hazel didn't say anything, and nor did he, and suddenly it occurred to him that Hazel might be finding meaning in this silence, meaning that was not there. 'There's nothing—' he began, but at the same time she said, 'Well, that's me done.'

She stood up abruptly, scraped the last of her pasta into the bin and piled up her plate and saucepan next to the sink. 'I'll wash up later, I promise. Sorry, were you going to say something?'

The moment's pause had given him cold feet. It was quite likely that she didn't care either way about the precise nature of his relationship with Clara. He hesitated. She folded her arms – impatiently, he thought.

'Nah,' he said, picking up his plate and moving towards the sink. 'Nothing.'

In her room, Hazel threw herself back against the cushions on her bed and lay there, bouncing gently, listening to the squeak of the springs. She stared up at the Artex, which collected in little bumps in this room rather than in sweeps and swirls like it did in Alfie's. Why had he dropped his ex into the conversation like that? It was as if he'd got her to talk about her date in order to grant himself permission to talk about his own.

It might not have been a date – it might have been a genuine case of meeting up with a friend, because Alfie was just that sort of guy, reasonable and level-headed enough to stay on good terms with his exes, not one to bear grudges or harbour resentments, and perhaps this was the message he had been trying to convey, and perhaps this message was part of a broader strategy to win her, Hazel, over.

But this line of thinking was rooted in vanity, not reason. Reason told her that if he'd wanted to win her over he wouldn't have gone near such a topic. More likely this ex was the woman she'd heard moaning in ecstasy the other week, or else she was *the* ex, Rachel Brightman, whose elfin features haunted his social media profiles and who had, likely as not, broken his heart. Probably this had been Alfie's way of telling her that their night together was in the past, and would remain there. After all, why on earth would he want anything more? She was a hopeless case. She was twenty-eight and she worked in a fucking *café*.

Her phone buzzed in her pocket. There were various messages waiting for her from Emily, jostling her for an answer about the move. If Alfie couldn't help she would ask their father instead. Hazel could see it: Jim taking the lead, thinking he was in charge, leaping out of the van to direct it into a parking space, delaying proceedings with advice about how best to lift things. She could feel the exasperation as keenly as if it was already happening. But if Alfie was there it would be awkward, which was worse. She was almost certain that Emily had only suggested he come because she thought she'd detected a hint of chemistry between them and wanted to play Cupid.

As she was deliberating over what to write, a Tinder notification slid down from the top of the screen. 'You haven't swiped in a while,' it said. 'Your profile will be hidden starting tomorrow. Swipe now to stay visible.' She had been on hiatus from Tinder, but now she felt the pull of intrigue. A date might not be so bad. A date might be just the thing. She had another notification too, an old one that she'd been ignoring, had stopped seeing, even. She looked at it now with fresh eyes. Somebody liked her, it said. Swipe right to find out who.

She opened Tinder and perused it for a while. It was disappointing. Everyone was trying too hard. Even the most attractive people let themselves down with self-aggrandising little spiels beneath their pictures that veered towards one of two poles, generic or pretentious. None of them was an Alfie. She wondered if Alfie himself would have been an Alfie if she had first encountered him in this way, given that his very Alfieness – the bubbling humour in his gestures, the eyebrow twitch when something amused him, the particular quality of his laugh – would have been impossible to convey. But there surely would have been *something* about him. Some clue, some hint of charm or originality. These people had no substance, no soul. They were empty boxes wrapped in shiny paper.

She was on the point of giving up when a picture appeared of a man whose face was half covered by an analogue camera, a black and silver Leica turned on its side, his finger poised to press the shutter. His one visible eye was closed, but he was grinning broadly. It was like a perfume ad: monochrome, high resolution, showing up a carefully cultivated crop of stubble, a dimple, and the slightest shadow beneath his cheekbone. In the second of his pictures he sat on a stool, laughing, another camera – a different one – on his lap. His hair was dark and he wore it swept up into a little bun. This picture, like the first, had been taken by a professional. Was he a model, then? If he wasn't, he could have been.

The other photos were less staged. In one he was sitting outside on the ground, wearing a hoodie and a scarf, an enamel mug in his hand. In another he was on a towpath, pointing and grinning at a canal boat that was also a second-hand bookshop. In the final picture he was crouching next to an enormous spider plant, several times larger than his own head, his face frozen in mock terror.

Beneath the pictures she read:

Miles, 29

Photographer. Londoner. Wannabe sourdough wizard. Fairweather runner. Incorrigible stone skimmer. Patti Smith fanboy. Houseplant dad. (Fave child: Joanna the spider plant. See pic. She huge.)

He sat more towards the pretentious end of the spectrum, that was clear, but she would take that over the generic end, if those were the only choices. Anyway, with a face like his, he could be forgiven all manner of sins. He was uncommonly attractive, a full ten. She swiped right.

Shortly afterwards Tinder notified her that she and Miles had matched. She felt herself smiling. So he liked her back. He was hot – objectively, head-turningly hot, and he liked her back. Actually, he had liked her *first*. Did that mean she was an equal rank of hotness? It wouldn't be illogical to assume so. Take that, Alfie.

Thinking of Alfie reminded her that Emily was waiting on an answer. She went back to WhatsApp and wrote, *Alfie says happy to help.* After all, why shouldn't he come? She had armour now. She was a hottie. Two point six miles away was another hottie who could vouch for it.

9

'THAT'S GOOD,' SAID Emily, wiping her face with a cotton wool pad and reading her phone at the same time. 'Alfie's going to help us out with the move.'

Daria was brushing her teeth and did not answer. She showed no sign of even having heard. She continued brushing, spat, rinsed her brush, scooped water into her mouth, gargled, spat again. 'Great,' she said eventually, with no expression in her voice at all.

All week she had been tense and irritable. Much of what she said was shot through with an undertone of exasperation. On Wednesday evening she had snapped at Emily for buying a new head of broccoli when there was one in the fridge already. On the train yesterday she had put her headphones on and closed her eyes and travelled like that all the way to Manchester, even though Emily could tell she wasn't really asleep. She cheered up when they arrived, happy to see her brother; the three of them had ordered a curry and drunk a bottle of wine. But now the strange mood was back.

The only explanation Emily could think of was that Daria was perturbed, more so than she would admit, by the thought of seeing Kamran's ejaculate. And fair enough: the act of insemination meant bringing her family into their bedroom; it meant enabling a strange indirect union between the genitalia of her brother and her wife. Emily couldn't imagine involving Hazel in an act of such intimacy. The thought was hilarious and horrifying. But she couldn't imagine it causing a mood of such sullenness or longevity either. Something else was going on.

In the morning Emily woke early. She lay on her back, listening to Daria breathing. The room was dingy; it was darker in the mornings now. She could hear Kamran moving about the flat, but although she enjoyed his company she didn't like the idea of being alone with him today, scrabbling around for something to talk about in full awareness of the task that lay ahead.

Instead she went to the bathroom and showered, and by the time she came out Daria was blinking awake. Emily leaned over to kiss her, smiling, and Daria smiled too, the tension gone from her face. But as Emily stood up straight again she burrowed back under the duvet, frowning slightly. Whatever it was that had been bothering her, she had remembered it.

The smell of coffee lured them out of the bedroom. Kamran was sitting on the sofa with his laptop open, wearing a T-shirt and pyjama bottoms.

'Morning,' he said, nodding towards a large cafetière, two-thirds full, on the kitchen counter. Daria flopped in an armchair and Emily poured the remaining coffee into two mugs.

'So,' said Daria. She took the mug of coffee Emily was handing her and stretched out her bare foot to prod Kamran in the knee.

Kamran grinned, stretched, shut his laptop. 'Yeah,' he said.

'How shall we do this?'

'You tell me.'

'I guess it's probably best to get it done as soon as possible, right?' Daria looked towards Emily, who nodded. 'When suits you?'

'Literally whenever,' said Kamran.

'Okay, I'll have a shower after breakfast. We'll go out for a walk and you can...' She waved her hand.

'Don't go for a walk on my account,' said Kamran. 'It's not necessary.'

Daria wrinkled her nose. 'Good for you,' she said. 'We'll go on our own account.'

They walked a route around Kamran's neighbourhood that took them down residential streets of terraced houses not dissimilar to the one they had rented in Norwich. At the end of one of these streets was a park, as Kamran had said there would be, and they did two laps of it, past a wide, shallow pond and a crowd of unwashed men swigging from lager cans. At one end was a play area crowded with children, crawling up scramble nets and sliding down slides, yelling at each other, chasing each other, falling over and getting up again. Parents clumped together on benches and at the boundary fence, talking and reading their phones, some with babies strapped to their fronts. Emily observed the scene with a throb of longing.

Longing had been a familiar feeling to her ever since the fateful dinner party in Melbourne, when a cuddle with someone's unsuspecting toddler had unleashed a sluice-tide of maternal urges. When they got home that evening she had wept for twenty minutes straight, astonishing both herself and Daria. Suddenly, and entirely without her permission, the lens through which she viewed the world had been swapped for a different one, drawing a bold line between the time before and the time after.

In the time before, she had thought of motherhood with ambivalence. 'Do I want kids?' was a question with a rotating cast of answers. Yes, definitely. Yes, but. Actually, maybe not. There was much to be gained (meaning, purpose, love); also much to be lost (sleep, liberty, brain cells). She imagined a beautiful, smiling infant, crawling into bed with them on Sunday mornings. Then she pictured a red-faced, angry infant, supine in some shop or other, bashing its fists and heels on the floor. The yeses vied for dominance with the noes, both camps equally matched.

In the time before, she had contemplated the kind of future that awaited any child born at this moment in history, and felt the No camp swelling to engulf its rival. She had pictured a world ravaged by uncontrollable climate change and concluded that people who procreated these days must be doing so in a state of blissful denial. It wasn't even accurate to call it climate change any more. There had been ominous changes in the terminology among certain sorts of people and publications; now it was climate *breakdown*, global *heating*. Her parents, if they ever read such publications or listened to such people, would be calling this *scaremongering*, as if the fear arose from the words used to describe the problem, rather than the stark facts of the problem itself. She herself had read several books about it. She knew there would be fire, fever, heat death, biblical floods, mass displacement, conflict, and if things continued the way they were going, extinction.

In the time after, she had driven herself mad trying to reconcile this knowledge with her non-negotiable desire to be a mother, before eventually resolving not to think about it. After all, nothing was certain. Who could say what lay ahead? The worst might not come to pass. Having a child would be an expression of hope. She wasn't naive, she wasn't one of those people who believed they would always live as they lived now; she was just refusing to be cowed by things that hadn't yet happened.

How wonderful! people would say, if they knew what she was planning. No one would say, Are you sure you want to have a baby when it might not have a future? any more than they'd say, Are you sure you want to have a baby when it might get cancer one day? Only rarely did people talk about the crisis as something so huge it gave you cause to rethink the trajectory of your life. Still, they were right, it *would* be wonderful, in the sort of simple, primal way that couldn't be undermined by fear or disputed by rational argument. It would be wonderful in the same way it was wonderful to have any of your primary human needs met, in the same way it was wonderful to be alive.

Kamran was waiting for them when they got back to the flat. 'I've got it in here,' he said, indicating the large front pocket of his hoodie.

'Right,' said Daria. 'Em, you'd better go and get ready.'

Emily shut herself in the spare bedroom and took off

her jeans and underwear. She spread a towel out over a pillow and lay on the bed with it propped beneath her rear end. The room was cold, so she arranged the duvet over her thighs.

'Ready!' she called, and Daria appeared moments later, holding a small plastic pot between thumb and forefinger.

'I think he's dripped some down the outside,' she muttered. With her other hand she opened her suitcase and took out an oral syringe, still in its packet. 'Let's get this over with, shall we?'

Emily winced. She opened her mouth to respond and then immediately reconsidered. She stared at the ceiling, trying not to be annoyed, while Daria crouched at the end of the bed. But the short-sightedness, the inability to see past the gruesome corporality of what they were doing! It was another indicator of the strange funk Daria was in. This was quite possibly the moment they created another human being, the beginning of the rest of their lives. And she wanted it *over* with.

Daria opened the pot and positioned the syringe. Emily, bisected by the duvet, was only visible from the waist down. She was shifting uneasily and the hairs on her legs were standing on end. Daria looked at the vulva before her as if seeing it for the first time. It was unmistakably Emily and yet also somehow not quite Emily. The arrangement of flesh was faintly ghoulish, she thought suddenly, like the *Scream* mask.

Once she had noticed the resemblance she couldn't unsee it. It *was* like the *Scream* mask! How fitting! Except of course it was really the *Scream* mask that was like *it*. A coincidence, or unconscious misogyny? She ought to write this down; she might get a conference paper out of it. *The Violence of the Vulva: Female Genitalia as a Symbol of Death in Twentieth-Century Popular Culture.*

'Daria?' said Emily, lifting her head from the pillow. She was frowning.

'Sorry,' said Daria, coming back to herself. She tried to put the image out of her mind. 'Are you ready?'

'Never been readier,' said Emily, so cheerfully that Daria couldn't tell if she was faking or being deliberately sarcastic.

Emily kept her eyes on the light fitting as the syringe did its work unseen, and then Daria was standing up, the pot between thumb and forefinger again, empty now, the syringe sticking out of it like a teaspoon.

'If we ever have to do this again,' she said, 'remind me to get some surgical gloves.' She opened the door and went out. Emily heard the tap running in the bathroom next door. When Daria came back in she smiled, but with effort, Emily could tell.

'You okay?' said Daria.

'Yep, fine. Bit chilly.'

'You could get under the duvet.'

'I might.'

'You going to stay lying down for a bit, then?'

'Yeah.'

'Okay. I'll go back out, see Kam. Say thanks.'

'Oh,' said Emily. 'Okay.' Multiple sources on the internet advised orgasm after insemination; it was supposed to help the sperm on its way. She had been hoping Daria would oblige. She had packed a vibrator in readiness.

'Do you want me to stay?'

'No, it's fine.'

'Love you,' said Daria, planting a dry kiss on her forehead and moving away.

Stay, thought Emily, *stay here with me*, but Daria was already out of the door.

10

HAZEL ARRANGED TO meet Miles on a Tuesday, for a canal-side walk and a coffee. Neither of them were working that day, Hazel because it was her day off, and Miles because he was an artist who presumably worked when he chose. Hazel took the tube to Bethnal Green and walked up Mare Street to the canal bridge, where she spotted him leaning against the wall by the steps down to the water, lit up fetchingly in the autumn sun. He was reading a paperback with the cover curled back on itself. As she approached he took a pencil from behind his ear and closed the book over it, like a bookmark. It was in French, she now saw.

'You must be Hazel,' he said, smiling. His teeth were perhaps not so gleamingly white as his Tinder profile had promised, but otherwise all was present and correct: the bun, the dimples, the cheekbones. Nervous excitement collected in her lower belly.

'Miles,' she grinned. He leaned over to kiss her, his stubble scratchy on her cheek. 'So,' she said, standing back.

'So,' he repeated, as they ambled down the steps towards the towpath. 'It's really great to meet you.'

'You too. What are you reading?'

'Oh,' he said, looking at the book as if surprised to find it still in his hand. 'Modiano, *Dans le café de la jeunesse perdue*. He's the guy who won the Nobel prize a couple of years ago.'

'You speak French, then?' said Hazel, who had never heard the name Modiano in her life.

'*Oui, mais pas très bien*,' answered Miles with a self-effacing laugh. 'It's a bit more effort, but it's worth it. It really loses something in the translation.'

'Impressive. I practically failed GCSE French.'

'Oh God, me too. Everyone does. It's pointless, what they teach you. *Je joue au tennis, j'aime les animaux, j'ai un chien qui s'appelle Rover*.' He pronounced Rover the French way, Rovaire. Hazel giggled. 'No,' Miles went on, 'if you want to learn a language properly you've got to move to the country, get stuck in.'

'Have you lived in France, then?'

'Paris, yeah. I did my masters there.'

'Masters in what?'

He made quotation marks with his fingers. '*Arts plastiques et visuels*. Art, basically.'

'Oh, nice,' said Hazel. 'That sounds amazing.'

'Mmm,' said Miles uncertainly.

'No?'

'It was okay,' he replied, with a shrug. 'But I guess just not really for me.'

'Why's that? I'd have thought Paris would be a great place to study art.'

'You know what, Hazel? You've hit the nail on the head. Paris is brilliant if you want to *study* art. It's literally *the* place to be if you're into art history. My trouble is, I never really wanted to study art, I wanted to *make* it. And Paris ...' He shook his head and sighed. 'Don't get me wrong, it was the epicentre of the modern art scene for ages, and I have so much respect for that, but the long and short of it is those days are gone. I mean, it's okay. It's still Paris, after all. But it's not super in touch with the zeitgeist nowadays.'

'I see,' said Hazel, nodding slowly.

'I should have gone to Berlin,' Miles continued. 'They're much more open to my kind of stuff there.'

'And what kind of stuff is that?'

'Mixed media, I guess you'd call it. I mean, my first love is film photography, but I do a lot of digital stuff too, and a bit of painting, and I've got massively into soundscapes this year. It kind of depends on the idea. Certain ideas need to be expressed in certain ways, I find. It's important to stay open-minded.'

Hazel nodded. 'Right, yeah, of course,' she said, with deep feeling.

'And,' he began, falteringly, as if on the point of admitting something momentous, 'I may as well tell you, I do some freelancing too. Stock footage, commercial stuff, you know, just to keep the wolf from the door. Selling my soul. Just in case you thought I was, like, *artistically pure*. Ha ha.'

Hazel turned her head to look at him. He appeared genuinely remorseful. 'I'm not judging,' she said. 'Good for you. I'd sell my soul too, if anyone wanted to buy it.'

'Yeah?' He gave her a lopsided smile. 'Who to?'

'Oh, anyone, if they needed an illustrator. Corporate bad boys. Fossil fuel companies. Arms dealers.'

He laughed uproariously, and she grinned. Secretly she wasn't at all sure she would be capable of refusing such people if they actually approached her for illustration work, so it was fortunate that none of them ever would.

'I did have a little look at your webcomic, actually,' began Miles.

'Really? Oh, God.' She thought of her most recent post, which was even more brazen than the one Irma had so enjoyed.

'Hey, no, I liked it!' he cried. 'You're really talented. It was very … educational.'

'That's one word for it,' said Hazel, and they glanced at each other, smiling. 'I can do other stuff too,' she went on. 'Other styles. I'm pretty versatile, actually. So if you hear of any gigs going …'

'I will absolutely let you know.'

Hazel immediately regretted saying anything. This was a date, not a networking event. 'Sorry,' she said. 'I'm not here to hustle for work. God, how gauche.'

Miles looked surprised. 'No, don't apologise,' he said. 'I mean it, I'll keep my ear to the ground. You're good. And us, you know, *creative types* – I sound like a wanker, but fuck it, that's what we are – we have to have each other's backs, right? Otherwise, what's it all for? This whole dog-eat-dog, every-man-for-himself thing, I can't stand it. Art is about human connection! If we trample all over each other, what's to separate us from those corporate lackeys we all hate so much? Do you see what I'm saying?'

'Oh, yeah. Absolutely.' She kept her voice serious, but she was thrilled. She felt like skipping. He wanted to help her. Apparently it would be against his principles *not* to help her. And he would have excellent contacts. He could probably introduce her to all sorts of useful people.

'Anyway, I'll get off my soapbox,' he said. 'Just a little bugbear of mine. Man, would you look at that!' He waved an arm at the water, which mirrored the canal-side buildings so perfectly it could almost have been a painting. 'I mean, that is *flawless*, no?'

He produced an old-fashioned film camera from his bag and crouched down, pointing it at the reflection of a gas tower against a stretch of blue sky. He fiddled with the settings and adjusted the lens and pressed the shutter again and again.

'Ah, *yes*,' he exclaimed when a canal boat went by, sending the dark lines of the gas tower jumping and wiggling. Hazel watched him out of the corner of her eye, feigning interest in her phone. Everything he was wearing – the tote bag advertising a bookshop in Berlin, the old woollen suit jacket, the ripped jeans rolled up at the bottom, the ankle boots, one of them laced with brown string – had been meticulously selected to appear as casually thrown together as possible. Still, he certainly knew what suited him.

'Hopefully there should be one or two that I can do something with,' he said eventually, standing up. 'Fuck, man! London is so inspiring!'

They started walking again. 'So, Hazel,' said Miles after a while, 'how do you feel about brunch?'

'I feel pretty good about brunch.'

'Me too. There's this place about ten minutes from here that I love. Cosy sort of vibe, pretty chilled, good coffee. Does that sound okay?'

The café, on a side street near London Fields, had exposed brick walls, filament light bulbs and a distressed wooden floor. They sat down at a corner table and scanned the menu. Everything on it cost more than Hazel's hourly wage. A waitress with a lip ring arrived to take their order and Miles, to her evident delight, made in-depth enquiries about the provenance of the coffee and the variety of available milks.

'Can I get you guys anything to eat?' she said, once his complex coffee requirements had been taken care of. Hazel ordered poached eggs with avocado, polenta chips and plum ketchup, trying not to think about all the brunches she ate for free at work.

'And I'll go for the shakshuka,' said Miles, smiling up at the waitress, who blushed and took their menus. Miles turned back to Hazel.

Suddenly, quite out of the blue, there was nowhere for her to look but at his face. No menu, no waitress, no canal. Just Miles's razor-sharp cheekbones, Miles's exquisite mouth and Miles's dark, perplexing eyes. He said something – she wasn't entirely sure what, but she burbled something in response and it seemed to be appropriate because he looked her in the eye and smiled. *Miles smiles*, she thought, out of nowhere.

Her armpits were prickling. She didn't know what to say next. They were on the brink of a deathly awkward silence; the seconds were ticking by, each one more painful than the last.

'A latte and an oat flat white?' said a voice behind her, and she started in surprise – visibly, no doubt.

'Amazing,' said Miles smoothly, treating the waitress to another smile. Hazel cleared her throat and stammered out her thanks.

Miles watched her expectantly as she took a sip. 'So?' he asked as she replaced her cup. 'What does the barista think of the coffee?'

'Excellent,' she said, nodding in approval. Miles feigned relief and laughed. Hazel laughed too, with genuine relief, silently thanking the coffee for guiding them through their conversational impasse.

'Tell me about your café, then,' said Miles. 'The one where you work.'

So she told him about Nish and Roisin and Irma, and the pornographic avant-garde French film the manager had decided to screen last Friday, and the man who sang off-key and earnest at every single open mic night. Miles was nodding and smiling, and then laughing – properly laughing, like she was actually being funny.

'That settles it,' he said when she'd finished. 'I have to experience this café.'

'Well, stop by.'

'I will,' said Miles, holding her gaze until she blushed and looked down at her cup.

Three days later, he messaged her. *Got some boring admin to do today. Was thinking it might lessen the tedium if I came and did it in your café. You around?*

Hazel had just opened up with Roisin when she saw it. 'Ro!' she cried.

'What?' said Roisin, alarmed.

'This guy I went on a date with is going to come here today!'

'Oh. Is that good, or …?'

'Yes, it's good! Shit! What do I do?'

'What do you mean what do you do? Just do your job. Do you like him, then?'

'Yes! He's *really* hot, Ro. Like *exquisite*.'

'So this business with your flatmate? Is that not happening? I thought it sounded like a goer.'

'Enh,' said Hazel, waving her hand dismissively.

'Right. So it's all about this dude now.'

'You'll like him! He's an artist.'

'I don't just automatically like all artists, Hazel. A lot of them are dickheads.'

'Miles isn't,' said Hazel, aware that Roisin would almost certainly disagree.

She left it an hour before replying, then told Miles yes, she was around; she was on the early, eight until four. She was wiping tables after the lunchtime rush when she heard his voice saying her name.

'Oh, hey!' she said, straightening up to kiss him on the cheek. She could feel Roisin's eyes boring into them from across the room.

'Good to see you, Hazel. Look, I know I should be being a bit cooler, a bit more aloof, you know,' he said. 'But life's too short, right?'

'Totally,' she said, reaching out to squeeze his arm. 'Let me get you a coffee. Oat milk flat white?'

'God,' he said, 'am I really that predictable?'

Hazel didn't want him to know she remembered his order from their brunch date, so she said, 'I just have a good coffee-sense.' Further conversation was curtailed by the roar of the coffee machine, and then a small flurry of customers appeared and demanded her attention. Miles withdrew to a corner table and stared intently at his MacBook, covering his ears with a pair of oversized headphones. Once or twice he looked up and caught her eye. When the café was quiet again she went over to his table.

'Is everything okay for you, sir?' she said. He looked up and smiled his winning smile, and she felt her cheeks warm up. She pulled out a chair and sat down across from him.

'So,' she said.

'So,' he replied. Then something seemed to catch his eye over her shoulder. 'Hey, is that ... are those ...?'

She turned around and looked at the row of framed cartoons that hung on the wall behind her. 'Original Hazel Phillipses?' she said, in a silly voice, so he'd know she didn't take herself too seriously.

'Original Hazel Phillipses! Are they for sale?'

'Oh! Well, yes. I mean, they've been there so long I just think of them as part of the furniture. But technically they're for sale, yeah.'

'How much?'

'Two hundred and fifty pounds,' she said quickly. 'Each.'

'Can I buy one?'

She looked at him. 'Really?'

'Yes, really,' he said, looking back at her, the corner of his mouth twitching upwards.

'Um, okay! Yeah, of course!'

He got up and inspected them one by one, chuckling. The final picture in the row made him laugh out loud. 'This is the one, man,' he said. 'So on point.'

He went out to the cashpoint and came back with a wad of notes. Hazel had trouble containing her excitement. 'Thanks!' she said as he handed them to her.

'No, thank *you*,' he replied. 'I've been looking for something for this one little spot in my flat. I was thinking maybe a lithograph or something, but this is perfect. Anyway, I like to support local artists when I can.'

Hazel, unused to being described as a 'local artist', simply grinned.

Miles stayed at his table for a further three hours and ordered a succession of flat whites. Eventually he stood up and came over to the counter. 'I'm off now,' he said. 'I've got to see a man about some pallets. But Hazel, listen, if you're free next Saturday evening, I've got this little exhibition opening.'

'Oh yeah?'

'It'd be great to see you if you fancy coming down. It's me and a couple of mates, a sound artist and a poet. Really great guys. We've been doing some collaborative stuff. It's our first exhibition.'

She nodded. 'Sounds cool,' she said, affecting nonchalance.

'Yeah? Well, no pressure. I'll WhatsApp you all the info and you can decide on the night.' He started walking backwards towards the door, her picture under his arm. 'Bring friends, if you come,' he said, pointing at her. 'The more the merrier.'

'I will,' she called, and he put his hand up to say goodbye. The bell jangled as the door closed behind him.

'You weren't lying,' said Roisin when he'd gone. 'He's hot.'

'He just asked me to the opening night of his exhibition next weekend,' said Hazel.

'Of course he did.'

'Will you come? I can't go on my own.'

Roisin groaned. 'Really, Hazel? Do you have any idea how many of those wanky-ass things I've been to in my life?'

'You should be jumping at the chance. Think of the net-working opportunities.'

'Oh, fuck *that*.'

'Please? As a favour?' Hazel turned to the pinboard inside the kitchen door and ran her finger down the rota. 'You're not working! And Nish ... Oh, Nish is working. I could try and persuade him to swap out.'

'I'll come if Nish comes,' said Roisin. 'Not on my own, no way. I'm not standing around like a lemon while you and Miles sneak out for a bit of hanky-panky by the wheelie bins.'

'Ro! Oh my God, as if!' cried Hazel, secretly pleased.

11

IT WAS MOVING day that weekend, so Alfie and Hazel got up early and took the train to a retail park in the furthest reaches of Bromley. They didn't speak much on the journey. Alfie thought he detected a degree of tension in the air, although perhaps it was just that they were both tired. As the train pulled out of London Bridge station he leaned his head back and pretended to doze, occasionally flickering his eyes open a fraction to observe Hazel from beneath his lashes. She was glued to her phone, and clearly unavailable for conversation. For the umpteenth time he thought back over that misstep of his in the kitchen, and wished he could undo it. They hadn't had a candid discussion since. This might have been a good opportunity to start one, but Hazel's expression was serious; something important was happening in the world inside her phone, and it didn't include him.

In fact, she was studying Miles's social media following. It was impressive, and she was envious. Many of them were people she herself followed but who had never followed her back. Miles had sent a photograph of her drawing the day before, leaning against the wall in his flat – all he needed was a hook, he had written; next stop, hardware shop! Now she was willing him to tweet the photo, and tag her in it. It could be a game changer. 'Picked up this absolute @zellips classic the other day,' he might write, or, 'This is @zellips, everybody. You're welcome.' She refreshed his Twitter feed compulsively, just in case he had somehow done it without her noticing. It was futile, of course, but there was nothing to distract her from it; Alfie had fallen asleep as soon as the train started moving.

Immediately after they arrived at the storage unit, Emily rang to say that she and Daria were running late.

'Typical,' sighed Hazel, putting her phone away. 'We've got some time to kill. What shall we do?'

They stood with their backs to the storage unit and surveyed the options. The car park was bordered on three sides by grey, hangar-like buildings.

'Pets at Home?' said Alfie.

'I was just going to say that,' said Hazel.

They crossed the car park and went inside, then made for the back of the shop where the animals lived. A large sign welcomed them to 'Pet Village'. They wandered down the rodent aisle, past children and their parents peering in at rabbits and mice and hamsters. Each inhabited its own modest section of what was, to all intents and purposes, a large display case.

'It's not exactly prime real estate in Pet Village, is it?' said Hazel.

'I don't know,' said Alfie. He waved an arm at the glassy surrounds. 'Studio flats with floor-to-ceiling windows? I doubt *we* could afford to live here.'

Hazel grinned. 'Well, when you put it like that,' she said. 'I suppose they're starter homes for rodents with rich parents.' Alfie laughed delightedly, and Hazel made an effort not to look too pleased with herself. She felt lighter, like she might start skipping.

'Toilets in the bedrooms, too,' Alfie continued, nodding at the sawdust, which was littered with black pellets. 'That's even more convenient than an en suite.'

'And meals on tap. You can eat and shit at the same time. They've got it better than we have.'

They bantered their way down the aquarium aisle, and on past the aviaries. Eventually they came to a large alcove with low lighting and the fittings done out in green.

'This is where the bad guys live,' said Hazel. All around were heaps of coiled-up snake flesh, the heads tucked away out of sight. In the bottom tanks were a few stick insects, and a tarantula, crouching on a pile of leaves.

Alfie pointed at it. 'I'll buy you a bar of chocolate if you put your face right up to the glass,' he said.

Hazel hesitated. She didn't mind spiders, so long as they kept their distance, but this one would be too close, mere centimetres from her eyes. Then again, it couldn't actually *touch* her. And it was a good opportunity to show Alfie that she could be gutsy and intrepid, as well as funny. And she was hungry.

'Okay,' she said. 'But make it a pastry. I didn't have any breakfast.'

'Deal,' said Alfie.

She crouched down in front of the tank and leaned in close, resting her elbows on her knees. It was far from pleasant, to have a spider take up so much space in her line of vision, but she forced herself to look at it with objective interest. She noted the heft of its body and the dusky red hairs on its legs. It was so furry, and so sturdily built, that she could almost kid herself it was another type of rodent. There was a languidness about it that suggested it wouldn't make any sudden movements. It seemed friendly, she decided, and once she had reached this conclusion she found herself pitying it. It could hardly enjoy being so visible to everybody. This was no kind of life, being peered and pointed at when you were trying to mind your own business.

All of a sudden there was something on her head. A spider – there was a spider on her head. She yelped loudly, sprang backwards away from the glass, and landed on the floor. Her hands flew to her hair, scrabbling frantically. But there was nothing there, of course. It had only been Alfie's fingers. She looked up and there he was, leaning against a pillar, clutching his stomach in mirth.

'I'm so sorry,' he gasped, as she sprawled there in astonishment, one hand over her racing heart. He was breathless with laughter. 'Oh my God – oh – I didn't think—'

'You little bastard!' she cried. 'You tricked me!'

'I'm sorry,' he said again, his voice full of gleeful remorse. He offered her a hand and hauled her up. 'I really am. I just couldn't resist. Is your arse okay? I'll buy you two pastries, Hazel. I'll buy you three.'

They hastened back out into the car park, away from the disapproving looks of the other customers.

'What a bad example to set all these children,' Hazel scolded. 'And you a teacher!'

'It was a good trick, though, you have to admit,' he said, and she shook her head at him, trying to suppress a smile.

They couldn't find anywhere to buy pastries, but there was a vending machine in the foyer of B&Q, so Alfie recompensed Hazel with an assortment of confectionery and a heavily iced cinnamon bun wrapped in cellophane. Then they wandered back towards the storage unit and settled themselves on the pavement outside, sharing a bag of Maltesers and swapping animal videos. Alfie contributed a masturbating monkey, Hazel a shamefaced golden retriever trying to hide eggs in its cheeks. This in turn reminded Alfie of the golden retriever dancing the merengue.

'What? No!' cried Hazel as she watched it. 'That's not possible! How is that possible?' On the screen the golden retriever was dancing, really dancing, on its hind legs, with a partner who was a man. Then the video stopped; Alfie had run out of data.

'Ah, fuck,' he said. 'Anyway, you get the idea.'

They were quiet for a while after that, woozy from all the merriment.

'I'd quite like to learn the merengue,' said Alfie eventually. By this he meant: Let's learn the merengue! She still had data; they could find a tutorial on YouTube. Who could say what might happen if they were standing up, face to face, their bodies inches apart?

'Do you like dancing, then?' said Hazel, missing his subtext entirely. 'I'm rubbish at dancing, nowhere near as good as that dog.'

'I like a bit of salsa now and again,' he said, and here, all of a sudden, he saw an opportunity to right his faux pas from the other day. He would have to tread carefully;

93

it was a risky strategy, but if done right it would negate the damage he had so clumsily inflicted, and of which her silence on the train had seemed to be the proof.

'I had lessons for a while,' he went on. 'With my ex. She was really into it. I got quite into it because of her.' He made a point of being offhand about it, so as to convey how inconsequential it was. Exes were not a threat, he wished to imply. It was normal to have them. There was no need to pretend they didn't exist.

There was a pause, and then Hazel said, 'Lucky. My ex made us go to an anarchist reading group.'

Alfie laughed, relieved. 'Let's do a skills exchange, then,' he said. 'I'll teach you salsa, you can teach me how to cause anarchy. We can start with salsa.' He stood up and offered her a hand.

'Seriously?' said Hazel, looking up at him. 'I'll tread on your toes, I guarantee it.'

'I'll live,' said Alfie, and she took his hand and clambered to her feet. They stood opposite one another and she looked up to meet his eyes. He lifted a hand, ready to put it on her waist; but she was distracted now, peering at something behind him. He dropped his hand and turned around. A large van was weaving its way through the car park towards them, hulking itself over the speed bumps. Emily was at the wheel, he saw as it approached. Behind it was a small blue car, driven by Daria.

'Saved by the bell,' he said. He looked at his phone. 'Only forty-five minutes late.'

'Emily'll blame it on traffic,' said Hazel. 'But I guarantee you they'll have stopped for coffee. Check the cupholders. You'll see.'

The convoy slowed down and pulled into adjoining parking spaces.

'Sorry!' cried Emily, jumping down from the van. 'Traffic was mad!' Hazel turned to Alfie and gave him a look of complicity. There was no need to even check the cupholders: Daria got out of the car with a coffee cup still in her hand. Alfie could sense that Hazel had noticed this too. They were sprung together by this knowledge, he felt, so that if they looked at one another they would bounce.

The two of them were tasked with unloading the van, which contained all the boxes that had been in Hazel's parents' loft, and packing as many of them as they could into the car.

'You see?' said Hazel when Emily and Daria had disappeared into the storage unit. 'They left so late they didn't even have time to pack properly. You'd think if they wanted this stuff in the car, they'd have put it there to begin with.'

Alfie didn't mind. He was full of energy. He felt strong and agile, leaping in and out of the van, hauling boxes in his arms. His eye hadn't twitched all day, and in his vivaciousness he forgot that it ever had twitched, and certainly that its twitching was a likely symptom of some sinister health condition that was to ruin his life and then end it prematurely. Today life was straightforward, it was proceeding exactly as he would wish, all promise and plenitude.

When they'd finished packing the car he and Hazel helped load the furniture and then the boxes out from the storage unit, and by the time they were done the van was full with barely an inch to spare.

'Who's going with who?' said Daria. 'Siblings in the van?'

Alfie would have liked to have gone with Hazel, but obviously you didn't just waltz into this kind of scenario and drive someone else's vehicle.

He and Daria waited for the van to start off, then followed it. 'Thanks so much for helping us,' she said as they pulled out of the car park. 'You must have better things you could be doing.'

'I have things I could be doing,' said Alfie, thinking of the stack of work waiting for him at home now that term was underway, 'but none of them are *better*.'

'Very diplomatic.'

'It's true.' He said it without emphasis, not wanting to give away the extent of his willingness to be there in case Daria began to suspect his real motive.

They couldn't play anything from Spotify because the car was too old, Daria said, but there were CDs in the glovebox and he could take his pick. He took them out obediently. The only artist he'd heard of was Philip Glass, who'd written the soundtrack to a strange film he'd seen once, late at night at a festival. His abiding memory of the occasion was his intense desire for it to be over; it had been uncomfortable sitting there on the grass, unable to change position without disturbing Rachel, asleep with her head in his lap. Now he wished he had paid it more attention.

At random he selected an album that turned out to be some sort of Cuban-Irish folk electronica. 'Whoa,' he said, as the first track got going. 'This is wild!'

'Isn't it!' said Daria, leaning over to turn it up.

There was no point trying to talk over the top, so he sat back and watched the road. The Cuban-Irish folk electronica lent itself very well to moving at speed, and when the album finished it left a residue behind it, an imprint on the silence. As they slowed down on the approach to some traffic lights Alfie said, 'Would you rather hear music playing every waking moment for the rest of your life, or never hear any music ever again?'

Daria laughed. 'Oh man,' she said. 'I don't know. Can I choose what's playing?'

'Yeah, you can choose whatever you want, it doesn't matter what it is, you just have to make sure music is playing constantly.'

'What about volume?'

'Always the same. Not so loud you couldn't talk to someone, but still too loud to ignore.'

'I think, probably … Agh, I don't know. Constant music could be torture after a while. Maybe no music. Oh, but then …'

'Which would you miss more? Music or silence?'

Daria looked anguished. 'This is really tough. I like both. You know what, I think I'd go without music, because that way I'd always think of it fondly. I think I'd rather miss it than hate it. And I could make music for myself. I could sing, I could whistle. You can make music out of silence, but you can't make silence out of music.'

'Profound.'

'Right?' Daria was nodding, pleased with herself. 'What about you?'

'I think I agree,' Alfie said. 'Silence seems like the pragmatic choice.'

'Okay,' said Daria. 'My turn. Would you rather … would you rather … Oh, I know! Would you rather eat food with no texture, or food with no flavour?'

They continued like this for an hour, going to great lengths to determine whether they would rather do without baths or showers, grass or trees, pillows or duvets; whether they would rather be teetotal or gluten-free, naked in an ice bar or wrapped up warm in a sauna, condemned to an eternity of horror films or an eternity of kids' TV.

Eventually Daria said, 'Would you rather stop for lunch or carry on driving?'

'Ha!' said Alfie. 'Stop, obviously.'

12

AT THE SERVICE station Emily demanded a selfie, and they all gathered by the van, looking up at themselves in her phone screen. Alfie and Daria grinned wholesomely; Hazel opened her mouth and eyes as wide as they would go; Emily turned her head just so and effected a subtle pout. She posted it straight to Instagram with the caption, *Truckin' through the home counties #movingday #norwich.*

Afterwards they walked across the car park to a complex of coffee shops and fast-food outlets. Hazel and Alfie went ahead, but not so far ahead that they couldn't be observed, with interest. Emily noted their tone and their gestures. They were familiar and flirtatious, clearly desirous of more from each other than they were yet allowed. She turned to Daria and raised her eyebrows meaningfully. Daria raised hers back, in understanding.

They purchased meal deals and coffees and vegan sausage rolls and sat down to eat them at picnic benches overlooking the car park and the motorway. Daria and Alfie's friendship appeared to have been galvanised by their trip.

'I've got a good one for later,' she said to him, without making any effort to explain herself, and he grinned and said, 'Excellent.' Neither Emily nor Hazel asked to be let in on the joke. Hazel was looking at her phone, smiling a little, her thumbs moving fast. What could be so interesting, Emily wondered, that it was more interesting than Alfie?

When she'd finished eating Emily went back into the service station in search of the toilets. They were cavernous, grey tiled, with a mirror on one wall. She caught sight of herself in it, and was disheartened by how much shorter and wider she was in reality than in the reflection she had recently grown used to, in the warped mirror at her mother's house, which made her look several inches taller than she was.

In the cubicle she was disheartened further. There was a smear of blood in her underwear. She stared at it blankly, then rooted in her bag for a tampon, reasoning away the disappointment. There was nothing to be surprised about, she reminded herself. She'd known this would happen.

When she arrived back at the van Hazel said, 'We're not in the Home Counties any more.'

'What?'

'Your Insta. We're in Suffolk now. Not a Home County.'

'Oh. Whatever. Shall we get going? It's pushing two.'

When she turned the key in the ignition *Hamilton* started playing at the exact place it had stopped when they parked. She snapped it off irritably.

'Hey!' cried Hazel.

'I'm not in the mood.'

'What's got into you?'

'Nothing. I just don't want any music on.'

'Fine,' grumbled Hazel, sliding down in her seat. There was quiet, the only sound the ambient roar of the engine.

Emily stared out at the road, an uneventful stretch of dual carriageway. There was a thickness in her throat, a heat around her eyes. Gradually, the grey of the road began to blur into the grey of the sky.

She blinked heavily, but her vision blurred over again. Her throat was clogged. She swallowed to try and clear it, sniffing thickly, as if she had a cold. In the passenger seat, Hazel stirred.

'Em?' she said. 'Are you all right?'

'Yep,' said Emily, wiping away the tears that were now trickling into the groove where her cheek met her nose.

'What's the matter? Do you want to pull over?'

'I can't!' cried Emily, gesturing at their surroundings. 'There isn't anywhere, is there?'

'Maybe another service station?' said Hazel, looking urgently at the road signs.

'No point. If I pull over, so will the others. I really can't be arsed explaining myself. I'm fine. Pass me a tissue, there's some in my bag.' Hazel obeyed, and Emily blew her nose a final time. She took a deep breath, blew it out sharply, and rolled back her shoulders.

'Do you want to talk about it?' said Hazel.

'I feel hormonal, that's all. I just got my period.'

'Okay.'

There was quiet again. They turned off the motorway and onto an A-road with an expanse of stubbly wheatfields on each side. After a while Emily said, 'The thing is, I was actually hoping I wouldn't get my period this month. I was hoping I might be pregnant.'

'What?'

'Yeah.'

'Oh my God! Are you serious? How?'

'Kamran, Daria's brother. He donated for us.'

'Fucking hell, Em! Why didn't you tell me? This is huge!'

'Well, not really,' Emily snapped. 'Since it's not actually happening.'

'Isn't it? Can't you try again?'

'Kamran's just moved to Bangladesh,' she sighed. 'He's joined Médecins Sans Frontières, I don't know if we said. So we had one go before he left. But obviously it hasn't worked. And now he's gone.'

'When will he be back?'

Emily shrugged. 'Not for a few months at least.'

'What are you going to do?'

'Use a sperm bank, I guess,' said Emily. 'I really didn't want to do it that way. I wanted us to use someone we care about.'

'Isn't there anyone else?'

'Not really. It's hard to find someone suitable. There are loads of boxes to tick. Anyway, no one can replace Kamran. It would have been so great. Daria could have been related to the baby. Her parents could have been the biological grandparents.' Emily felt her lip trembling, and bit it.

'He won't be in Bangladesh for ever, though, right?'

'Who the fuck knows, Hazel!' Emily cried, suddenly desperate to change the subject. 'Anyway, I can't wait around until whenever he deigns to come home. It's got to be plan B. Now will you just let me concentrate on driving, please?'

Hazel raised her eyebrows at this injustice, but did not protest.

They pulled up in front of the new house in the middle of the afternoon. It was part of a long redbrick terrace and had three old sash windows, two upstairs and one down, and a tiny paved garden separated from the street by a low wall. By the early evening the sofa was set up in the living room, the table and chairs in the kitchen and the bed in the master bedroom. The boxes were stacked neatly at the edges of each room, the cutlery was in a drawer, and the van stood empty in the street outside.

Emily said she'd go to the little supermarket round the corner for a bottle of wine.

'We've got a bottle of wine,' said Daria.

'I know,' said Emily, looking at her pointedly. 'But a spare won't hurt, will it?'

'I'll come with you,' said Daria, sensing that this was what Emily wanted her to say.

As soon as they were out of earshot of the house Emily said, 'It didn't work.'

'Oh,' said Daria. 'Oh, no.' She swallowed hard and looked down at the pavement in a display of disappointment that wasn't entirely feigned. A shoot of regret at the passing of this, their first and simplest chance of becoming parents, was emerging tentatively from the vast barrenness of her relief. She held it carefully in her thoughts and willed it to grow, its existence a relief in itself.

'Hello?' said Emily, irritated.

'Sorry,' Daria replied. 'I was digesting. Come here.' She caught Emily's hand and pulled her in towards her, kissing her hair. More than anything she wanted to talk about this strange and confusing paradox she now found herself in – to be relieved at the presence of an emotion precisely because it was not relief – but this was a long way from what Emily wanted or needed to hear. 'We'll think of a new plan,' she said instead. 'We'll have you pregnant soon. Maybe by Christmas, maybe even sooner.'

Emily nodded into her shoulder, sniffling. 'I just really wanted it to work *this* time.'

'Yeah. Me too. But it usually takes a few tries. It doesn't mean there's anything wrong with you.'

'I know that,' Emily said, standing back from Daria and wiping her eyes. 'It was just hard not to get my hopes up. I did try not to.'

'You're only human, sweet pea.'

'I'm going to get *so* drunk tonight,' said Emily as they resumed walking.

Later they ordered pizza from a vegan place that made ricotta out of cashew nuts. Emily, her spirits rising in direct proportion to her wine consumption, took count-less pictures of the living room, and of them in it, and of the pizza, and of them eating it. Alfie said the pizza was delicious, possibly even the best pizza he'd ever had, the cashew nuts were so creamy, really nothing like cheese but so much *better* than cheese, and the garlic broccoli, the caramelised onion, fucking Christ, he was beside himself. Emily beamed and said could she take a video of him saying that for Instagram, so Alfie started saying it all over again. He was trying to make it sound improvised but he broke down laughing before the end.

'Try saying it to the camera,' said Emily, and Alfie com-posed himself and faced her phone head-on.

'Okay, so I love cheese,' he said. 'I really fucking love cheese.' He held up his slice of pizza and said, 'But this pizza, which is entirely *devoid* of cheese, is possibly the best thing I have ever tasted.' He took a bite and groaned with intoxication.

This might have been the funniest thing Daria had seen all week. Emily and Hazel were speechless with mirth. Played back, Alfie's voice was tinny, and in the low light his wine-stained teeth looked grey. They waited, grinning, for the two-dimensional Alfie to say 'entirely *devoid* of cheese', and then they collapsed against the moving boxes and onto the floor, tears running down their cheeks. Later Daria checked Instagram and saw the video in her feed, captioned: *You heard the man #vegan #govegan #veganism #plantbased #vegansofinstagram #whatveganseat #vegan-foodporn #crueltyfree #berwickstreetpizza.* She watched it again, but it wasn't quite as funny the second time.

13

HAZEL LAY AWAKE for hours that night. She was on a camping mattress in the second bedroom; Alfie was downstairs on the sofa. For some time she considered what might have happened if there hadn't been a second bedroom, or if it had been too full of boxes to be slept in, and they'd both had to spend the night in the living room. She imagined the tips of Alfie's fingers finding the tips of hers in the darkness.

We shouldn't, she would have whispered as they reached for each other, moved towards each other.

Right, he'd have whispered back. Pause. Then: We could be quiet.

And the warmth of him there, the smell of him, the roughness of his cheek in the gleam from the streetlamp. She would lean into him, persuaded, and they'd do it and she'd have a monumental orgasm, and afterwards she would have to share his sleeping bag because her own would be sopping wet.

As it was she fumbled alone and felt sad afterwards. She thought back to their conversation outside the storage unit. This ex, whoever she was. He was always bringing her up. Was it the same one each time? Did he miss her so much that he thought about her even as he flirted with other people? Because they *had* been flirting, Hazel refused to believe they hadn't. Perhaps he'd loved this woman so much that nobody else could eclipse her, even if he wanted them to. Probably he wished he could move on, but found that other people only reminded him of what he'd lost. Or else it was more calculated – perhaps the ex was a device he employed when he wanted to keep a flirtation in check, an antidote for when things went too far. A way to balance the books, as it were, like going for a run to neutralise an excess of junk food.

To make herself feel better Hazel had messaged Miles in the van, a simple 'what you up to?' that led to a coy back-and-forth stretching out over several hours. Somehow she had promised him she would attend his exhibition opening the following weekend regardless of whether or not her friends were free to go with her. She wasn't entirely sure how it had happened. She dreaded the thought of turning up friendless and alone, desperate for Miles's company.

Fortunately, Nish managed to swap out of his shift, and Roisin kept her word. When Hazel arrived at the studio they were there already, smoking by the entrance, Roisin tall and impossibly glamorous in a boat-necked black dress that glided over her breasts and fell seamlessly to the floor. She wore a denim jacket over the top; white plimsolls peeped out from underneath when she walked. Her short bleached hair was slicked back.

'You look like Lee Miller,' said Hazel, who was wearing ripped, high-waisted jeans, a midriff-skimming T-shirt and a shiny green bomber jacket from the nineties, all in an uncharacteristic attempt to look fashionable. Next to Roisin she felt the social power of this outfit ebbing silently away.

The studio was a large room with a paint-spattered floor and huge, draughty windows, dozens of little square panes of glass stacked up and across, each one dripping with condensation. They hung up their jackets, visited the drinks table and consulted the flyer that someone had handed them. One side was mostly taken up with a black-and-white photograph of an apple, which sat in the palm of a tiny, spindly female hand. In the top left-hand corner were the words *and still I diminish* – handwritten, carelessly jotted down as if in a notebook. Underneath the image it said:

miles newman • liam robinson • daniel miller
consumption and embodiment
a poetic exploration

content warning: terminal illness,
eating disorders, miscarriage

On the other side was a paragraph introducing the exhibition, followed by three short artist biographies. Hazel skipped straight to the most interesting part, which read:

miles newman is a photographer, painter and sometime videographer. he studied fine art at goldsmiths, continuing his studies at université paris-dauphine before returning to his beloved london to make art on his own terms. the work on display here is the culmination of a longstanding artistic and philosophical interest in the human body and its meanings.

Surprisingly, given her earlier disdain, Roisin was now looking around with interest. She moved away and started studying the pictures on the wall with a concentrated intensity that seemed to signal a desire to be left alone. Nish and Hazel exchanged glances, turned their backs on her, and made for the exhibits on the other side of the room.

The first thing they came to was a pair of headsets hanging from the wall. Nish put on one and Hazel put on the other. She found herself listening to a harrowing recording of a woman coughing, violently and ceaselessly, unable to fully get her breath. There was a gentle rubbing noise, like a hand on a back, and the voice of a man saying, 'It's okay, love, it's all right, you'll be fine, there, that's it, it's okay.' Eventually the coughing subsided and was replaced by laboured, rattling breaths. The man asked if the woman wanted a cup of tea and the woman grunted yes. Then she started coughing again, and Hazel took off the headset and put it back. She read the small white label beneath it and learned that this was a recording of some people called Graham and Maureen Lampeter, at home in 2015. A larger panel of text informed her that:

maureen lampeter worked at millers in bradford from 1975 to '82. in 1979 renovation work took place in the store, later understood to have caused major disturbances to the blue asbestos in the wall cavities. maureen was one of at least seven former employees to be diagnosed with pleural mesothelioma in the decades since the renovations. she died in early 2018.

'Jesus Christ,' said Hazel under her breath. Nish replaced the other headset.

'That was fucking traumatising,' he said.

'Don't listen to this one, then,' Hazel told him. She described the recording, and Nish made a dramatic gesture of distaste.

'Walking away,' he said, and set off in the direction of the drinks table.

Hazel continued without him. The next thing she came to was a series of close-up images of Maureen Lampeter herself: her lined face, a thin hand on a teacup, Graham kissing the top of her head. At the end of the row of photos, a poem had been printed directly onto the wall:

please let the air in
oh i long for you even
as you finish me

Hazel stared at it. She didn't know anything about poetry. Perhaps someone who knew about poetry would be able to tell her why this poem deserved to be printed on a wall.

Then came more photos, black-and-white this time, each one depicting parts of a young woman's body: hands, hips, neck and shoulders, all of them deathly thin, bone and sinew protruding through the papery skin. The woman's face did not appear. In one image, a hand was held up in front of a sunny window and the light shone through it. Another Hazel recognised from the flyer: the apple in the spindly hand. Some appeared to have had paint added to them: crude black lines, outlining the body, others running straight across and straight down, like bars at a window. One had a poem handwritten over the top of it, but this one Hazel did not read.

In the corner near the images a woman was standing on her own, frowning, speaking quickly and quietly into her phone. Hazel thought she caught the words 'dehumanising' and 'prettify', although the woman might equally well have said 'revolutionising' and 'Spotify'. Then she heard her own name and turned around.

'Miles!'

'You came,' he said, smiling and leaning in to kiss her on the cheek. 'You look amazing.'

'Thanks!' She gestured vaguely at the room around her. 'This is great. Really impressive.'

'You wouldn't have said that two hours ago,' he said. 'It was an unbelievable shitshow. I'll spare you the details. It actually got to the point where I hoped you weren't coming so you wouldn't see what a total mess I'd put together. But I'm really glad you did.' He caught her eye and smiled again, then said he'd better go and mingle; there were a couple of collectors and gallery owners in the room somewhere. 'I'm totally shitting it,' he said, and put a hand on her shoulder. 'Stick around, though, yeah? We can catch up properly in a bit.'

Later, Hazel was listening to a recording of a pregnant woman at her first ultrasound scan, thinking of Emily, when someone started speaking into a microphone. Miles and his collaborators had appeared on the platform at the end of the room. Slowly, everyone started moving towards them. The one at the microphone introduced himself as Danny, the sound guy, and then pointed to the other one who wasn't Miles and said his name was Liam and he was the poet. Then Danny said, 'And finally this is Miles, our photographer, painter and generally just annoyingly talented guy.' Everyone laughed, and Miles grinned sheepishly and shook his head as if to say, Stop, you're embarrassing me.

Danny thanked everyone sincerely for turning out on this really quite chilly night, and then expressed further heartfelt thanks to a lengthy list of individuals and organisations who had shown 'support', presumably financial. Then he invited their friend Lars to the stage. Lars was tall and sandy-haired and had the slightest hint of a foreign accent, maybe Swedish. He said he was sure everyone here would agree that the exhibition had been fascinating, extraordinary. He invited the room to join him in a round of applause.

Then the discussion began. The four of them sat in a semicircle on the platform, little microphones clipped to their T-shirts. Lars asked questions and Miles, Danny and Liam nodded seriously and said things like 'something I've been thinking through recently', and 'at the time I was getting a bit obsessed with the theme of', and 'I think we were all drawn to the possibility of using that as a framework for'. Hazel noticed that Liam had an estuary accent and said 'mate' a lot, but occasionally forgot himself and let slip a plummy vowel.

Danny started talking about the themes of the exhibition, consumption and embodiment. The decision to investigate these themes, it was implied, was all his idea. He explained that his wife's pregnancy had been the impetus for some 'in-depth thinking' about the way 'consumptive forces' act on the body. The result of that thought process, he said, was what they saw around them.

Miles and Liam appeared restless, and as soon as Danny had finished they both started speaking at the same time. Miles stopped and let Liam continue, which was gallant, Hazel thought. Liam stressed that in a happy coincidence, his own practice had at that time been taking him in a similar, if more morbid, direction. He'd been thinking a lot about Maureen Lampeter (a friend and neighbour of his parents, it turned out), and it was starting to colour his poetry. He talked about the nature of Maureen's condition, pleural mesothelioma, and how the simple act of breathing had made the cancer proliferate faster. This idea would not leave him alone, Liam said, because he felt it provided the perfect metaphor for consumption more generally, in so many contexts: the way we must consume and yet simultaneously we are consumed. Hazel thought of Maureen Lampeter, letting herself be recorded in a moment of suffering and indignity. Is that all she is? she thought. A *metaphor*?

Then Miles got his turn, and when he'd finished explaining how he, in another happy coincidence, had himself been reflecting on exactly these themes at exactly this time, Lars took over again and asked the audience if they had any questions. Hands went up; a microphone was passed around. Hazel felt a hand in hers and Nish's hot breath in her ear. 'Blah blah blah,' he whispered, as Danny responded to a question. The woman in front of them looked round, and Hazel shushed him hurriedly.

On the platform Lars was pointing, saying, 'Yes, lady at the back there.' There was a pause while the microphone was passed from person to person, and then a voice began asking a question. Hazel and Nish looked at each other in surprise. It was Roisin.

'I was just wondering,' she said, 'what you think about the fact that we as an audience have been put in a position tonight where we essentially have to consume other people's pain? Specifically women's pain? Do you find that troubling at all?'

An uncomfortable hush fell over the room. Miles, Liam and Danny exchanged glances, each of them evidently hoping another would volunteer to answer the question. Then Miles began, tentatively, to speak.

'Thanks,' he said. 'Thanks for that. Yeah, it's an important question. It actually sort of intersects with something I've been thinking about quite a bit myself, which is how do we relate ideas of consumption and embodiment to the experiences we've been having this evening, in this room?' He started to speak faster and more surely, warming to his theme. 'We've all been consumers tonight. We're all owners of bodies. So the exhibition space is a site at which those themes are played out on multiple levels.'

'That's not really what I—' came Roisin's amplified voice, but Miles held his hand up and spoke over the top of her.

'I think it's interesting to explore what it means to consume some of these artworks,' he said. 'Essentially, as you say, we're consuming someone else's pain. And certainly we have to ask, is that something we're okay with?' He raised his hands questioningly. Liam and Danny and Lars looked thoughtful.

'Er, no?' said Nish, more loudly than he realised. Several people turned around this time, some of them smiling.

114

'Sometimes,' Miles continued obliviously, 'your body doesn't *want* you to consume it. I mean, I'm sure I'm not the only one who had a really visceral reaction to that recording of Maureen Lampeter – my heart was pounding, I felt a bit nauseous. And so there are these layers of, sort of, *embodied* acts of consumption, if you like. And in this case there's a moral ambiguity to that, which I find really fascinating.' Nish snorted; Hazel pinched him.

'And just to add,' put in Danny, 'that obviously, all of this material has been used with the full consent of the subjects involved.'

'Well, thank God,' came Roisin's amplified voice. 'That doesn't automatically make it ethical, though. Sorry.'

Hazel and Nish looked at each other. Nish was grinning in amazement. 'What the fuck!' he whispered, delighted.

'We'll take another question now, I think,' said Lars, but Liam held up a hand to stop him.

'Hang on a second,' he said. He looked in what must have been Roisin's direction. 'What exactly are you suggesting?'

'What am I suggesting? Okay, well, put it this way. Say a woman consents to sex. Technically she wasn't raped. It doesn't always follow that she wasn't violated, though, does it? Or that she wasn't used or exploited. Or that it didn't make her feel like shit.'

Miles, Danny and Liam looked at each other, eyebrows raised. 'Whoa,' said Miles. Around the room people stirred and shifted.

'Sorry,' said Liam, 'are you comparing this exhibition to rape?'

'That's really fucking offensive, actually,' said a woman with a septum ring standing near Hazel.

'It's interesting you should say that,' Roisin replied, 'because personally, I was quite offended to see a pimped-up anorexic body on display like some kind of freakshow porn.'

'Oh, come on,' said someone.

'Stop being a dick,' said someone else.

'Look,' said Miles, holding up his hands in a pacifying gesture, 'I'm sorry you didn't get what we're trying to do here. But if you didn't enjoy the exhibition that's your prerogative. You're free to leave at any time. In fact, it might be best for us all if you did.'

Hazel and Nish followed Roisin out. When they got outside she was already lighting a cigarette.

'What the fuck was that?' said Hazel.

'I know, right? They've never had any of their own pain so they have to fetishise other people's.'

'No,' said Hazel coldly. 'I mean you.'

'Oh, *I'm* the problem?' said Roisin. 'What are you, embarrassed?'

'What do you think? I asked you here for moral support and then you go and bloody well kick off in front of everyone!'

'Please. It was hardly kicking off. Don't exaggerate. What did you expect me to do? Just ignore all my principles and let them get away with peddling that shite?'

'I assume by that you mean, say, being polite? Not insulting people in public? I didn't realise that would be so difficult for you!'

'Oh my God, listen to yourself, Hazel. That's fucked up. Would you expect me to be polite if you took me to some nice jolly of Miles's that turned out to be a far-right rally?'

'Um, kind of,' muttered Nish, 'because otherwise you might get killed.'

Hazel ignored him. She stared at Roisin in fury. 'What – why the – how have you got from a mediocre art exhibition to a far-right rally? It's a totally fallacious comparison! Why do you have to be so extreme all the fucking time?'

Roisin sighed, as if it was all very simple. 'Hazel, I'm just trying to illustrate that it's very problematic of you to try and prevent me calling someone out just because you've got plans to fuck them later.'

'No, Roisin,' said Hazel. 'You're aggressive, and you enjoy making people feel uncomfortable.'

'Oh, I'm sorry, did I make the rich white boys uncomfortable? Well, personally their shit art made me pretty uncomfortable too, so I guess we're even.'

Hazel said nothing. Her mouth was set, her breath jagged.

'Guys, guys,' said Nish. 'Let's all calm down. Why don't we go and *consume* some more beverages?' He grinned expectantly, but no one laughed.

'I'm going back inside.'

'What? Oh, come on, Hazel. Let's talk this out. You surely don't still want to have sex with that joker.'

'Excuse me?'

'Whoa,' said Nish, taken aback. 'I just mean – yeah, maybe Ro was a bit inappropriate. But that Miles guy … He just seems … well, like a bit of a wanker.'

Anger flared in Hazel's chest. 'It's *irrelevant* whether or not he's a wanker,' she said, making an effort to keep her voice steady. 'It's *irrelevant* whether or not I want to have sex with him. The point is that this was a unique opportunity for me, and Ro just did her best to fuck it up. When have I ever had an in with a crowd like this? Who knows what they could have done for my so-called career?'

There was an uncomfortable silence. 'Is that why you wanted to come?' said Nish, abashed. 'You should have *said*.'

'Well, it wasn't the only reason,' she said. 'And anyway, I thought I could be casual about it. I didn't realise Ro was going to try and burn all my bridges before I'd even *met* anyone.'

'Look, Hazel,' said Roisin, grinding her cigarette into the ground with her foot, 'I know this kind of crowd, and I know you, and trust me, you're not a match. These aren't your people, I promise you.'

'It might have been nice,' replied Hazel tartly, 'if you'd given me the opportunity to make that decision for myself.'

Roisin shrugged, saying nothing. There was quiet again, and for a moment it seemed like the worst was over, like somebody might be on the point of saying sorry. But this only deepened the urgency of Hazel's argument. She wasn't ready to forgive or forget.

'The one good thing about what you just did, Ro,' she declared, 'is that you didn't stand next to me when you did it. So you go and *consume some more beverages*. I'll just be back here, salvaging whatever the fuck I can out of the train wreck you've engineered. Okay?'

14

EMILY HAD GOT a job at a company that developed software systems for vertical farms, big warehouses that grew vegetables in stacked-up tanks under lights. The company marketed itself as a leading light in the Green Revolution, which went some way towards counterbalancing her unease about procreating on a planet as beleaguered as this one. On Fridays she worked from home, but the commute during the rest of the week was as forewarned: tedious and exhausting. She got home at seven thirty at the earliest. Daria, though she still doubted the wisdom of this routine, nonetheless benefited from it, because it meant she could have two evening therapy sessions a week without Emily wondering where she was.

Her therapist was a comfortable woman called Janet, whose office was full of plants and photos of her children. She had a ready supply of tissues, and encouraged Daria to make use of them. Daria learned from Janet that she was punishing herself for feeling the way she did, and that this was unproductive. Her phobia was not to be dismissed, Janet said; it was perfectly rational. Really what she was feeling was an extreme version of what all prospective parents ought to be feeling, if they had any sense. Of course, when anything was taken to extremes it became a problem, but she thought that if they had a few sessions together, they could work on bringing things a bit more into balance.

Janet taught her some breathing exercises, and she had been practising these on the sofa one evening, feeling exceedingly relaxed, when Emily came in and said, 'You'll never believe this. Hazel's going out with some hipster!'

'What? No!' said Daria, sitting up. 'What about Alfie?'

Emily flopped on the sofa beside her and showed her a picture of Hazel that appeared to have been taken by a professional. She was in someone's kitchen; behind her there were saucepans hanging on a wall, and to the side, a silver coffee pot on a stove. Hazel herself looked as though she had just woken up. She was wearing an oversized T-shirt and her hair was tousled. She smiled gently, a smudge of yesterday's mascara outlining her eyes, both hands clasped around a large mug.

The photo had been posted by someone called Miles Newman, whose social media profiles were all open in various windows on Emily's phone. He was an East London Adonis, all teeth and cheekbones. His most recent Instagram offering was a series of pictures captioned *A few of the afterparty*, several of which also featured Hazel: deep in discussion with fashionable people, turning to look coquettishly over her shoulder, standing by a large window with a whisky glass in her hand. On Facebook and Twitter he had posted links to an esoteric-looking event in Hackney Wick, accompanied by comments like,

Join me, @miller_daniel and @liamr_poet for a mixed-media exploration of human corporeality. Hazel had liked one of them.

'So?' said Daria. 'Did you ask her about it?'

Emily nodded. 'They're seeing each other. They met on Tinder, apparently. He's an artist. She didn't give much else away.'

'Fuck,' said Daria. 'Poor Alfie.'

'I know!' cried Emily. She was acutely disappointed. Alfie was kind, and funny, and unpretentious. He was exactly what Hazel needed. He would have slotted into their family like he belonged there. And now, to be pipped to the post by this angular showpiece, this 'artist'! It wasn't fair.

'I suppose we don't know for *sure* he likes her,' said Daria.

'Oh, come on! He gave up an entire weekend to help us move. He barely knows us. Why, if not to spend more time with her?'

'I don't know, because he's a nice bloke? Because he enjoys our company?'

'But the way he was with her!'

'Well, the way they were with each *other*. I thought for sure she was into him. Maybe we just imagined the whole thing.'

'In our vicarious desire for blossoming romance,' said Emily, with a bitter laugh.

'Exactly,' said Daria, putting an arm around her. They snuggled into each other, and were quiet for a while.

'Guess what,' said Emily, tracing a line on Daria's palm with her finger. She had deliberated for some minutes over whether to say this out loud.

'What?'

'Well, my period's due,' said Emily. 'And I haven't had any backache, or any spotting. If it doesn't come by tomorrow I'll officially be late.' Two weeks previously they had taken the morning off work for a trip to their nearest fertility clinic, where Emily had lain with her knees in the air while a nurse injected her with semen. She had reluctantly accepted that there would be no adoring super-uncle to visit and babysit and send birthday cards. Instead, anonymous sperm from a freezer and a donor they may or may not meet one day, depending on whether the child decided to contact him when it turned eighteen.

To Daria's dismay, her dominant feeling, in reaction to this news, was dread. She supposed she hadn't yet had many sessions with Janet, and it was unreasonable to expect immediate progress. Still, it was disappointing. She gave her best impression of a smile, and hoped Emily would be convinced by it.

But to Emily the smile looked like what it was: the stretching of a mouth in imitation of a fitting reaction. She shifted in her seat, uneasy. She shuffled down on the sofa and put her head on Daria's shoulder, the sounds of the room half obscured by the rub of her ear against fabric and the brisk thumping of the heart underneath it.

Daria got up to cook dinner, and to distract herself, Emily scrolled through pictures of Hannah Fox and her family. Since her Facebook faux pas back in September she and Hannah had embarked on a tentative course of acknowledging each other's existence. Hannah had started it, liking an article Emily had shared as if to imply that she didn't mind Emily having trawled voyeuristically through her ancient photos. A few days later she liked something else, which Emily took as confirmation that the first like had been sincerely meant. After that she felt emboldened to like something of Hannah's, and a cautious back-and-forth ensued. Then Hannah followed her on Instagram, and Emily reciprocated, and now there were likes to be dealt out there too. It was Emily who took it to the next level, commenting on a picture in words. 'Gorgeous family', she had written beneath an image of Hannah, her partner and their baby, and Hannah had replied, 'Thanks :) :)'.

Now she was gearing up to send Hannah a proper message. She wanted to know how they had conceived, who had carried, why they had made the choices they had. She was collecting stories like these. She opened Messenger and wrote:

Hey! Long time no see. Hope you're doing well – certainly looks that way. Congrats on the recent arrival. My wife and I have just started trying so hoping for one of our own in the not too distant future. Would be great to chat more about your experience at some point if you're up for it. I'm full of rookie questions.

When she'd sent it Daria called that dinner was ready. Emily laid the table in silence, the memory of Daria's fake smile looming once again in her mind.

'You'll never guess what a student said in my Crisis seminar this morning,' said Daria as they sat down to eat, with what seemed to Emily like a manufactured level of cheer. Daria was convening a final-year module called 'Literature in Times of Crisis', which she had developed herself while they were in Melbourne. 'She said in fifty to a hundred years' time, when we're living in some apocalyptic climate-change hellhole, literature will basically just be the glacé cherry on top of a big pile of shit. If it even still exists. Isn't that good? I might incorporate it into one of my slides.'

'That is good,' said Emily. 'What did you say?'

'I said, excellent image, but couldn't it be argued that that's been literature's predicament since the dawn of time? And this kid Evan, he said, maybe it's better to say literature is the seams of gold running *through* the shit, and if ever it gets relegated to glacé cherry, that'll be a problem.'

'Your students sound pretty switched on.'

'Those two are. They're head and shoulders above the rest of them.'

'Don't hate me,' said Emily, her fork hovering in the air, 'but that glacé cherry thing. It sounds pretty accurate to me.' This was a move of deliberate provocation. It wasn't clear to her what she hoped to gain from it.

'I don't know. I think I prefer seams of gold.'

'But imagine in, say, 2100, when you can't leave the house in summer because you'll fry to death, and there are millions and millions of climate refugees, all trying to get into northern Europe and Canada, only no one wants to let them in, so most of them die, and the bees are extinct, so there isn't much food, and what there is isn't nutritious any more, and you can't jet off to the Med for a week because it's a desert, you can't even go for an old-fashioned British seaside holiday because all the beaches are gone, submerged, beaches are these historic things that only old folks remember—'

'Okay,' said Daria. 'I get the picture.'

'Well, how is literature going to help?' said Emily, finally eating the food on her fork.

Daria smiled like a besieged politician. 'Literature is a way of *communicating*. It's a way of creating *empathy*. We'll need it more than ever if the climate full-on breaks down. There'll be civil unrest. Society will start to unravel. People will be in competition with each other for the most basic necessities. We'll need reminders to stay human, even when the world's beyond saving. *Especially* then.'

'But why do those reminders have to come from literature? There's so much content now that could serve the same purpose. Look at TV. TV's really good these days.'

'Well, it takes all sorts. I'm not saying literature's got a monopoly on empathy.'

'No,' said Emily. 'Although you do have a vested interest in it staying relevant. I'm just playing devil's advocate,' she added as Daria looked up from her plate, affronted.

'You're being pretty aggressive with it,' muttered Daria.

'What? Oh, come on.'

'Anyway, if the future's as hopeless as you think it is, why are you so desperate to have a baby?'

Emily put down her fork with a vigour she had not quite intended. 'Why am *I* so desperate?' she cried, at once angry and triumphant. 'As far as I was aware we both wanted to have a child. Is that not the case?'

'Jesus Christ, of course it is. What is this? Why are you being so volatile?'

There were umpteen reasons. Daria wasn't telling her something. Daria had asked her a pointed question to which there was no satisfactory response. An ache had started in her lower back and abdomen.

She shrugged. 'No reason. Only that I sometimes feel you're utterly unbothered about this whole thing.'

Daria blinked in surprise. '*What?*'

'Well, do you remember what you said at Kamran's? You said, "Okay, let's get this over with."'

'Did I? Well, it was gross. It was my brother's *jizz*, for Christ's sake.'

'Yeah, and your brother's jizz was our future child! We were creating a whole new human life! I mean, we weren't, obviously, but we didn't know that.'

'Well, I'm very sorry I haven't been showing Emily-approved levels of reverence. Next time we go to the clinic I'll walk out backwards.' Emily opened her mouth to protest. 'I mean *if* there's a next time,' Daria added quickly.

Emily shook her head. 'You're not even excited.'

'I *am*!'

'I don't know what upsets me more,' Emily said quietly. 'The fact that you're hiding something from me, or the fact you think I won't notice.'

An anguished look came over Daria's face. 'I don't know what you mean.'

'Don't you?'

Daria said nothing for a long time. Emily waited, and as she waited, a familiar warmth began moistening her underwear.

'Listen, Em,' said Daria, then went quiet again. Emily was suddenly having trouble concentrating. Time was short. She was still in her work clothes, and the kitchen chairs were cloth-covered.

'The thing is, I've been—'

Emily held up her hand. 'Can you just hold that thought?' she said. 'I'll be right back. I really want to hear this.'

She went upstairs to the bathroom and dealt with the blood smeared over her underwear, then went back to the kitchen and sat down heavily in the chair.

'Are you okay?' said Daria.

Emily looked across the table at her, letting gravity drag down on all the muscles in her face.

'Oh, babe. Oh, no,' said Daria, understanding, and there was such sadness and compassion in her voice that Emily immediately regretted her earlier accusations. She no longer wanted to hear what Daria had been going to say. A gnawing disappointment was demanding her attention instead. There was a thumping in her ears, an obstruction in her throat.

'I really thought this was it,' she said.

Daria got up and stood behind her. She put her arms around Emily's shoulders and nuzzled into her neck.

'I'm sorry I was shitty,' said Emily.

'You weren't shitty. Well, only a tiny bit.'

'I'm sorry I said you weren't excited.'

'It's okay, sweet pea.'

'I feel like shit.'

'I know.'

Daria wouldn't let her do the washing-up, so she curled up on the sofa and hugged a cushion. A quick glance at her phone revealed that Hannah Fox had replied to her message – a chatty reply, it appeared, with exclamation marks and emojis – but it would be a while now before she had the heart to read it.

15

HAZEL FELT A little murmur of unease in her stomach whenever she thought about Miles's exhibition. At first it was easily attributable to embarrassment at the scene Roisin had caused, but as the days passed, it took on a different quality. If looked at directly it might have been recognisable as shame; if allowed, it might have blossomed into acknowledgement that Roisin had been right, and that the extremity of her reaction had blinded Hazel to the wisdom of her argument. But Hazel did not look at it directly, much less allow it to blossom. It was easy to put it from her mind: she had only to look at the contours of Miles's face, whether in person or in a photo, to conjure up a sense of wonder that anyone could be so beautiful, and, moreover, that anyone so beautiful could be desirous of *her*.

They frequented his flat and his neighbourhood because they were so much nicer than hers. The neighbourhood was quiet yet happening, comfortable yet edgy. The flat was like nothing Hazel had ever seen in real life: part of a converted warehouse with bare brick walls, polished concrete floors and enormous windows on two sides. Miles had been pestering to be allowed back to her place, but she had so far resisted, thinking of the tired furniture and the mould in the bathroom, of her single, squeaky bed and the undignified sounds that drifted where they were not welcome. Of Alfie, too. There was no real need to introduce him to Miles, so why bother? Anyway, it was fun to play at being wealthy.

She had first seen Miles's flat the evening of the exhibition. He was hosting the after-party there, and had introduced her to a lot of serious people whose names she mostly failed to remember. Without exception, they declared Miles and his co-exhibitors to be 'really talented guys' or 'really interesting guys' or 'really great guys'.

'What about that ruckus at the end, though!' said people.

'Oh my God, *so* inappropriate,' said other people.

'Who *was* that?' many of them wanted to know, and Hazel stared into her drink, hoping none of them had seen her talking to Roisin.

To her relief nobody seemed to make the connection, or if they did, they didn't say so. She told them all she was an illustrator, which gave her a thrill. She could feel herself acquiring a certain gravitas, taking up more space in their thoughts. She half expected to be caught out by someone who recognised her from the café, but this only added a pleasant frisson of danger. Several people followed her on Instagram, right then and there, laughing promisingly at what they saw.

She and Miles didn't have a moment alone together until most of them had left. By then the remaining guests were sprawling on the sofas and making relaxed conversation; quiet music was emanating from a record player in the corner. Miles poured her a glass of whisky and led her to stand by one of the enormous windows.

'Well, I have to say, I'm pretty pleased with how that went,' he said, looking out at the lights in the distance.

No thanks to me, thought Hazel guiltily. She braced herself, and came clean.

'Miles, I have to apologise,' she said, and he looked at her quizzically. 'It's really embarrassing. My friend Roisin. She was that one during the Q&A.'

'Oh, her!' said Miles, as if Roisin was a distant memory. He laughed. 'I *thought* she looked familiar! She works at your café, doesn't she?'

'Yeah. Fuck. I'm so sorry. I don't know what I was thinking, bringing her.'

'You're cute, Hazel. You don't need to apologise. You can't be held responsible for your friends behaving badly. Anyway, it's always good to have a bit of a debate. It's *healthy*.'

'Okay,' said Hazel. 'Phew.' There was a pause. They looked at each other, and then away again. Hazel turned to the window, which gave on to the River Lea and the Olympic Park. Miles stood beside her and they sipped their whisky in silence. Then Miles said, 'Hazel,' and she turned back to face him. 'I'd really like to kiss you,' he said, taking a step closer. 'How would you feel about that?'

They spent the rest of the evening holding hands conspicuously, hoping that the guests would take the hint and leave. Hazel surveyed each piece of furniture in turn and wondered which of them they would have sex on. There was the kitchen table, which had metal legs and a wooden top and benches along each side. She supposed the wood had some kind of finish to it, for the avoidance of splinters.

The granite worktops might be an option if they were the right height, although they would be chilly at this time of year. The seagrass mat in the living-room area would be too knobbly, but one or other of the sofas would probably do very well.

In the end, however, Miles led her upstairs to his bedroom, which was littered with cameras and tripods and screens. One wall was given over to a vast mirror that doubled the room in size, and the bed – a mattress resting on two pallets – sat opposite it, so that Hazel kept catching sight of herself in various poses and states of undress. The effect was odd, but not altogether unpleasant.

At first the sex was good. She was astride him, in control and enjoying herself. Then, deciding perhaps that this had gone on long enough, he flipped her onto her back without warning and began thrusting vigorously. She made an effort not to appear put out, then realised he wasn't looking at her anyway, but at the wall just above her head. His jaw was set in determination, as if he were struggling to postpone the inevitable. When it could no longer be postponed he slowed to a shuddering halt and fell against the pillows next to her. Then he turned on to his side to face her and reached up to stroke her cheek with his finger.

'Hey,' he said softly, holding her gaze. He took her hand, brought it to his mouth and kissed her palm. 'How was that for you?'

'It was great!'

'Did you come?'

'Not quite, but—'

'Ah, man,' said Miles gravely, reaching out to touch her hair. Immediately she wished she had lied. 'Shall I rectify that for you?' he said.

'That's a kind offer,' said Hazel, 'but it's really fine.' The moment had passed; there was no chance of retrieving it now.

'I've been told I'm quite good in that department.'

'Really, I—'

'It's no skin off *my* nose,' said Miles, propping himself on one elbow and kissing the base of her neck.

'Miles ...' she began, but he was already brushing his lips over her breasts, and then her stomach, and then, with tiresome inevitability, his head found its place between her legs, where for a full fifteen minutes it performed a sequence of tepid tongue acrobatics that put her in mind of being tickled with a wet sponge. She gave occasional cursory moans and hoped that Miles would soon tire. It was nearly three in the morning, she noticed when she turned her head absentmindedly towards the bedside table. But her orgasm was obviously a point of personal pride for him, and he had no intention of letting himself be beaten by a stiff neck or an aching tongue. She thought about asking him to stop, but she didn't want his hurt feelings to sour the atmosphere. In the end she panted, arched her back, kicked a little, and gave a final, conclusive moan.

16

EMILY WAS NOT the only person who had noticed Miles's photo of Hazel. Alfie had noticed it too. He had considered pressing her for details, had even rehearsed his options in front of the bathroom mirror, which were: 'So who's this Miles character, then?' and, 'So you've got a boyfriend now, I gather?' and, 'So when's the wedding?' In every variation he sounded like a creep. It was pointless asking, anyway, when it was obvious what the answer would be. More pictures were appearing, and if ever Alfie got up to pee in the night he often saw Hazel's door standing open, the bed empty.

He went back over their conversations in his head and tried to pinpoint the moment at which it had all gone wrong. He kept stumbling over the times he had mentioned his exes. Perhaps the second instance had not, after all, negated the damage done by the first. But Hazel had exes of her own. She'd mentioned one of them, and anyway, he was certain that a person like her – worldly, experienced, interesting – was more likely to be deterred if he did *not* have exes than if he did. Which led him to wonder, had he imagined their chemistry? If not, had she led him on deliberately? He refused to believe in either scenario. In the end only one conclusion remained, gut-wrenching, yet almost pleasing in its simplicity: she had liked him, but she liked Miles Newman better.

Alfie spent several masochistic hours trawling Miles's online profiles – not just the usual places but also hireanartist.com, artistprofile.de, milesnewman.co.uk. It was an education, following which he felt he understood completely what type of man Miles was. On milesnewman.co.uk he found a series of black-and-white photos called 'hibernus': a leafless trees and frosted grass-type affair, moody skies over broad open fields, that sort of thing. By way of an introduction Miles had written:

winter. n. // a death of sorts. melancholia /
contentment. tangible stillness. hard ground, crunch
underfoot. seeping chill & things buried.

all shot on a leica M4-P 50mm. prints available from
the shop.

Later Alfie mashed potatoes for dinner with a fury like he was mashing Miles's head. 'Seeping chill *ampersand* things buried'. Why couldn't he just write *and*?

Alfie might have taken refuge in the conviction that Hazel was misguided, unable to recognise her own desire, and would come to her senses if taken by the shoulders, looked in the eye, and told: But you love *me*! Sadly, this was a fantasy in which right-thinking men could no longer justifiably indulge. Only Hazel knew what Hazel wanted. If she wanted Miles Newman, it was not for Alfie to persuade her otherwise.

It was lonely without her. He perked up when the front door slammed, but it only ever seemed to be Tony. He lingered in the kitchen in hopes she would walk in, but when she actually did he hastened away, lost for words. He could be sure neither of them would mention Miles, yet he would know Miles existed, and she would suspect he knew Miles existed, and the weight of all this unspoken knowledge and suspected knowledge would drag down on their conversation until it sank. Better to say, 'I'll leave you to it,' and slope away.

Alfie's eye twitch had by now gone away, but had been replaced by a lingering cough that he feared would turn out to be lung cancer. He didn't smoke, but the air in London was full of carcinogens thanks to all the people who drove cars without any possible justification for it. He had once seen a headline, emblazoned across the *Metro*, which said living in London was the equivalent of smoking twenty cigarettes a day.

To distract himself he messaged Jasmine and asked if she wanted to go for a drink at the weekend. She told him she was meeting up with friends but he was welcome to join them, so he said, *Okay, that might be nice.* They went to a pub in a neighbourhood Alfie had once frequented and now avoided where possible. There was no music, but it was loud. There were tables and chairs, but no one was sitting at them. People put their coats on the chairs and their empty glasses on the tables and gathered in little circles nearby, shouting at each other. Jasmine's female friends wore their hair long and drank through straws. Her male friends slugged pints and draped their arms around the women. What conversation Alfie could hear consisted mainly of anecdotes about other nights like this one. The woman next to him told the story of a venue so posh one of their number had felt compelled to steal the handcream. This was met with shrieks and bullish laughter and hands clamping over mouths.

'And then we googled it,' she went on, 'and it was literally forty pounds! The handcream! Like, *forty* pounds!'

Alfie was just considering going to the toilet and not coming back again when he felt Jasmine's hand on the small of his back; then moving down, finding the hem of his T-shirt, sliding up under it. She was two drinks in, or maybe three.

'Let's get out of here,' she demanded to the group. 'I want to dance.' They threw back their drinks and rummaged for their coats. Out in the street Alfie and Jasmine hung back, and as the others tottered off towards some club or other she took his hand and pulled him into the doorway of a Pret A Manger, where she kissed him fulsomely, pressing her hips into his.

'I thought you wanted to dance,' said Alfie.

'I'd rather fuck,' she replied. She moved her hand towards the button of his jeans, as if ready to fuck right here in this doorway.

Alfie ordered an Uber and took her back to the flat. She kissed him on every landing, a few times on the stairs, and then again when the front door closed behind them. At this point he was almost distracted by a light under Hazel's door, the sound of voices in her room, but he slid a hand inside Jasmine's coat and corralled his thoughts back towards the business at hand.

*

Jasmine was loud, like the other time. At first she did all the work, while Alfie lay back and looked up at her breasts. Then she asked him if he would like to take her from behind.

'Sure,' he said.

'But, like, *behind*.'

'Oh, right!' He laughed, surprised. 'Okay.' He'd done this before, just once, with Rachel. She had quickly vetoed any further attempts, saying the pleasure was outweighed by the uncanny feeling of shitting yourself in reverse, but Jasmine lay on her front and parted her buttocks for him, waiting patiently while he fumbled, out of his comfort zone.

He thought he had heard her at her loudest, but he had severely underestimated her. The high-pitched moans he was used to were nothing to the noises she made now, wailing and bellowing, writhing beneath him like an animal in pain. He stopped, certain he was doing her damage, but she panted at him to carry on. Through the wall he heard the music from one of Tony's video games, the volume raised pointedly. Hazel would be hearing it all too, as would whoever she had in her room with her. She *requested* this, he thought, as if it were possible to convey the message to them all telepathically. She *likes* it. Please don't think you need to be concerned for her welfare.

Later, when Alfie stepped outside his bedroom door, he heard a rhythmic squeaking coming from Hazel's room; a few quiet sighs too, if he strained his ears. He stood for a moment, perfectly still. Then he realised what he was doing and hurried guiltily into the bathroom. At least the sounds he and Jasmine had made together hadn't totally turned her off, he reasoned as he brushed his teeth. At least she was enjoying herself. He did want her to enjoy herself. He tried to brush his tongue, and gagged.

In the morning Alfie woke with a numb arm. He was aware of it from the depths of his slumber, and was woken by a kernel of dread spreading steadily out from his abdomen. Then, coming to, he registered the warm weight of Jasmine's head on his shoulder and a wave of relief washed over him, so delicious that he kissed the head in gratitude.

He got up and went into the kitchen to make coffee, massaging his arm as he waited for the kettle to boil. He felt the twang of a nascent cough in his chest and registered it with irritation. Could he not go five minutes without having some sort of symptom? When the coughing fit started he bowed his head and directed it under his T-shirt, his breath moistening the bare skin of his chest. Just as it began to decrescendo, a globule of phlegm shot out of his mouth and landed in the space between his nipples.

'That sounds like a nasty one,' said Hazel from behind him. He turned, wiping his mouth with his forearm. She was pulling out a chair, sleepy and beautiful.

'Yeah,' he said. 'Sorry. Be right back.' He strode past her, making for the bathroom, but the bathroom was occupied. He searched the kitchen cupboards for paper towels, and found none. The phlegm was worming its way down his torso, but he tried to ignore it. He poured hot water over coffee grounds, reached for the mugs.

The toilet flushed, a door opened and closed, and Miles Newman appeared in the kitchen doorway. He was tall, in the flesh, though perhaps not quite as tall as Alfie. His hair was tousled and hung to his shoulders.

'This is Miles,' said Hazel. 'Miles, this is Alfie.'

'Hey, man,' said Miles, reaching to shake Alfie's hand and clapping him convivially on the shoulder. 'Good to meet you.'

'You too,' said Alfie, hating him. The phlegm must by now have made contact with the fabric of his T-shirt. He dared not look.

'Can we borrow your coffee pot?' said Hazel.

'Sure,' said Alfie. He did not wish to facilitate their intimacy in any way, but it would have been pointlessly ungracious to refuse. He poured the coffee out into a mug each for himself and Jasmine and pushed the cafetière across the counter towards them. 'All yours,' he said.

'Thanks, man,' said Miles. 'You're a lifesaver. Can you believe there's a barista in the room who doesn't even own one?'

'I get my coffee free at work,' said Hazel with a shrug. Miles grinned and ruffled her hair.

Alfie was finally heading for the bathroom when the front door banged. They all heard it. He faltered, halfway across the kitchen.

'Shit, man!' said Miles. 'Was that your lay?'

Hazel looked at him. '*Lay?*'

'What?' said Miles, surprised.

'Probably just Tony,' said Alfie, before Hazel could explain her objection. 'He works on Sundays.' This was true, but he and Hazel both knew it was far too late for him to be leaving. Hazel turned towards him, and he felt himself shrinking under her gaze. Her eyes flicked to the two mugs of coffee on the counter, then back to his face, then to an undefined spot in the region of his abdomen, presumably the damp patch that must by now be adorning the front of his T-shirt. She said nothing.

He turned back for the coffee and went straight to his own room. It was empty. The only indication that Jasmine had ever been there was the imprint of her head on the pillow.

'Nice,' muttered Alfie to himself. 'Classy. Really fucking classy.' He took off his T-shirt, wiped himself with it, threw it into the laundry pile, and got back into bed. He stayed there until Hazel and Miles left the flat, drinking both mugs of coffee himself.

17

IT WAS OF some surprise to Hazel that she was still seeing Miles, several weeks after their first encounter. She did not quite think of them as a couple, but apparently everyone else did, which seemed, by and large, to make it so. Her orgasm count had by now risen to one, although Miles believed the total to be rather higher. The fakery set an unhealthy precedent, but also maintained a certain equilibrium. Without it he would be disappointed in himself, which really meant he would be disappointed in her. To deprive him of the appreciation he felt was his due, given the practised nature of his sexual technique, would be to burden their relationship with a layer of complexity that it might not withstand.

Hazel avoided thinking too hard about Miles himself. She was physically as well as professionally attracted to him, and for the time being this was enough to inure her against his foibles and missteps, such as being monstrously wealthy and making artworks that capitalised on the pain of the less fortunate, or that attempt at man-to-man solidarity in the kitchen with Alfie. The sex wasn't ideal, but it might yet improve.

The week after their encounter with Alfie, Miles invited her out for dinner.

Heeey-zel :) This new curry place just opened near Vicky Park if you fancy getting hot and sweaty with me Fri or Sat night?? ;) ;) Vegan + GF, 5*s in Time Out?

She replied with a thumbs-up emoji, suggesting Friday. This tendency in Miles was one of the flaws she was, for the time being, prepared to forgive: his being a trend fol-lower, a bandwagon jumper, predisposed, for example, to rate a place on its vegan-gluten-free credentials despite being neither vegan nor gluten intolerant himself. He also did yoga, collected succulents, drank oat milk, wrote in a Moleskine, carried a reusable coffee cup, bought albums on vinyl, supported local micro-breweries, avoided bread unless it was sourdough, and kept a bike with drop handle-bars in his living room. That some of these things were also true of Hazel did not ease her suspicion that on him they formed a carapace, a lamina, were deliberately arranged to conceal a core that was not there.

Miles had been to India, and considered himself, there-fore, to have a modicum of authority on its cuisine. For this reason, when their dinner date came around, it was he who took charge of the ordering, requesting dish after dish for them to share, consulting Hazel only in the broadest terms. 'You like jackfruit, yeah?' he asked her, and, 'Chickpeas, yay or nay?', and, 'How spicy are we thinking?' The assumption was that she would opine in moderation but not to excess. She told him she wanted the spiciest of the dishes, the ones with four chilli symbols next to them, not because she really did, but because she felt an overwhelming need to test his limits.

'Babe, trust me, I don't think that's a great idea,' he said, and then gave several further variations on this same theme until she, aware that there was a real risk of him capitulating, stopped asking. When the food arrived she was forced to admit that he had chosen well. They ate voraciously, and when the bill came they split it neatly, fifty-fifty, as they always did, because bill-splitting was a core principle of feminism to which Miles, in spite of his wealth and her relative poverty and his having chosen all the food, liked strictly to adhere.

She refused to stay with him that night because the curry had done bad things to her insides. She told him she was getting her period and he said, 'Oh, poor baby,' and insisted on putting her in an Uber even though she could just as easily have got the bus. She looked out at East London passing by the window and toyed with the idea of breaking up with him, imagining the conversation she might have with Nish the next day.

'I'm wondering about ending it with Miles,' she would begin.

'How come?' Nish would ask, and she would reply: 'He's failing my fart test.'

'Your *what*?'

'My fart test. I just invented it. Basically, let's say it takes the average couple six months before they feel comfortable farting in front of each other—'

If Roisin had been talking to her she might have come over at this point.

'Six months?' they would echo in astonishment, because it probably took Nish closer to six days and Roisin most likely never farted in front of anyone at all, ever.

'Well, however long,' Hazel would continue. 'What I mean is, most relationships go through a fart-free period, which I would *guess* lasts an average of six months, maybe more, maybe less. Anyway, this is the test: is the pleasure you get from being with the person worth the abdominal discomfort? Of holding them in, I mean?'

'Never,' Nish would probably declare, and Roisin might raise an eyebrow and say, 'Sounds to me like you both need to go to the doctor.'

She grinned to herself, thinking of it. It was a good idea, too good to waste. When she got home she opened her drawing pad, intending only to sketch out a few ideas, but by the time she put down her pencil she had completed an entire cartoon, ready to be inked and put on Instagram. In it, two women were discussing a boyfriend.

'Do you like him?' said one.

'Yes,' said the other. 'I mean, I think so.'

'Does he pass the fart test?' said the first, and explained this concept exactly as Hazel had imagined doing, to Nish and Roisin. In the last panel the second woman concluded, 'I guess I need to break up with him, don't I?'

She fell asleep happy, but woke up wretched, barely five hours after she had gone to bed. She pressed snooze on her alarm several times. When eventually she dragged herself upright and into the kitchen for breakfast, she found that someone had used her milk without asking, leaving a gratuitous drop in the bottom of the bottle so that she wouldn't notice until she tried to pour it over her cereal. She took longer in the bathroom than usual because of that stupid curry, and because the water pressure in the shower kept cutting out. Then the front tyre on her bike needed pumping. When she arrived at work, fifteen minutes late, she found Roisin setting up on her own.

'Sorry,' said Hazel, and almost launched into an explanation, but remembered just in time that they were only speaking when absolutely necessary. She was ready to forgive the scene at the exhibition, just as soon as Roisin apologised, but Roisin appeared to have no intention of doing any such thing.

'Nish is off sick,' she said now, without making eye contact.

'Brilliant,' said Hazel, because it was Saturday, and they needed him.

The day did not improve. She and Roisin were rushed off their feet and sullen with each other. The customers were impatient and unsympathetic. The waiting times were unacceptable, they said. More than one threatened to leave a bad review on TripAdvisor. A man left his suitcase sticking out and then tutted at Hazel when she tripped on it, slopping hot coffee onto her hand and forearm. As she made a fresh cup she saw him inspecting the case pointedly for damage. Then she delivered the coffee to a woman with large earrings who said, *'Finally*, thank *God*, I'm *gasping.'*

By lunchtime Hazel felt bruised and brittle, beset with resentment at the shitness of everything. Where was Irma, she wondered, or the nice old man with the mini dachshund? She hadn't seen either of them in days. She sent messages to Nish, Alfie and Emily, desperate for a friendly word from someone, but none of them responded. Nish probably wasn't ill at all, she thought resentfully. 'Ill' was just as likely to mean 'horny'. Probably he had an important assignation under a duvet. Emily would be busy doing something grown up, like washing her car or buying a cat or getting herself pregnant. Alfie would be preoccupied with something or someone more important than her – marking or lesson planning or another of his 'lays', as Miles had so charmingly put it.

Later, when things were quieter, Miles himself walked in. He caught her eye from across the café and smiled at her, and she walked over and hugged him, right there, in the middle of the room. 'What a welcome,' he said, and kissed the top of her head. It was a relief to be wrapped in the arms of a person who appreciated her, even a person who had been examined and found wanting according to an infallible metric of her own invention.

'I just stopped by,' said Miles, 'to ask if you fancied coming over later. Just to chill, listen to some music, drink a bit of wine. I'll cook.'

'That sounds lovely,' she said, her face still against his chest. 'Can I bring anything?'

'No,' he replied. 'Just your beautiful self.' He took her chin in his thumb and forefinger, raised her face to his, and kissed her.

When she arrived at his flat she was greeted by the smell of chicken roasting in the oven. He poured her a glass of wine and put Ella Fitzgerald on the record player. She gave an account of her day and he was outraged in all the right places. The chicken was succulent and flavoursome, and for dessert there was tiramisu from an organic patisserie in Stoke Newington that he had visited especially. Afterwards they drank loose-leaf tea and watched a slow, subtitled film starring Isabelle Huppert, which lulled Hazel into a pleasant doze. When it was over Miles led her upstairs, gave her one of his T-shirts to sleep in, and curled around her as she fell rapidly back to sleep.

At home the next day, she remembered her cartoon. She opened her drawing pad and studied it for a while. She considered inking it, but it didn't seem quite so clever as it had when she'd drawn it, nor so truthful. She no longer felt certain that Miles failed the test. Anyway, she couldn't post a cartoon inspired by the thought of breaking up with him if she was not, in fact, breaking up with him. She shut the pad. She would have to shelve it.

18

CHRISTMAS CAME AROUND, inevitably. Alfie spent it in Northampton with his father, just the two of them that year. Ordinarily they would have visited his father's family – Auntie Yvonne and Uncle Steve and Alfie's cousins Tom and Jess – but they were all out of the country: Jess was studying in Sydney for a year, and the others were visiting her. If Alfie was honest, it was a relief to be rid of them. He liked his aunt and cousins, but Steve was a yearly trial. He always started drinking early, so that by the time Alfie and his father arrived he was primed and ready to get a bee in his bonnet about the State of Things, backed up by spurious theories from dark corners of the internet. He referred to Black people as Alfie's 'brethren', to Yvonne as 'she who must be obeyed', and he could be relied upon, over the course of the afternoon, to slap someone on the back and command them to 'drink up, you miserable cretin!' Frequently his political diatribes left Tom and Jess hunching over their plates with embarrassment, and Alfie with deep welts in his palms from clenching his fists beneath the table.

Alfie always liked to imagine how these occasions might be playing out in a parallel universe, one in which his mother was still alive: the two of them catching each other's eye across the table, communicating in their own private language of eyebrow twitches and slow blinks, tallying up the affronts in a silent game of Uncle Steve Bingo. Or more likely they wouldn't be there at all, because his mother would not allow it. Alfie himself had suggested they break the tradition on the grounds that Steve had incontrovertibly racist inclinations which he struggled to conceal in Alfie's presence. His father said yes, Steve was a racist, but he was an everything else-ist too, and he himself didn't much enjoy being called a 'pansy' for refusing a fourth beer, as it happened. The best course of action was to grit your teeth and keep your head down. They went for the sake of Yvonne and the cousins, didn't they? And it wasn't right to punish them, was it?

'Mum wouldn't have made us go,' Alfie muttered, and his father responded with a quick and heavy sigh that turned into a growl at its close.

'*Don't* bring your mother into this, *please*,' he said.

Alfie might have continued protesting, but for over ten years he had been using the fact of his father's 'needing' him at Christmas as a subconscious excuse to avoid visiting the other branch of his family. This consisted of his maternal grandfather, Sam, and Sam's second wife, Doreen, and all the various step-aunts, -uncles and -cousins Alfie had acquired as a result of their union. He hadn't seen any of them in a long time. His grandmother had died when he was seven and Sam and Doreen's marriage had happened far too soon after her death for Alfie's mother's liking, so soon as to be *fucking disrespectful* and an *insult* and a *slap in the face*. Alfie could remember hearing these words, spoken furiously to his father, and not knowing what they meant; he remembered understanding that a ferocious row had occurred somewhere out of earshot, that scenes had been caused, feelings hurt, things said that could not be forgotten, and that this was why he no longer saw his grandpa. A few years later, his mother's own illness brought about a fractious truce, and Grandpa Sam reappeared in his life under the shadow of their new circumstances. Then his mother refused a final offer of death-delaying chemotherapy, and Grandpa Sam clashed with Alfie's father over whether to respect her decision, or try to persuade her to change her mind. His father took the view that it was her life and none of them had the right to make her prolong it against her wishes; Sam that she had a duty to her son to stay alive for as long as she possibly could. They hadn't spoken since the funeral.

Once, before the tradition of going to Yvonne and Steve's was properly established, Alfie had spent an uncomfortable Christmas at his Grandpa Sam's. He was eighteen and his mother had been dead for a year and a half. His stepfamily did their best to make him feel welcome, but by then they'd been part of Sam's life for the best part of a decade, and Alfie was the only one who didn't know all the codes and rituals and in-jokes. They didn't mention his mother once, which was probably because they didn't want to upset him, but which seemed at the time to demonstrate how little she had meant to them, how unaffected they were by her absence. A gulf had grown up between Alfie and his grandfather, too, and it wasn't closed by their shared grief. Sam was visibly more at ease with his step-grandchildren than he was with Alfie, although with hindsight Alfie attributed this to his own sullenness and unwillingness to communicate. He hadn't forgotten his childhood Christmases in the same house, and had throbbed with resentment to see relative strangers making themselves at home in it without a thought for the people they had replaced.

He turned them down the following year, and the year after that. The year after that the invitation became general, rather than specific. He was always welcome, they said, a reassurance reiterated at wider and wider intervals until eventually it ceased altogether. The distance between them had calcified, and now it was simply the way of things.

This year's arrangement was probably the best of all possible worlds, Alfie thought: just him and his father, drinking beer, heating things up in foil trays, pulling six crackers between the pair of them. They had a turkey meal for two from Tesco with Bisto and boiled carrots, and afterwards they watched *Paddington*, which made them laugh, and *Mrs Brown's Boys*, which didn't. Naturally, bigger and better Christmases beamed themselves in over Instagram. People opened presents in their pyjamas and festive knitwear and prepared delectable things in their large kitchens. They draped themselves over their furniture, played charades in front of woodburners, gathered around jigsaws and Monopoly and novelty card games that would never again see the light of day. Alfie's step-cousins had documented the festivities at Sam and Doreen's, so Alfie knew that Sam had spent much of the day in his favourite armchair, the reclining one that no one else was allowed to sit in, and that someone had given him a copy of *Sapiens*, and that he'd fallen asleep with his hands folded on his belly and a paper crown slipping down over his eyes. Recently Alfie had begun his own private tradition of angsting about their estrangement, and this year he gave over Boxing Day evening to it. It followed the same pattern it always did. He started by castigating himself for having been such unpleasant company on the Christmas they'd spent together – over ten years ago now – and then moved on to blaming Sam and Doreen for letting him hide away from them. They had been the adults, after all; they should have insisted he come back the following year. Then he went back further and blamed his father and Sam for fighting, his stepfamily for existing, and his mother for having been so ungracious about their existence – because if she had accepted them, mightn't they all have been one big happy family by the time she died? Then he raged at her for dying, and his grandmother too, and from there he segued into a state of morbid fear that he, too, would die a death like theirs.

The season was supposed to redeem itself on New Year's Eve. Alfie had rented an Airbnb in Edinburgh with a group of university friends, one of whom had received some sort of craft beer subscription for his thirtieth birthday and kept sending everyone pictures of his new favourite IPA. But on New Year's Eve morning Alfie – packing in a haphazard, last-minute sort of way – plunged his hand into a rucksack containing nothing but an unshielded razor, and shredded the tips of two fingers. He spent the rest of the day in A&E, feeling his fingers throbbing and imagining that he had given himself blood poisoning. The hour of his train approached, and then passed. He participated in the pre-trip WhatsApp frenzy from the waiting room, sending gruesome pictures of his fingers and wry observations about the other patients, videocalling with sympathetic, disappointed friends as they sat on trains and drove up the motorway. Eventually everyone arrived in Edinburgh, his phone stopped buzzing, and at five in the afternoon he went back to his own flat, his fingers stitched up and bound fatly with gauze.

When he got in he found Hazel, Emily and Daria drinking red wine at the kitchen table. Emily and Daria had invited themselves down to London at the last minute, having neglected to plan anything because they had poured all their energy into hosting one of the picture-perfect Christmases Alfie had envied on Instagram. They asked what his plans were, and he told them that he had none, they'd been scuppered, thanks to this (he held up his fingers). He told them the story, adding a pinch of self-deprecating humour, and they were gratifyingly shocked. Oh *no*, they all clamoured, oh *fuck*. They pressed drinks on him and said they were thinking of walking up Primrose Hill to try and catch a glimpse of the fireworks, if that had any appeal as a Plan B. Alfie said it did, and Emily raised her wineglass and said, 'Yeah, the London crew!', which gave him a warm feeling that made his injury seem almost worth it.

They spent the early part of the evening playing Scrabble, but a special raucous version where you had to drink if it took you longer than two minutes to put your letters down. By the second drink Alfie felt certain that he was having as much fun as he would have had in Edinburgh, quite possibly more. But then, during a lull in the hysteria, Hazel looked at her phone and said, 'Oh. Does anyone mind if Miles comes over?'

There was quiet while they contemplated this seemingly casual request, which was actually something approaching momentous.

'Sure,' Alfie said, which (he realised after the fact) was a clever way of saying he did mind, but making it sound like he didn't.

'We're desperate to meet him,' said Emily, and Daria nodded.

'He was supposed to be in Berlin,' said Hazel. 'But he had this horrible cold, so he couldn't go. He says he's feeling better now. Well enough to see the new year in.'

Brilliant, thought Alfie. Just when things were looking up. Now Miles was coming to ruin it, and bringing germs with him. He grinned and said, 'Berlin's loss is our gain!' He thought he sounded sincere, but Hazel looked at him sharply, without smiling.

Miles arrived before the game was over. He had a red nose and a hoarse voice that unfortunately did not detract from his good looks. He shook Emily's hand, then Daria's. Alfie did not particularly want to shake the hand of a person with a cold, but Miles was already reaching out to him.

'Hey, Alfie, how're you doing?' he said jovially, gripping Alfie's hand and slapping him on the shoulder. Then he sat down next to Hazel, kissed her, and looked at her letters. They conferred quietly, smiling at each other. Later, when Hazel claimed victory, Miles punched the air and put his arm around her. Emily and Daria exchanged meaningful glances, battling – it seemed to Alfie – to keep from grinning. It was hardly a fair win, given that she'd had help from her wingman, but Alfie did not want to be the person who pointed this out.

After Scrabble they opened another bottle of wine. Miles sat on the floor in front of Hazel's armchair with his long legs stretched out in front of him and asked Emily and Daria all manner of highly personal questions, like how long had they been married and had their families been supportive and could he see their wedding photos. Alfie was appalled, but Emily and Daria answered him with sincerity, seeming not to mind. Emily handed him her phone so he could look at the photos. Miles made noises of approval and said, 'Oh, yeah. Nice. Beautiful. This is all so creative. Look at those place markers!'

'Do you like them?' said Daria. 'I did those.'

'You did? This design?'

'Yep.'

Miles looked around at Hazel. 'You're not the only artist in the family, then.'

'Never said I was,' replied Hazel.

'You could go into business,' said Miles, turning back to Daria.

'Pff, no,' said Daria, waving him away, but she was smiling.

'*Oh* yeah,' said Miles, moving on. 'Here she is!' He zoomed in on a photo and held it up for a better view. Then he looked back at Hazel and nodded. 'Hot.'

'Shut up,' she said, shoving him gently with her foot, but she was smiling too.

*

The front door banged; there was a shuffling out in the hall. 'Hi, Tony,' called Hazel, clearly in a benevolent mood. 'Happy New Year's Eve.'

Tony appeared at the living-room door. He was in his work uniform: black trousers and a sweatshirt from Games Workshop. He wore a black leather jacket over the top that creaked even as he stood still. 'Thanks,' he said uncertainly. 'You too.'

'Do you want a drink?' said Emily, holding up the bottle.

'Oh,' said Tony, flushing. 'Well. Okay. Sure.'

Emily shifted along the sofa to make room for him and he sat down, pressing himself into the arm as if to ensure he didn't accidentally touch her. He sipped his wine and said nothing, occasionally reaching up to brush away fronds of Alfie's bamboo palm, now bursting out of its assigned corner. The conversation was dominated by Miles, Emily and Daria, still discussing the wedding; also Miles's brother's wedding, at which he had been best man; also weddings in general, and the expense of them, the petty politics, the hard work. Hazel chipped in with the occasional anecdote. Tony stared into his glass, his hair falling forward to screen them all out of his peripheral vision. Evidently he had nothing to contribute. Nor, for that matter, did Alfie.

When the time came to leave the flat it seemed rude not to invite Tony to go with them. He accepted, to the quiet surprise of all except Alfie, who had observed his subtle attempts to look at Emily sideways through the curtain of hair. On the way to the tube the party naturally divided itself up into pairs. Hazel walked with Daria and Emily with Miles, leaving Alfie and Tony to bring up the rear. This formation continued when they got to Primrose Hill, as if it had been agreed in advance that Alfie would step up as babysitter. But he had never consented to such a sacrifice. They surely couldn't imagine that he was walking with Tony for his own enjoyment. Had they forgotten him, then, or were they leaving him out on purpose? He wasn't sure which was worse.

He and Tony had lived together for several months now and knew each other with an unwelcome intimacy. They had had close encounters with the remnants of each other's meals, encrusted, skin-topped and viscous. They had seen each other's skidmarks in the toilet bowl, and their bodily detritus mingled in the vacuum cleaner and the rubbish bins like some foul, dusty soup. But for all that, they were as good as strangers. This might have been the occasion to learn something of one another, but Tony was no conversationalist, and when they spoke it was to make small talk as laborious as it was uninformative.

Shortly before they turned into the park Tony stopped to tie his shoelace. The others didn't notice, and powered on ahead. Alfie waited for him impatiently, fearful of losing them in the stream of revellers flowing up the hill. Tony tied the lace on one shoe, then knotted it, then knotted it again. He started to rise, but changed his mind and turned his attention to the other lace for good measure, untying and retying it with the same care he had afforded to the first.

'We should probably ...' began Alfie, gesturing at the park. Finally Tony got up and they resumed walking, their progress now frustratingly slow.

'Alfie,' Tony ventured.

'Yeah?'

'Those two.' He nodded towards the rest of their group, still just visible in the crowd.

'Which two?'

'The two women.'

'Oh. Emily and Daria. Yes?' Alfie wondered if the lace-tying had been a ruse to get them out of earshot.

'They're, like, together, right?'

'Yes.'

'Like, a couple?'

'Yes.'

'Cool,' said Tony. Alfie waited for him to elaborate, but he did not.

Eventually they caught up with the rest of them, but no one turned around; no one, it seemed, had even noticed they were missing. They approached the top of the hill, weaving in single file through the groups of people already in position until they found a spot generous enough to accommodate them. The others stood entwined in their pairs and Alfie hovered near them, uncertain of his place in the tableau. He looked sidelong at Hazel, who was standing closest to him. He could have reached out and taken her hand, drawn her in close, kissed her head through her beanie hat. But Miles had fenced her off with an arm about the shoulders, and she was leaning into him, her hand in the back pocket of his jeans.

Below them was a sweep of dark trees, then the lights of central London. The BT Tower, top heavy like a sonic screwdriver; the Shard off to the left, tiny from this distance; the arc of the London Eye glowing green, blue, red.

'Fucking hell,' said Miles. 'London, man. What a fucking beaut.'

Alfie had been trying to muster the sense of awe the sight deserved, but this proclamation, and the murmurs of agreement from the assembled company, made him resent not only Miles, but London too. It might look pretty from this vantage point, but the twat to non-twat ratio was higher here than anywhere else in the country, possibly even the world.

After a minute or so Alfie realised that Tony was not beside him. He turned and saw that he had set himself further back, out of line with the rest of them, probably so he could watch the silhouettes of Emily and Daria without their noticing. Alfie rolled his eyes and turned back. When the fireworks began he found they did not evoke the hope and promise of a new beginning, so much as the explosive masturbating Tony would undoubtedly engage in, once returned to the safety of his bedroom.

19

LATER, WHEN EVERYONE in the household had retreated behind closed doors, Emily waited for Daria to finish brushing her teeth and scrolled through social media to keep from falling asleep. Her feeds were overrun with posts of merriment and oblique self-congratulation – variations, all of them, on a theme of marriage and babies. There were engagement rings and champagne glasses, a #wild glass of orange juice held aloft over a baby bump, and a collage of holiday and wedding photos captioned, *BEST. YEAR. EVER.* There was a new picture of Hannah Fox, sitting on a sofa with her wife, the pair of them cuddling their baby. Emily knew now that Hannah had carried him, following three injections of sperm donated by a childhood friend. Birth was 'fucking intense', Hannah had written, but the insemination sessions had been 'actually sort of fun'. Emily did not like to dwell on this now that she had been through four of them, none of which could be described as anything more generous than bearable.

She scrolled on until she came to a photo of a baby fresh out of utero. He belonged to her old university flatmate,

Martha, so she liked the post and left a comment wishing them well. It was Martha's second child, which was interesting because she and her husband had struggled to conceive the first. Emily knew this because after the baby was born they had taken to social media to document the drama preceding its arrival – the false hope, the miscarriages, the failed rounds of IVF. Martha would presumably get down from her soapbox now, Emily thought meanly, and relinquish her post as self-appointed spokesperson for the infertile.

Daria came back in, smelling of toothpaste and facewash, and burrowed in under the duvet. Emily took her turn in the bathroom, still thinking about Martha and her rapidly expanding family. The first baby could not be much over a year old. How had she produced a second so quickly? Was it usual to continue with fertility treatment even while you nursed a newborn? Or perhaps the second had been an accident. Maybe they hadn't bothered with contraception, thinking they couldn't conceive unassisted. And then, whoops! – as if the first pregnancy had begotten the second, as if their bodies had rewarded happiness with more of the same. Was it possible, Emily wondered, that the anxiety and distress of the preceding years had not just been a result of their troubles but also, in some way, their cause?

Can stress reduce fertility, she asked Google as she sat on the toilet, and Google gave her a broad spectrum of replies. Some websites said no, not in itself, although certain stress-related behaviours might. Others said the jury was out; others said yes, probably, it could. She was too tired and too drunk to pay serious attention to the scientific credentials of each one. Instead she thought back through their insemination sessions, trying to call to mind an occasion on which she had felt relaxed, but admitting instead that they had been fraught and tense, all of them – increasingly so, in fact, because the stakes grew higher as their attempts increased in number. She had learned to greet her period with enforced calm, but she wouldn't be able to continue much longer without growing desperate.

She peeled herself off the toilet seat and returned to the living room, hoping to discuss it with Daria. But Daria was in a deep, boozy slumber. Emily climbed in beside her and stared at the ceiling, wide awake. She was comforted, to a degree. Perhaps the problem of her non-pregnancy (or was it too early to call it a problem?) might yet prove easy to solve. But the foil to this was that stress didn't just go away when you told it to. At present it showed every sign of mounting. What if her ability to conceive was diminishing as her anxiety grew? Each attempt, if this were true, would have a lower chance of success than the one before.

She turned this thought over and over in her mind until, sick of the ceiling and of the slatted blind glowing orange from the street light, she got up and went into the kitchen instead. She stood by the sink and looked out over the roofs of the houses below, wondering idly how many people were having sex in them. Perhaps her chances of conception would improve if she could relax and enjoy herself, like they all were – like Hannah Fox, apparently, had been able to. How many babies were conceived by mistake, as by-products of their parents' carefree, spontaneous fun? Millions, presumably.

Maybe it was true, then, that watched pots took longer to boil. The injustice of this now struck her. For how could *she* stop watching? How could she ever relax and enjoy herself, when she had to drag herself to a clinic in the early morning before work and let a stranger in disposable gloves administer labelled semen not long defrosted?

Just then a voice behind her made her gasp violently in surprise. 'Jesus fucking Christ,' she said in a loud whisper, slapping a hand to her heart.

'Shit,' somebody whispered in response. 'Sorry, I didn't mean to scare you.' The person moved soundlessly towards a cupboard, took something out, and came forward into the pool of street light. It was Alfie, holding a glass tumbler. 'I've got the thirst,' he said.

She moved away from the sink so that he could fill the glass. He slugged back the contents in an instant, then filled it again and sipped more slowly. 'Are you okay?' he said. 'What time is it?'

'Dunno,' she said. 'Late. I can't sleep.'

'That sucks. Did you have a good night, at least?'

'Yeah, I did, thanks. Did you?' She remembered guiltily that he had been stuck with Tony all evening, and interjected before he could respond. 'Thanks, by the way. You kind of took one for the team there.'

'Did I?'

'You know, looking after...' She inclined her head towards Tony's room.

'Oh!' whispered Alfie. 'Right. Well. No problem. Happy to do it.'

'Let's go for brunch tomorrow, if anywhere's open. We owe you one.'

'That'd be nice. I'm sure there'll be somewhere.' He filled up his glass for the last time, then took a step towards the door.

'Night,' he said. 'I hope you get some sleep.'

'Night,' said Emily, smiling after his retreating silhouette. She was terribly fond of him, she realised. How nice it had been of him, to stick with Tony like that the whole evening, making sure he was included and entertained. They would buy him something lavish tomorrow, and it would be no more than he deserved.

20

THE APPROPRIATION OF Alfie began the next day at two in the afternoon. The clouds sat heavy in the sky, ushering in an early dusk. Daria, Emily and Alfie had been waiting for Hazel and Miles for an hour, but Hazel's door remained firmly closed and no one behind it appeared to be stirring. Emily decided they had waited long enough, so the three of them took a bus to Hackney Central in search of brunch. They had chosen this neighbourhood for its high density of suitable cafés, but even there they found most of them closed. They settled for a place halfway down Mare Street, staffed by a woman with a visible hangover. She greeted them sleepily from behind the counter, sprinkling spinach over something yellow.

When they had settled themselves and ordered coffee, Emily said, 'Can we please talk about Miles?' There was a loaded pause; they looked at each other, all of them hoping someone else would volunteer to speak first.

'Alfie knows him better than us,' said Daria.

'Not really,' said Alfie quickly. 'I've only met him once before.'

'So how did he compare? The second time?'

'Well, the first time I barely saw him. Just said hi and shook his hand. So no comparison, really.'

'Hmm,' said Daria, unsatisfied. 'I'll start, then. He's not *not* pretentious.'

The other two snickered in complicity. 'I'd even go so far as to say he's really very pretentious indeed,' said Emily.

'He has got a fairly high opinion of himself,' Alfie conceded.

'And he's a mansplainer,' said Daria. Between them, she and Emily recounted the trip up Primrose Hill, during which Miles had talked at length of the atrocities habitually committed against farm animals, and of the numerous Netflix documentaries that exposed them. He had spoken so fervently on the subject – about how fucked up it all was, how sadistic, how morally reprehensible – that they had been surprised to learn he ate meat, although he was about to embark on his third Veganuary.

'We were like, mate, we're vegan,' said Emily. 'We've been vegan for seven years. Do you think we don't know all this stuff? You're just vegan-curious!'

'Yeah, and don't think you've absolved yourself of all wrongdoing because you only buy meat once a week and it has to be organic,' said Daria. 'Hello? *It's still meat.*'

'Right!' went on Emily. 'Something still had to die for the sake of your taste buds, sweetie.'

'So he's a hypocrite, basically,' said Alfie, happy now to speak plainly, and Emily and Daria whooped, delighted.

The hungover waitress appeared with a tray of coffee. 'Amazing, thank you,' fawned Daria, checking the acerbic tone in her voice. 'Choose what you want, guys, quick.'

They speed-read their menus and settled on tofu scramble – all three of them, even Alfie. But the tofu had run out, the waitress informed them. There was nothing else vegan on the menu, so Emily and Daria ordered fry-ups with all the meat and eggs removed.

'Just beans, mushroom, tomato, hash browns, toast?' said the waitress.

'Yes, but no butter on the toast,' said Emily. 'Unless you've got vegan spread.'

'I'll check,' sighed the waitress, and turned to Alfie.

'I'll have the same,' he said.

'Oh, hey,' said Emily, worried that they had shamed him into choosing a brunch more to their liking than his. 'You can still ... we didn't mean ... you don't have to—'

'It's fine!' said Alfie. 'Maybe I'll do Veganuary too.' He nodded at the waitress, who was waiting, impatiently, for confirmation.

When she'd gone they returned swiftly to the topic of Miles. Emily touched Daria's forearm, her forehead creased in a pretence of caring concern. 'So you're a lesbian?' she asked sweetly. 'How does your family feel about that?'

'Oh my God, I thought that was a bit off!' cried Alfie. 'Only, you seemed to be okay with it!'

'Did we?' said Daria. 'For God's sake!' She turned to Emily with a look of exasperation.

'We're pushovers, that's why,' said Emily. 'We're far too forgiving of inappropriate questions.'

'Actually, speaking of inappropriate,' said Alfie, but then pulled back, seeming to think better of finishing his sentence. They clamoured for him to continue; he waved them away, but they clamoured on until he gave in. 'Okay, what the hell,' he said. 'I'll tell you, but don't judge me.'

'We won't,' said Daria.

'So the first time I met Miles, we were all in the flat. I'd had a sort of … one-night stand. And the woman – you're not going to believe this. I got up to make coffee, and while I was making it, she walked out on me.'

Their eyebrows were raised; their jaws dropped. A noise of outrage escaped from Emily's open mouth.

'Yep, just got up and walked out. Anyway, I was in the kitchen making coffee, she's still in my room, Miles and Hazel are in the kitchen with me, and then the front door bangs. And I'm like, wait. Was that …? Did she just …? And Miles just looks at me and goes—' Alfie affected an air of hipsterian aloofness and said, in a softened voice, '"Shit, man! Was that your lay?"'

'*Lay?*' echoed Daria and Emily.

'Lay,' confirmed Alfie, laughing. 'I actually think he was genuinely concerned. I mean, poor guy. He was really feeling for me there. And then he opened his mouth, and *that* was what came out.'

After the meal, Alfie went to the bathroom and Emily watched him retreat. 'God,' she said, with longing, 'he's *so* much nicer than Miles. I should have known Hazel would never go for someone so perfect for her.'

'But you heard what he said,' Daria replied. 'He had a one-night stand. Doesn't sound like he's pining after her, does it? Maybe they genuinely just don't fancy each other.'

Emily sighed and pouted. 'Guess not. Guess we read it all wrong.'

'Wishful thinking?' said Daria, smiling wryly and taking her hand.

'I suppose. Hey.' Emily's downcast expression had transformed. She leaned across the table, grinning, and said in a loud whisper, 'Don't you think he'd make a good sperm donor?'

'Alfie?' said Daria, eyebrows raised in amusement. '*Not* what I was expecting you to say.'

'Well, think about it,' began Emily, but Daria cut her off.

'Shh. He's coming back.'

They feigned interest in their phones as Alfie made his way across the café towards them. He was extremely pleased to have found himself vindicated, and to have found, moreover, that his place in the affections of Emily and Daria had not been usurped, as he'd suspected.

'So,' he said as he sat back down, 'I was thinking, the pubs will start opening soon. There's one on Broadway Market that has board games. Just putting it out there.'

Daria and Emily nodded. They had nowhere else to be. 'Why not?' said Daria.

As they walked they strategised about how to get Hazel to join them without Miles, and concluded that there was nothing for it but to message her and hope for the best. In the end, however, Hazel replied that they were just too late, she and Miles had agreed to meet some of his friends somewhere else, and perhaps they could all catch up later.

At the pub Daria and Emily bought beer and crisps, and for Alfie – just in case they had given him to believe that they disapproved of him in any way – a packet of pork scratchings. Alfie and Miles were not held to the same standards, they wished to imply, because Alfie did not make a pretence of being more ethical than he really was.

'Oh, ha, thanks!' he said. 'So much for Veganuary!' He looked almost disappointed.

They played Ticket to Ride and then Catan and then a round of Would You Rather, but Daria's mind was only ever partially on the game. Her thoughts strayed frequently to Emily's comment in the café. *He'd make a good sperm donor.* Had she meant it? It was a radical change of position, yet not entirely off-piste. Their current mode of baby-making wasn't at all to Emily's taste. 'It's so clinical,' she had said more than once. 'And don't say that's because it's a clinic. You know what I mean.'

Daria didn't like the clinic either, but for different reasons. It wasn't just the thrum of anxiety, which was starting to feel like background noise, but something else, something more surprising, that inflected it. It was resentment, she had realised. She resented having to sit on the sidelines and watch somebody else inseminate her wife. She resented being nothing more than a hand holder, a spewer of encouraging words. She resented the fact that her presence there had no bearing whatsoever on whether or not Emily ended up pregnant. It was an illogical way to feel, she confessed to Janet, given that she had taken the helm once before without in the least enjoying it. In fact, she had willed it to be over. But Janet said no, it was perfectly logical. It was natural to feel attached to your own small area of jurisdiction when everything else was outside your control.

'Try and think of the nurse as part of a system,' she said. 'A cog in a machine. She's not part of your marriage, she serves it.'

'Yes,' said Daria, 'I know that.' In a lengthy jumble of incomplete sentences she explained that she didn't want to actually *overcome* the resentment. It was an achievement, of sorts. It was so right and so proper, so befitting her situation, that she couldn't help feeling satisfied by its existence.

'It's like, ego and superego, you know?' she said, abashed to be referencing Freud in front of a person trained in psychology. 'At one level I'm just feeling it, and at some other level I'm watching myself feel it. And enjoying it, I suppose.' It was the same with the disappointment that bloomed whenever Emily's period arrived. Suspended somewhere above the feeling itself was the appreciative eye that observed it, the spotlight that trained on it, as if light would make it grow.

What if they stopped going to the clinic, she wondered now – if they found a sperm donor and did it themselves? Would she be pleased to take back the control she had relinquished? She excused herself from the game and shut herself in a toilet cubicle, closed her eyes and tried to picture it. The pot of white goop, warm to the touch, possibly a little sticky. Emily's knees pointing at the ceiling. She, Daria, the master of ceremonies, agent of Emily's future pain.

She thought she could do it better than last time. It would be different, because she was different. She still had her fear, but she was learning to manage it. She would just have to focus on the end goal: a child with the woman she loved, a donor who cared about them. Lovely Alfie, an outpost of their family.

It hadn't occurred to them to consider him before. They had listed every man they knew, but not one of them had been suitable. Their commitments lay elsewhere, or they lived abroad, or they were unreliable, or else, for some

ill-defined but unassailable reason, they just *weren't right*.
Back then Alfie had been too much a part of Hazel's world
to be brought so irrevocably into theirs. But he was their
friend now, too. And if Hazel had no claim on him after
all? If they really were just flatmates, and nothing more?

When she arrived back at the table, Alfie took a drinks
order and disappeared in the direction of the bar. 'Em,'
said Daria urgently, sitting down, 'did you mean what you
said before? About Alfie?'

Emily looked over her shoulder to check he wasn't within
earshot, then leaned in close. 'I hadn't really thought it
through. But kind of, yeah. Why, what do you think?'

'I'm not against it.'

Emily grinned. 'No?'

'I mean, there's a lot to discuss. And he might not want
to do it.'

'Right. But in theory?'

'In theory, I think … Yeah, it could work, couldn't it?'

'I've got a good feeling about it. He's so nice, you know?
So decent.'

'And he's a primary school teacher.'

'Oh yeah, of course he is! So he's good with kids.'

'And if him and Hazel aren't a thing …'

'He's fair game.' They sniggered guiltily. 'I've been
thinking,' Emily went on. 'I want to see if I can enjoy the
donation sessions. I feel like it might help my chances. I
don't want it to be stressful. Stress is so damaging. It could
be a vicious cycle, for all we know.'

'How do you mean?'

'Well, say stress affects your body's ability to conceive.

Hear me out,' she said as Daria's expression changed to one of incredulity. 'It's perfectly possible. Stress is really powerful. It can cause heart attacks, for Christ's sake.'

'Yeah, but, like, in combination with other things.'

'But hypothetically, say stress has a negative effect on your fertility,' Emily persisted. 'And the more you try, the more stressed you get. The longer you go on trying, the less likely you are to conceive. You see?'

'I see.'

'So why not try and enjoy it? Pump it in, and then have sex? For example.'

'I see where you're going with this.'

'We can never, never, *never* have fun at the clinic, Daria. It's just not possible.'

'I agree.'

'And it's so expensive.'

This was true. They would soon be due a difficult conversation about how much longer their savings would last.

'We shouldn't ask Alfie just because he'd be *cheap*,' said Daria uncertainly.

'Of course not. It wouldn't be the main reason. But it'd be another pressure off, wouldn't it? If we didn't have to worry about money?'

'Well, yeah. For sure.'

'If Alfie was our donor we could get an Airbnb, take the day off work. Make it into a sort of mini-break. Just … relax and enjoy it.'

'I mean, it depends on my teaching. I can't just take a day off in term time.'

Emily sighed. '*Details*. Do you see what I'm saying?'

'I do. Yeah, why not? It certainly wouldn't do any harm.'

'And that way we'll get to have a donor we know, and the kid will get to know where it comes from, and Alfie will make a really sweet godfather, uncle, whatever ...'

'Godfuncle.'

'Godfuncle! Yes!' Emily giggled, pink in the face, euphoric.

'Shh,' said Daria. 'He's coming back.'

Emily took a deep breath to calm herself. Alfie was moving slowly, holding three pints. Daria watched him approach and thought how strange it was, the way ideas slid into place sometimes, just like that, tongue into groove.

Part II

21

THE FEUD BETWEEN Hazel and Roisin carried on into January. Nish was bored of it, and told Hazel so on one of Roisin's days off. Hazel put her hands up in self-defence and said she was perfectly willing to forget all about it. All Roisin had to do was apologise for causing a scene at Miles's exhibition.

'Yeah,' said Nish, 'but she's never going to do that.'

'Why not? She was out of order! She knows she was!'

'She says she was standing up for her principles.'

'She was being a dick.'

'She says you've come down on the side of politeness and it's disappointing.'

'Disappointing? Oh, please. Am I not the person she thought I was?'

Nish shrugged. 'I dunno, Hazel. If you want to resolve this you might have to be the bigger man. Person, I mean.'

'Why should I? She started it!'

'That's what it means to be the bigger man, though, isn't it?'

'She's just so fucking stubborn,' said Hazel.

'Well, yeah,' said Nish. 'But so are you.'

Hazel thumped the jug of steamed milk on the counter-top with more than usual vigour, slopping some over the side. Nish said nothing, but handed her a cloth. When she was back from delivering the coffee he changed the subject with effortful cheer.

'How's the drawing going? You haven't been posting much lately.'

'Ugh, don't remind me,' Hazel grumbled. 'I'm all out of inspiration. I haven't drawn anything in weeks.'

Ever since rejecting the fart test drawing, she had been short on ideas. Or at least, short on ideas that could be executed without repercussions. There was another dormant cartoon in her drawing pad, uninked, which she couldn't post unless she broke up with Miles first. In it, a woman lay naked and expressionless on a bed, a man's head working away at the intersection of her splayed legs. A second panel showed the top half of the man's face, framed by thighs, frowning, with speech bubbles to indicate grunts and slurps. The woman glanced towards the clock, then looked back at the ceiling, then grinned and shrieked, saying it tickled. The man persisted until she oh'd and ohhh'd and ohhhhhh'd, but her expression was detached and indifferent. Then he came up for air, chin glistening. 'You bloody love it, don't you, you little minx?' he said, and the woman grinned at him, her two thumbs in the air.

The man in the cartoon didn't look anything like Miles. But even if Miles could be convinced that it was not about him, he would only wonder why she was drawing cartoons about receiving cunnilingus from someone else. She had sensed him bristling once before when she began a sentence with the words 'my ex', and had not felt him relax even as she continued with, 'used to do this really annoying thing'. It was always the same with men, she thought. They wanted to be Columbus, wanted to plant their flagpoles, hated being reminded that the land mass in question was already on the map.

Like Nish, Miles had noted the infrequency with which her Instagram was being updated. She told him she had a bit of writer's block, and he looked grave.

'It's interesting you should say that. I've been thinking. I wonder if it's time for you to branch out a bit.'

'Branch out how?'

'Well, everything you do is really great, right, but – and don't take this the wrong way – it's also kind of … well, narrow. As in, it's just about the experience of being, like, a twenty-first-century white woman.'

'Erm, okay,' said Hazel, frowning. 'But I don't think I can really draw about the experience of being a twenty-first-century woman of colour.'

'That's not what I'm suggesting. I'm suggesting you could broaden your horizons way beyond the experiential. The world is wide, Hazel! There are so many things you could draw cartoons about.'

'But this is what I do. It's who I am. I'm a woman in the twenty-first century, and I draw silly cartoons about it. The funny bits and the awkward bits. The embarrassing bits. What's wrong with that?'

'Oh, Hazel, hey, nothing's wrong with it. I'm only saying there might be new avenues for you to explore. Like, maybe you could be a bit more politically engaged?'

'You could say what I do already is politically engaged. As in, the personal is political.'

'Mm, yeah, but I mean *actually* political. What about climate change? Have you ever done a cartoon about climate change? Or the refugee crisis, or child poverty?'

'No, because none of those things are funny.'

'What's so good about funny? Why does everything have to be funny? I'm sorry, but hoiking a massive clump of hair out from between your arse cheeks when you've finished shampooing? No offence, but that isn't funny either, Hazel. It's actually pretty fucking gross.'

Hazel opened her mouth to respond, but nothing came out. 'It was supposed to be gross,' she stammered eventually. 'That was the point.'

'Okay, but what am I supposed to take from it? People are gross? Great, I feel so much better for knowing that!'

'What are you trying to say? I thought you liked my cartoons. You paid two hundred and fifty quid for one of my cartoons.' As she said this, she realised that he had never actually put it on the wall.

'I do like your cartoons, Hazel. I'm just trying to challenge you. You've got so much fucking talent! You could really be using it for good, you know?'

'I wasn't aware that I was using it for bad.'

Miles took both of her hands in his. 'Babe, you're not. You're absolutely not. It's just that you're so amazing. You're a force to be reckoned with. You could change the world if you wanted to. I mean it. You just need to think big.'

Perhaps he was right, she thought later, staring at a blank page in her drawing pad. She never really thought about the wider world when she drew. Perhaps it was irresponsible of her. She had a platform; she ought to make better use of it. There was so much to be angry about, and to fear. The rising tide of intolerance, the floundering of democracy, the disturbing changes in the weather. Never, never had there been so vast a catalogue of problems to surmount. When you thought about it – really thought about it – you couldn't help wondering how it was that everybody was still standing. They were like surfers on their boards, working to stay upright while a swelling current of chaos troubled the surface beneath them.

And there it was! There was her image. She started drawing: just one large panel, a beach scene, people surfing on a choppy sea. Some stood upright, others paddled on their stomachs, others had fallen into the water. When you looked closely you saw that the waves and eddies and currents spelled out things like 'take back control' and 'the 1%' and 'climate anxiety'. Behind the surfers was a gargantuan wave about to engulf them, suspended like Hokusai's, the words 'the sea' picked out in the curling foam at its crest.

She took a photo of it and sent it to Miles. Five minutes later he rang her.

'Yes, yes, fucking yes!' he cried.

'You like it, then?'

'Hazel, it's brilliant! It's exactly the sort of thing I meant!'

She grinned. 'Thanks for the pep talk. It kind of unblocked something.' You're a mental laxative, she almost said, but stopped herself.

'I've just got one suggestion.'

'Go on.'

'A shark fin. But shaped to spell out the name of some capitalist supervillain. Maybe Mark Zuckerberg? Or is that too long? Oh, oh! Jeff Bezos!'

'Mm,' said Hazel. 'Okay. Maybe.'

'I promise you, Hazel. Just add it in. It'll be brilliant. The finishing touch. You'll see.'

Hazel hung up, intending to think about this some more. But immediately she noticed the voicemail symbol in the top left-hand corner of the screen. She hated voicemail. Nobody ever left a voicemail unless they wanted to talk about something serious.

She dialled in to listen to the message. It was from Emily. 'Hi, Hazel,' she said. 'Can you call me back? Don't worry, it's nothing bad. I just really need to talk to you.'

22

HELLO, BEGAN THE coolest, strangest, most momentous email Alfie had ever received in his life.

> We've got a proposition for you. But it's a bit
> unconventional, so maybe read this sitting down.

Alfie rubbed a hand over his hair, frowning, and sat on the edge of his bed obediently.

> For the past four months, we've been trying for a baby.
> Originally the plan was to use sperm donated by Daria's
> brother. (Emily will be the one carrying btw!!!!) We
> managed to do one insemination that way, only then he
> moved to Bangladesh to work in a Rohingya refugee
> camp, the selfish prick. Since then we've been going to
> a fertility clinic, but we're not mad keen on conceiving
> that way. We would really like the donor to be someone
> we know and respect, and if it can't be family, a friend
> would be the next best thing.

Alfie's heart began thumping in his ears. He read on so quickly that he skipped several sentences and had to start over.

We're not looking to get into some super modern co-parenting set-up. We'll be the parents, full stop. But our view is, the more people in a child's life who love it, the better. So ideally our donor will be someone who takes an interest in the kid's development, sends birthday and Christmas presents, babysits occasionally and generally acts as a sort of godfather/uncle or, if you will, a GODFUNCLE.

Now we come to the crunch. Alfie. We haven't known you long, but you feel like an old friend. We respect and trust you, and we would be honoured if you would consider being our donor. At this stage the commitment would entail:

Going for a full check-up for STIs and letting us know if there are any medical issues in your family history that might give cause for concern.

Being available once a month to provide us with the – ahem – necessary substance. Exact dates will depend on when Emily's ovulating so some flexibility would be required (though within reason, of course).

And that's it!

We cannot emphasise enough that there is absolutely NO pressure WHATSOEVER, and if you have any doubts or misgivings we would rather you turned us down, whether now or later on. If you're at all intrigued, get in touch and we can talk about it some more. But please also feel free to tell us to fuck off. By the way, we've discussed it with Hazel, since you were her friend first, and she's given us her blessing.

Take care,

E&D

xxx

Alfie sat for a long time on the edge of the bed, too surprised to move. Then he got up and went out into the hall. 'Hazel?' he called.

Hazel was in her room, grappling with a cartoon. She had been reading a lot of news lately and it was taking its toll: the night before she had dreamed that everyone residing in Britain was made to take a new points-based test to determine whether or not they were allowed to be there. Alfie, Daria and Nish had all failed it because you got fifty points subtracted if you weren't 'indigenous'. The dream had given a flavour of trepidation to her whole morning, and now she was trying to put it to good use. But the cartoon was turning out turgid and sanctimonious, and she was on the point of giving up.

She got up and went to the door, grateful for the distraction. Alfie was outside, pacing. He stopped and faced her. 'I ... I got this email,' he said.

'Ah,' she said, opening her door fully and leaning on the frame. 'I think I might know what that was about.'

'Okay. I mean. Wow. What do you think?'

'The question,' said Hazel, 'is what *you* think.'

'I don't know! I'm stunned!'

'Good stunned or bad stunned?'

'Just … stunned. I don't know! I don't know what to think.'

There was a pause. They stood, looking at each other. 'Why don't you go and sit down,' said Hazel, 'and I'll make us a cup of tea?'

Alfie obeyed, and when Hazel joined him in the living room a few minutes later he was sprawled in his preferred armchair, staring intently at the wall.

'Tea,' she said, holding out the mug, and he blinked like he was coming out of a trance. She sat on the sofa and curled her feet up under her. 'What are you thinking?'

'Okay,' he said decisively, sitting forward in his chair and putting his elbows on his knees. 'So, it doesn't fill me with *horror*. It's not a definite no. It's *definitely* not a definite no. But it's also not exactly what I had in mind for, like, my thirties. Well, not just my thirties. My life. It's just not what I had in mind, full stop. But then, that doesn't necessarily mean it's a bad idea, does it?'

'Not necessarily.'

'And anyway, what *did* I have in mind? It's not like I've got a life plan.'

'I don't know. Did you want to find a partner one day? Have kids of your own?'

He blinked. 'Why, because … you think I wouldn't be able to do those things? If I did this?'

'I'm not saying that. It just makes it more complicated.'

'I don't think I'd want to be with anyone who couldn't handle it,' he said pensively. 'If someone was a dick about it, I'd know they weren't for me. It'd be a good test.'

'Right.'

'And I can't say I'm not pleased to be asked,' he went on. 'I'm definitely flattered. I like Emily and Daria a lot. It's nice to feel they appreciate me. And what they're suggesting actually sounds quite cool. I think I'd probably enjoy being in that sort of set-up. You know, a bit of babysitting, a bit of hanging out, a few bedtime stories. Uncle Alfie. I can see myself as Uncle Alfie.'

'You mean Godfuncle Alfie,' said Hazel. 'Daria invented that. She's extremely proud of it.'

'I think Alf Godfuncle works better,' he replied. Hazel stared. 'You know, like Art Garfunkel.'

'Ohhh,' she said, nodding. She smiled wryly. 'Nice dad joke there.'

'Ha,' said Alfie. 'Probably not very PC to call it that, in the circumstances.'

'Probably not.' They grinned at each other. 'Sounds like it's all falling into place, though,' Hazel went on, taking a swig of her tea. 'Like maybe you want to say yes.'

'Agghh,' said Alfie, hugging himself and looking scared. 'Maybe? I mean, yeah, there's something appealing about the idea. I'm an only child, so I never expected to be an uncle. And now it's come up, I'm thinking, You know what, that might actually be really nice? It's just … Oh, I don't know.' His face twisted into an expression of unease.

'What?' said Hazel.

He was quiet for a while, as if searching for the right words, then said: 'It's just that thing they said about disclosing any medical issues in my family. Stuff that might be of concern.'

'Oh?'

'Well, there is something in my family. Something quite significant. It might actually rule me out. Because my mum and my grandma, right, they both died of breast cancer. And the thing is, my mum had this test when she was ill, like a genetic test, and it turned out she was carrying this faulty gene. A cancery gene. I forget what it's called. She got the test for my sake, so I could find out if I was carrying it too, if I wanted. But I haven't ever been able to face it.'

'Oh,' said Hazel. 'Shit.'

'Yeah.'

'That's pretty heavy.'

'I guess.'

'You'd be all right, though, wouldn't you, if you had it? Men can't get breast cancer, can they?'

'They can, actually,' said Alfie. 'It's rare, obviously. But I think I'd just be more at risk of cancer generally. Maybe my risk of prostate cancer might be higher. I can't remember. I looked it up once but I didn't really read the information properly, it made me too anxious. Anyway, the point is, if I had it, and Emily had a little girl, and then *she* had it ...'

'Yeah,' said Hazel. 'Right. I see.'

'I guess I'd just have to take the test,' he said blankly. 'Maybe I should be taking it anyway.'

Hazel chewed her lip. 'It'd be better to know, I'd have thought?' she said. 'One way or the other?'

He shrugged. 'Maybe.'

They sipped their tea, both staring into the middle distance.

'Say it was all fine, though,' said Alfie. 'Say I found out I wasn't carrying it. What would you think about me being their donor?'

Hazel sighed. 'I just want my sister to be happy,' she said. This wasn't precisely true, it wasn't *just* this that she wanted, there were other things.

'And this would make her happy, you mean? You mean you'd want me to go for it?' He wondered suddenly if he would be able to refuse Emily without disappointing Hazel.

She shrugged, torn. The thought of Alfie biologically tying himself to her family made her uneasy, but there was no way to tell him this without admitting to feelings she had been doing her best to conceal. 'I think you need to decide,' she said.

Alfie stared for a while at the coffee table, then raised his eyes to meet hers. 'It's complicated, though, isn't it?' he ventured. 'Even without all the cancer stuff it feels ... well, complicated.'

It was clear to Hazel that this was an admission of particular significance. His voice was slightly tremulous, his face almost fearful. She held his gaze, thrumming with adrenalin. Of course it was complicated. They had unfinished business, and the fact that they might be on the point of admitting this out loud seemed immediately to recalibrate everything. The way he had brought up his ex. The way she had raged about it, taking to Tinder in revenge. It suddenly seemed possible that he had meant it with no more weight or consequence than she had, when mentioning her own ex to Miles. A smile played at the corners of her mouth, and she fought hard to suppress it. Her hands trembled, so she sat on them.

'How do you mean?' she said, making an effort to remain calm, because she needed to be certain she was reading him correctly before she gave herself away.

For several seconds they stared at one another. Alfie's heart was pounding, so hard he felt sure she must be able to see it. But he detected no sign of agitation in her. She appeared entirely unruffled, gazing at him placidly with an affected innocence that he read as pity. She was even smiling a little, though whether in mockery or embarrassment he couldn't tell. He looked away. 'Well,' he mumbled, 'maybe not for you.'

'I'm confused,' she said, with a slight laugh, and Alfie thought, Of course you are, because for you it's simple: you don't want to be with me, you never did, you don't care that this will be it for us, it's all the same to you if you never kiss me or touch me or sleep with me again.

He shook his head. 'Never mind,' he said, standing up. 'I've got some serious thinking to do. Have you finished with that mug?'

'Not quite,' said Hazel, stunned. He wasn't actually *leaving*?

But he was. On his way out of the door he turned and said, 'You cooking tonight?'

'I brought leftovers back from work,' she said, without looking at him. 'I'll probably just watch some Netflix.'

'Cool.' He left, and Hazel remained where she was for some time, staring into the space where he had been.

23

EMILY WAS A nervous wreck. They had sent the email on Saturday afternoon, but by Sunday morning there was still no reply. She looked at her phone so many times during breakfast that Daria confiscated it.

'Drink your coffee,' she said firmly. 'And let's have a conversation.'

'Why hasn't Alfie messaged us back?' Emily wailed.

'He will, babe. Give him a chance. It's all news to him. He hasn't been thinking about it obsessively like we have.'

The reply didn't come until the evening, and even then it didn't give an answer. Alfie expressed both great pleasure and extreme surprise. He was flattered and delighted that they saw fit to entrust him with such a responsibility, he said; still, he needed a few more days to consider whether or not he could accept it. It wasn't that he was reluctant, only that one shouldn't rush into a thing like that. He was sorry to leave them in suspense, but he was sure they would understand.

'He's sorry to leave us in suspense!' cried Emily. 'He has no idea!'

'It's good, though,' said Daria. 'We wouldn't *want* him to rush into it, would we?'

'Well, *no*,' said Emily, rolling her eyes at Daria's unshakeable good sense. 'But *still*.'

While they waited, Alfie sought advice from trusted friends, of whom – he now realised – he did not have many. He went through a mental list of everyone who had provided a listening ear during the Rachel saga, and found, to his surprise, that he didn't much want to open up to them this time. It was all too intimate, too fearsome. In the end he told two people: Hector, his oldest friend from school, who lived in New Zealand now and could only talk at awkward hours of the night, and Jamie, his housemate from university, who had revealed himself to be a kindred spirit in the very early days of their tenancy by seeking Alfie out and confessing in a panic that he had found blood in his stool. (A burst haemorrhoid, in the end.)

It seemed increasingly clear to Alfie that he did want to be the donor, partly because he found himself wishing that he could just go ahead and do it, without worrying about all this other baggage, and partly because he couldn't bear it when his friends made arguments against the idea. He became irrationally furious when Hector asked if he was sure he wanted to 'shackle' himself to these 'randoms'. What made him hesitant was not the idea of getting embroiled in a serious, irreversible commitment with people he hadn't long known, or the frankly bizarre notion of bringing a living, breathing offshoot of himself into the world: it was the thought of getting tested for what he thought of as 'the cancer gene'. *Would* it be better to know, as Hazel had said? Hector said it wouldn't, no way, not in a million years. What if he had it? Wouldn't the anxiety drive him insane? And it was true that knowing he had it would be an entirely different thing to suspecting that he might. But then, if he didn't!

'*Imagine* you find out you aren't carrying it!' Jamie said. 'Mate, the *relief*!'

This was very seductive. Alfie punctuated his uneasy thoughts with little fantasies of the post-anxiety utopia that might be waiting for him just over the horizon, and it was this, in the end, that persuaded him to seek out the medical paperwork his mother had left behind, and make a phone appointment with his GP. His GP said she could refer him to the genetic testing unit at a hospital in central London, and he should look out for his appointment letter in the post.

A week and a half after his first message, he emailed Daria and Emily again. Daria was upstairs marking essays; Emily was lying on the sofa, scrolling through the headlines after a day working from home. When the message appeared she sat up suddenly. Her thumb hovered over it for half a second, trembling. Then she opened it, skimmed it for keywords, leapt to her feet, and dashed towards the stairs.

'Daria!' she cried, taking them two at a time. She burst into the spare room, which now doubled as a study; Daria stared at her in shock.

'What is it?' she said. 'Are you okay?'

'Check your phone!' cried Emily.

'Oh, shit.' Daria stood on her chair and reached for the highest bookshelf, where she had stowed her phone for the avoidance of distraction. 'Is it Alfie?'

'You fucking bet it's Alfie,' said Emily.

Daria read the message standing on the chair. It was brief, but to the point. He had been thinking about it very hard, he said; he was sorry it had taken him so long to email. He felt they ought to discuss it properly before they reached a final decision, but in principle he liked the idea very much. There was just one hurdle, which might turn out not to be a hurdle at all, he wasn't sure – but he would tell them all about it when they spoke.

'"I've always felt slightly ambivalent about parenting,"' read Daria, '"but I feel very good about godfuncling! Great word, by the way!"' Her voice rose with pleasure; her face broke into a self-congratulatory smile. Emily shook her head fondly and reached for Daria's hand, pulling her down from the chair to kiss her.

'It sounds promising, doesn't it?' she said.

'Yeah, I'd say we're a step closer,' said Daria.

'I wonder what the hurdle is?' said Emily, and Daria shrugged and said there was only one way to find out.

They WhatsApp-called with Alfie after dinner. At first they were all nervous with each other, uncertain how to act or what to say in the new roles they had invented for themselves.

'I don't even know where to begin,' said Alfie, raising his hands in a gesture of good-humoured defeat.

'Well, shall we just sort of give you an *overview*?' said Daria, and, switching into university-lecturer mode, proceeded to explain the legalities. If Alfie did 'come on board', she said, his being the biological father wouldn't count for nothing, but he wouldn't be a primary parent. He wouldn't be on the birth certificate, or have any financial responsibility. Daria, though not biologically related to the child, would be the second parent by default, because she and Emily were married.

Then there were the details of their own particular arrangement. 'We've been reading up on this,' said Daria, 'and the advice is to write a sort of contract, which we all sign, about our expectations for how this is going to work. It wouldn't be legally binding, just an expression of our intentions. So that if, down the line, there were disagreements, we could refer to this document, or a judge could—'

'A *judge*?' interjected Alfie. 'What sort of disagreements were you expecting us to have?'

Daria laughed and said he wasn't to worry, it was purely precautionary, but it was best to be prepared because life threw you curveballs sometimes. As she understood it a lot of disagreements came about because the donor wanted to be more or possibly less involved in the upbringing of the child than the parents felt was appropriate. But the contract would be a way to guard against that, Emily pointed out. A disagreement was far less likely to arise if they were clear from the outset about how they expected things to work.

'We'd need to define this word "uncle",' said Daria, and privately everyone acknowledged the absence of her favourite portmanteau as a marker of how serious this all was. 'So that we're sure we're on the same page.'

Alfie gave a short laugh and said, 'Well, *my* uncle's an arsehole. Whenever I see him I'm mostly just wishing he'd shut the fuck up. But obviously that's not the sort of uncle we're talking about.'

'What did you envisage, then?' said Emily. 'How would you see this working? What kind of relationship would you have with the kid?'

'Well,' said Alfie, 'obviously I'd send birthday and Christmas presents. Maybe I could be there on birthdays even, if you wanted. Maybe it could come and spend the weekend with me sometimes, when it got older. Hopefully I'd have a better flat by then. And we could go to McDonald's and the zoo and – or, actually, maybe we'd do more vegan-friendly things. The Science Museum, say. Sorry.'

He was abashed. All that time he'd spent thinking about it, and it hadn't *once* occurred to him that he oughtn't to suggest going to McDonald's or the zoo. Fortunately, Daria and Emily were smiling and shaking their heads as if to say, Don't worry about it.

He stumbled on. 'And I suppose … I suppose I could try to be a bit of a mentor, you know, in the awkward teenage years. If it was a boy I could give it advice about – you know, boy stuff. And it'd be quarter-Jamaican, wouldn't it, so I guess I could sort of talk to it about its heritage and stuff like that.'

Emily and Daria were nodding and mm-ing in encourage-ment, as if this was exactly what they'd been hoping to hear. 'Would you want to introduce it to your folks?' said Daria.

'Well, not my mum, because she's dead,' said Alfie, and Daria winced.

'I'm so sorry,' she said. 'I didn't realise.'

'It's fine!' said Alfie, too cheerfully. He meant that it was fine for Daria to say 'folks', not fine that his mother was dead, but he decided against explaining this. 'My dad, though,' he continued pensively. 'I'd tell him about it, I guess. If he wanted to meet it I suppose that could be arranged. And the rest of my family … That's difficult. I don't know. I'd have to think about it.'

'Totally fine,' said Emily. 'It'd be entirely up to you.'

'What about if you had kids of your own?' said Daria.

'Oh. Um. I don't know. That's not really on the cards at the moment.'

'Not at the moment, but maybe a few years down the line. You never know.'

'I ... hope they'd be friends, I suppose. Like cousins, really.'

'So, say our child has been the only child in your life for a few years. And then you find out you're about to have one of your own. How would you make sure our kid doesn't feel sidelined?'

Alfie gaped. 'I ... I ... well—'

'Sorry to put you on the spot,' said Emily. 'You don't have to answer that.'

'No, it's okay. I suppose I'd make sure I still spent time with it, just the two of us. And I guess I'd get it involved – let it hold the baby, I mean, even feed it, maybe. So it feels important, you know? So there'd be no room for doubt. That I trust it, I mean. That I love it. That we're all family.'

Daria and Emily looked at each other, impressed. 'You really know how to deal with kids,' said Emily, turning back to the screen. 'You know what makes them tick. It shows.'

'Oh,' said Alfie, smiling modestly. 'Well. Thanks. I do my best.'

'To be honest, it sounds like you'd do this perfectly,' said Daria. 'But was there something you weren't sure about? Some kind of hurdle, you said?'

'Oh,' said Alfie. 'Yeah. That.' He sighed deeply. The fantasy child had loomed so large over their conversation that he'd almost forgotten he might be prevented from

197

fathering it. 'It isn't that I'm not sure about whether I want to do it,' he went on. 'I am. I do. It's just what you said about my family medical history. If there's anything that might cause concern.' They frowned at this, worried, and it was painful to know that what he was about to say would not in any way reassure them.

He braced himself and said: 'There's a chance I might be carrying a dodgy gene. BRCA1, it's called. My mum had it, and she died of breast cancer. So did my grandma, which means she was probably carrying it too.'

'Oh, Jesus,' said Daria.

'Yeah,' replied Alfie, nodding slowly. 'So, you know. I might have something I wouldn't want to pass on. Which throws a spanner in the works a bit.'

'Fuck,' said Emily.

'Is there a way to rule it out?' said Daria. 'Some kind of test?'

'There is, as it happens,' said Alfie. 'And actually, I've already spoken to my GP about it. She's referred me. I got my appointment letter today. I'm going for the test next week, and then it'll be a couple of weeks after that before I get the result.'

'Oh!' said Daria. 'Wow. Okay. Well, that's good, I suppose!'

'I think so.'

'So we'll just have to wait and see, and if it comes back positive we'll … I don't know.'

'We'll think about it if it happens,' said Emily firmly. 'We'll just put it all on hold for a bit. We won't finalise anything, until we know.'

'And you're sure you want to do the test, Alfie?' said Daria. 'It'd be quite a lot to handle, wouldn't it, if you got a positive result? You'd be higher risk for cancer yourself, presumably?'

'Yeah. But I do want to do it. I've been angsting about it a lot. My whole adult life, really, not just this past week. But I've decided now. I want to know. If I've got it I could work on minimising the risk. And if I haven't, well. That would be fucking *sweet*.'

They smiled at that, but the news had troubled them, he could tell. It had inflected the mood, like dye billowing through liquid. They seemed at a loss for words.

'I did have one other question, actually,' he said, keen to change the subject. 'Unrelated.' They nodded in encouragement, and he continued: 'Say it was all fine, and we decided to go ahead. What would happen if your brother came back? Would I still be the donor, or would he?'

This took them by surprise. Kamran's contract had been extended for another six months, and he had expressed no intention of coming back any time soon. He'd taken his most recent holiday in India. They were now so accustomed to his absence that the possibility seemed abstract and remote.

'I don't think we need to worry too much about that,' said Daria. Emily looked at her.

'He's right, though,' she said. 'We ought to think about it, since we're taking all these precautions.'

'I'd completely understand if you'd rather use him,' said Alfie. 'It's only natural. He's family. He was always your first choice, right?'

'Yes,' said Daria, 'but—'

'You don't need to worry about hurting my feelings or anything,' he continued. He felt this needed to be expressed as a matter of some urgency. 'I totally get it.'

'That's extremely grown up of you,' said Emily.

'Just the kind of guy I am,' said Alfie, grinning.

'I suppose, if it came to it, we'd probably prefer to use him,' said Daria. 'Because of the biological link. Not just for me, but my parents too. Not that biology matters all that much, at the end of the day. But if we had the choice, biological link or no biological link ...'

'Oh, yeah. Totally. I get that.'

'But as I say, it's not likely to happen,' said Daria hastily.

'Well,' said Alfie, 'that answers my question, anyway.'

After that there wasn't much more to discuss. It was useful to have established their position on Kamran, but the world in which they might have such a choice to make felt very distant. Alfie's sobering reminder of human mortality and misfortune lingered like a heavy cloud, and he was sorry to have soured the atmosphere. Yet being the bearer of news rather than the recipient of it had given him the illusion of being in control, which left him feeling calmer than he had all week. He would do this fucking test, he thought to himself with new resolve. And afterwards he would get on with his life, and he would enjoy it too, whatever the result.

24

IT GOT HARDER to maintain this attitude as he waited, first for the appointment, and then for the result. The test itself was quick and painless, but still a great ordeal because it was conducted in a medical establishment, and Alfie hated medical establishments. He could always detect in them a lingering scent of bad news. He was not a person who needed leaflets to remind him that he might one day be struck down by pains in his chest, or find blood in his urine or lumps in his testicles. He knew things rotted and wasted and atrophied; he knew his insides might turn on him, and for that reason had always regarded them with wariness, like strangers in his house. This medical establishment was worse than usual, because the majority of its awareness-raising literature was concerned with disturbingly named genetic conditions that he'd never heard of, let alone considered worrying about. He left the place alarmed, as he often was, to be in possession of a body.

In the weeks that followed he ate erratically and slept far less than was healthy. Hazel had heard about the test from Emily, and asked him over WhatsApp how he was feeling about it. Alfie sent her a gif of a man breathing into a paper bag and captioned it 'a lot like this'. Work consumed all his energy and attention during the day, so that he could go hours without thinking about what might lie ahead. But his stomach plummeted as soon as the bell rang, knowing he would shortly be left alone with his thoughts. He had never been so reluctant to let his class go, or so grateful to see parents waiting in the corridor for 'a quick word'. In the evenings he delayed going to bed, untempted by the thought of lying there, sleepless, in a stew about the test, which might at this very moment be sitting in a lab with a label on it, or being written about in an official letter, soon to be pushed through his front door. He stayed up late working instead, or else watching TV shows on his laptop. Sometimes he fell asleep with his laptop still open and woke up with a stiff neck, still in his clothes.

He left home each day before the post arrived, so walking up the stairs in the evenings, then along the corridor and in through the front door, was a moment of great trepidation. Every day he opened the door with his breath held, expecting to see an envelope waiting for him on the doormat. More than once he tore open an official-looking letter with trembling hands, and found it related to taxes or pensions. Even when there was no post at all he remained uneasy until he had checked the kitchen table and his own bedroom, in case someone had slid something under his door.

And then one evening, there it was. There was no mistaking it. The NHS logo was in the corner, the words 'private and confidential' along the bottom. He stooped to pick it up. It was very slim; evidently there was just a single piece of paper inside. This was a good sign, surely? The envelopes containing bad news were presumably stuffed full of supportive leaflets. He stuck a finger under the flap, and ripped. 'Dear Alfie Berghan,' he read, as he unfolded the page, and for a moment everything seemed to pause. Through the open door of the living room he could hear the buses pulling up to the stop outside, and from the kitchen, the scrape of cutlery against china. He felt very still. *It's the moment we've all been waiting for,* the narrator would be saying if this were a reality TV show, *the moment Alfie gets news that will shape the course of his life.* Then he unfolded the remainder of the page, and the verdict was before him. He didn't read a word of it, aside from the bit that said 'pleased to inform you' and the bit that said 'negative'.

He was embarrassed later, to think how he had reacted, running into the kitchen and pulling Tony – Tony! – into a hug, telling him everything in short, breathless bursts, moving all the while, punching the air, dropping to the floor to do push-ups, leaping up and hoisting himself on to the countertop, propelling himself off again. He would go and buy beer, he declared, there had to be beer, would Tony join him for a beer? Tony was evidently astonished, but he agreed, and when Alfie returned to the flat with two four-packs of Corona he found him sitting at the kitchen table, waiting. Alfie was calmer by then, and apologised for having gone slightly mad, but Tony was very forgiving.

'It's fine,' he said. 'You can go mad. You've got a good excuse.'

'It's just the *relief*,' said Alfie. 'I can't even describe it. After all this *time*.'

'The cycle is broken,' said Tony.

'Exactly! That's exactly it! The cycle is broken!' cried Alfie, surprised to hear his disordered thoughts summarised so pithily, and further surprised that it was Tony who had summarised them.

They opened their beers and drank them. Neither of them said anything for a long while. Alfie might once have been unnerved by the silence, but not today. The adrenalin was leaving his body, and he was pleasantly sleepy. Everything felt luxurious.

'My dad actually died of cancer,' Tony said then, very matter-of-factly. 'I don't think it was a hereditary thing, though. I think he was just unlucky.'

Alfie sat up straighter. 'Shit,' he said. 'I'm sorry, man. I never knew. Recently, or ...?'

'Nah, ages ago,' said Tony. 'I was fifteen.'

'You're kidding,' said Alfie. 'I was sixteen.'

Tony nodded sagely and took a swig of beer. 'Fun times,' he said, and Alfie laughed in surprise.

There was quiet again after that. Then Tony asked Alfie if he felt like ordering a pizza, and Alfie said he thought that was an excellent idea. He wasn't sure if Tony would venture any more information about his father, or indeed about anything at all. But it didn't really matter. They could just sit and eat their pizza, a pair of half-orphans, not saying anything, and that would be perfectly fine.

25

EMILY AND DARIA were euphoric to hear Alfie's good news, and euphoric again, a few days later, when he got clear results in the sexual health tests he had taken at Newham Hospital. By now they had drafted the agreement that he was to sign, and had even had it looked at by a solicitor friend of Emily's. Alfie was struck by how thorough it was. He'd had a nagging feeling that they hadn't really meant what they said about wanting to include him in the child's upbringing – that he would end up hovering awkwardly on the periphery of their family, which, he thought bit-terly, seemed to be the position he was destined to occupy in families generally. But according to the agreement, his role would be very clearly defined: peripheral, yes, but not awkward, and while he naturally would not be an *insider*, he wouldn't be an outsider either. The child would address him as '"Uncle Alfie", or else just "Alfie"'; he would have in-person contact with the family approximately once a month, and he would endeavour to participate in 'activities of a familial nature including but not limited to attending birthday parties, going to restaurants, games and playtime, reading bedtime stories, etc.' He made no changes, and queried nothing.

They agreed to meet up and sign the document in Colchester, which would inconvenience everybody equally because it was about halfway between Norwich and London. Hazel was to be witness, and she was so quiet, both on the train and on arrival, that Alfie wondered what could be wrong with her. She appeared to consider herself a bystander rather than a participant, even in matters that had nothing to do with the baby. The four of them strolled around the town and ticked off its highlights; Emily declared it to be an odd mixture of old and new, elegant and ugly, and Daria agreed, saying yes, even with its merchants' houses and Roman remains, it did not quite add up to the sum of its parts. Alfie said they were right, that was exactly it. Hazel, a sullen pair of eyes, said nothing.

They found a pub for lunch, and as soon as the drinks were in, Daria withdrew a folder from her rucksack containing three copies of the agreement. 'Before we get too drunk,' she explained, handing them around. They signed and dated in their designated spaces, then raised their glasses 'to the baby'.

After that nothing remained but to set a date for the first donation. Emily would next be ovulating in two weeks' time, they said. The ideal date, in so far as it was possible to tell in advance, was March 6th. They would stay somewhere in East London and could pick up the donation whenever was most convenient for Alfie. Emily was going to take time off work. Fortuitously Daria had no classes that day, although she did have to be back in Norwich the following afternoon to give a paper at a research seminar.

Alfie looked at the calendar on his phone and saw that the sixth was Parents' Evening.

'Oh, crap,' said Daria.

Emily looked crushed. 'I guess maybe the seventh, then?' she said doubtfully to Daria. 'I could, sort of, do it on my own?'

Daria shrugged. 'I suppose.'

'It's okay,' said Alfie. 'I can do the sixth.'

'But—'

'We can do it after Parents' Evening. Or, actually, even before. School finishes at three fifteen. We usually get rid of the kids within half an hour. And Parents' Evening doesn't start until five. You'd just need to come by the school and pick it up before then.'

'Really?' said Emily. 'Isn't that a bit tight?'

'I'll manage.'

'Are you sure?' said Daria. 'It's not ideal, is it?'

'Honestly,' said Alfie. 'I should have an hour. That's plenty of time.'

'Well,' said Emily, 'if you really don't mind.'

He said he really didn't, and they thanked him warmly, marking the 6th in their diaries.

Hazel, who had observed this exchange with her arms folded and one eyebrow raised, now leaned forward and said: 'So – sorry, just so I'm clear – you're going to be coming up with the goods in a *primary* school?'

They all looked up from their diaries. 'Well – yes,' said Alfie.

'Okay,' said Hazel, smirking. She lifted her glass and took a casual swig.

'There won't be any children around, doofus,' said Emily.

'There must be a disabled toilet or something, right?' said Daria.

'Of course,' said Alfie, glaring at Hazel. 'It'll be fine.'

The sun was shining, so after lunch they set off on a walk along the river towards a pub Emily had found online. Alfie and Daria walked in front, Emily and Hazel behind. The latter pair walked so slowly, and made so many stops for Emily to take photographs of boats and clouds and snowdrops, that Alfie and Daria soon found themselves far ahead. It was harder than usual to think of things to say. Everything seemed trivial in comparison to the momentous events now beginning to unfurl.

Eventually Daria said: 'So are you still basking in the glory of that test result? Must feel pretty good, I'd have thought?'

'Pretty good, yeah,' he said, smiling. 'I hadn't realised how worried I'd been about it. But I guess it was sort of always there in the back of my head, even when I wasn't thinking about it.'

'I'm not surprised,' said Daria. 'It's quite a thing to have hanging over you.'

'I mean, I might have had it, and been fine,' he added. 'I wouldn't have been in the highest risk category, what with not having breasts or ovaries. But my risk of cancer generally would have been higher than average, I think. Which alone is enough to freak me out. I'm a massive hypochondriac.'

'Are you really! I didn't know that about you.'

'Oh yeah, very much so. Not just about cancer either, about everything. You sound surprised.'

'I am a bit. I don't know why, though. It's hardly surprising, given the situation. I suppose you just always seem pretty relaxed.'

'Ha,' said Alfie. 'Well, I'm not. I'm a crazed neurotic. I've had multiple sclerosis, motor neurone disease and about five types of cancer in the last year alone.'

He spoke cheerfully, but Daria suspected it was all a front: an attempt to convince himself that his fears were entirely baseless, or else an insurance policy against other people's derision. 'Do you think it'll get better now, though?' she said. 'Now you know you don't have this extra risk factor?'

Alfie sighed. 'I'd like to think it would,' he said. 'But realistically, I doubt it. Right now I'm still on a bit of a high from the result, but the novelty's going to wear off eventually, and then I'll just go back to worrying again, probably. Because even without that gene there's still a fucking *smorgasbord* of diseases I could get. And probably the odds of me getting any individual one of them are low, but when you add them all together, and you realise how many painful, debilitating ways there are to die, you start to think, Well, when's it my turn? I can't avoid disease for ever. How have I even made it this far? How is my body still functioning? *Is* my body still functioning, or is something going wrong right this minute? And that's before you factor in air pollution and pesticides and microplastics and all the other stuff that's probably shortening all our lives. So really, you're just waiting. And then when you get a symptom you think, Right, well, this must be it.'

There was quiet for a moment as Daria absorbed this. Finally she said: 'Alfie, look, I don't know if it's okay for me to say this, but have you ever considered therapy?'

Alfie blinked in surprise. 'Oh,' he said. 'Ha ha. Not really. I did go for counselling after my mum died, for like a year. But not since. Why, do you think I should?'

'I only ask,' she said, turning to check Emily and Hazel were out of earshot, 'because I'm in therapy right now, and it's been pretty helpful.'

'Oh? What for? If you don't mind me asking.'

'For my phobia of pregnancy.'

'Whoa,' said Alfie. 'Wait, what?'

'Yeah, I know. I've got a phobia of pregnancy and childbirth. But a really severe one. Like, panic-attack inducing.'

'Shit,' said Alfie. He felt suddenly as though he had missed some crucial piece of information. 'But … are you … I thought … Isn't Emily the one carrying the baby?'

'Yep,' said Daria. 'You'd think that'd make it better, wouldn't you?'

'So it's the same level of fear, even when you're not the one going through it?'

'Yep.'

'Wow,' said Alfie. 'Does Emily know?'

'Nope.'

'Oh.' He held back, unsure how much probing was permissible, but Daria carried on of her own accord.

'I am going to tell her. But I'm waiting until she's actually pregnant. I don't want to burden her before then. She's already stressed out. When she's pregnant she'll be so happy, it'll be easier for her to take it in. I've discussed it with my therapist,' she added, as if Alfie might be about to dispute her reasoning.

Alfie's initial thought, which he was ashamed of later, was that it would be quite nice to be afraid of something that couldn't actually do you any physical harm. How pleasant it must be to be burdened only with irrational fear that could be explained away, as opposed to rational fear, like his, which was a function of facing up to what was true. He would swap phobias with Daria, he thought, any day of the week.

But as Daria continued talking he heard the edge in her voice, and recognised it as the sort of edge that forms in the voice of a person who is braking, hard, against the plunge into abject panic. She was telling him about the dream she had had once or twice, in which the baby got stuck on its way out, and the doctors stuck sharp instruments up inside Emily so that they could bring it out in bits, limb by limb, like a ship in a bottle but the other way around. He felt afraid himself, in sympathy, and with recognition came pity. Fear was fear. They were both scared of pain and death and things that grew slowly in the dark.

'Do you know where it comes from?' he said.

'Oh, yeah,' said Daria. 'Easy. My mum nearly died when she had my brother. Pre-eclampsia. It took me a long time to bond with him because of it.'

'That'll do it,' said Alfie.

'And then when we watched a childbirth video in sex education, I was so horrified I fainted. And I read a lot of classic novels as a teenager, which made me think death in childbirth was more common than it actually was. Confirmation bias, you see. My therapist helped me work that out.'

'Ah. Clever.'

'I know,' she said, smiling. 'I was really pleased with myself.'

They walked on in companionable silence. The pub was now just visible in the distance.

'So is therapy making the fear go away?' said Alfie after a while.

'I wouldn't say that, exactly. But it's helping me understand it, and manage it better.'

'What are you going to do when it comes to the birth?'

Daria shrugged. 'Do my breathing exercises. Medicate, if I have to. My therapist says we should have a second birth partner, to take the pressure off me. That'll be Hazel, I guess. And I'm lucky, because there's an end point. That helps. I won't have to deal with any of this once the baby's actually born.'

'You'll just have to worry about keeping a tiny human alive instead,' said Alfie, and Daria laughed.

'Right,' she said. 'No biggie.'

'But seriously, if you ever want to offload,' he said. 'You've got my number.'

'Likewise,' said Daria. 'And don't rule therapy out.' She took a gulp of river-scented air and sighed it out again contentedly. 'Thanks for listening to me. I do feel better for letting someone in on it, actually.' It was true. She felt calmer than she had in days. There was a pleasant sort of downward drift happening inside her, a steadying of something agitated, like sediment settling on a riverbed.

26

HAZEL HAD SPENT much of the day feeling petulant and doing her best to hide it. Her question about masturbating in a primary school had been successfully disguised as sarcasm, but on the walk along the river she had more trouble containing herself.

'Your cartoons have got all serious lately,' said Emily.

'So?' said Hazel. Nish had remarked on this too, as had some of her followers. The trend now emerging was that the new cartoons received approximately half as many likes as the old ones. No wonder, said Miles – they were deeper and more challenging. They would not be everybody's cup of tea.

'So nothing!' said Emily. 'I was just *saying*.'

'I'm trying something new, that's all.'

'Whose idea was that?'

'Mine, obviously!' snapped Hazel.

'Okay,' said Emily, shrugging.

'I mean, I did discuss it with Miles,' Hazel admitted. 'He liked the idea of me going in a more political direction.'

'Right.'

'*What?*' cried Hazel, detecting judgement in her tone.

'Nothing! God, you're touchy!'

Emily crouched down to take a picture of something – more as a way of punctuating the end of the conversation, Hazel suspected, than because she actually wanted the photograph. Hazel waited, saying nothing. She did not want to hear anything against Miles; nor did she want to entertain the possibility that she had made a mistake by taking his advice. Her regard for him was a fragile structure and she was at pains to avoid thoughts that might compromise it. She wanted to be happy with him, because this would mean that she was happy without Alfie.

She was glad Alfie wasn't carrying the cancer gene, of course. She wasn't a monster. Nevertheless, she'd been so keenly aware of its enormity as an obstacle to proceedings that it had seemed fanciful to imagine it might be overcome. Alfie, her sister's sperm donor! She had felt very comfortable in her certainty that it would never happen. Only then it *was* happening, and the blow to Hazel was a little like what she had felt after the Brexit vote or Donald Trump's election. This was an inappropriate comparison, she knew – an *offensive* comparison, no less, because the central principles of this event were joy and openness and love. Still, it was seismic: a shifting of relations, an upending of the status quo, a declaration that nothing would ever be the same again.

Alfie, it was now clear, was not interested in her. She was embarrassed to recall the conversation they'd had in the living room. She had drastically misread him, and was glad, at least, that she hadn't revealed the extent of her delusion. What he'd said about it being 'complicated' had obviously been a reference to the legalities of the situation, not to mention the notion of fathering and loving a child, and yet also not being its father. She cringed to recall her replies. How naive she must have seemed.

He had a certain quality about him now, a new glow of benevolence that robbed him, somehow, of his tangibility. Emily and Daria had offered him a task of profound purpose, and in accepting it he had moved from his earthly plane to another, loftier one, which Hazel observed at one remove. The new, altruistic Alfie ejaculated not for his own immediate gratification but to secure the future happiness of others. If she herself had wanted anything from him – which she did not – it would have seemed base and unworthy by comparison.

When they reached the pub Hazel bought the first round, which although democratic was nonetheless unfair, because she only earned the minimum wage and was here as a favour to the rest of them. Emily should have stepped up, she thought, and bought it for her. Back at the table she watched them all talking and pictured them as characters in a cartoon that she would never draw, much less post. In the cartoon Emily and Daria would be regarding Alfie with the adoration of disciples, and Alfie himself, on closer inspection, would turn out not to be a man at all, but an angel.

Outside, dusk fell. They considered leaving and walking back along the river, but decided that it was already too dark. They would settle in, stay for dinner, then take an Uber back to the station. The windows darkened until they could no longer see the river outside. They ordered more drinks, and somebody located some menus. Emily and Daria were quick to choose because there were only two vegan options. Hazel deliberated silently for some time over whether to have what she really wanted, which would cost a lot of money and potentially cause offence, or something more modest and less controversial.

When the waiter came to take their order she made up her mind and said, 'I'll have a steak, please.' Emily watched her, smiling and frowning at the same time, as she specified medium rare, with garlic butter. 'What?' said Hazel defensively, when the waiter had gone.

Emily rolled her eyes. 'Nothing!' she cried. 'What is *wrong* with you today?'

'I just don't appreciate you getting all judgy over my meal choices.'

Emily opened her mouth in outrage and looked to Daria for back-up. Daria held up her hands and said, 'Don't look at me.'

'I didn't say anything!' said Emily, turning back to Hazel.

'You didn't have to,' said Hazel.

'Why, because you read my mind?'

'No,' said Hazel, 'I read your expression.'

Emily shook her head and took a swig of wine. 'You're imagining things.'

'Nice gaslighting, thanks.'

'Oh, for fuck's sake.'

'Well, come on then,' said Hazel. 'Look me in the eye and tell me you don't disapprove. Go on, I dare you.'

'I don't give a fuck what you eat,' said Emily, and Daria touched her hand, as if to stay it.

There was a brief pause. Daria looked wearily across the table at Alfie, who grimaced, and opened his mouth to change the subject. But Emily, more riled by the silence than by the talking, spoke first. 'You really want to have this conversation, don't you?' she said, narrowing her eyes. Hazel folded her hands beneath her chin as if to say, Bring it on.

'Fine,' said Emily. 'I admit, I'm curious to know why you've been posting all these earnest cartoons about climate change if you're going to turn around the next minute and have a steak.'

They're not my cartoons, Hazel thought. She tried not to think it, but she thought it anyway. I'm just doing what I'm told, because I'm pushover, and a lousy feminist. Out loud she said, 'I see. You think I'm a hypocrite.'

'I didn't say that.'

'Personally,' Hazel continued, 'I reckon that since I'll probably never have kids, I can eat all the steak I want.'

Emily opened her mouth, but nothing came out.

'I mean, what's the carbon footprint of having a child in the developed world? Fifty-eight tons per year? Fifty-nine?'

'Okay,' Daria interjected sharply. 'Can we drop it now?'

Emily was livid, but she had no counter-argument, no statistics to hand that would exonerate her. She excused herself, and left the table. After that nobody knew quite what to say. Daria looked up at the ceiling, Alfie down at his plate, and Hazel, emerging from the state of tunnel vision in which she had conducted the argument, was suddenly, acutely ashamed.

'Sorry,' she murmured, without looking at them.

'Go and make it up with Emily,' said Daria stiffly. 'Then maybe the evening won't be totally ruined.'

Hazel got up and went in search of her sister. She found her hunched on a picnic bench outside, elbows on her knees, staring out into the quiet blackness of the river.

'Em?' she said, and Emily looked at her without smiling, then looked back out at the water. Hazel sat down beside her.

'I'm sorry,' she said. 'I was a dick.'

'Yeah, you were. What is it about today? Were you actively planning on spoiling everything, or was it an accident?'

'Accident,' said Hazel in a small voice.

There was quiet, except for the lap of the water in front and the gentle hubbub in the building behind. 'I should have dropped it, I suppose,' said Emily, after a while. 'I was a bit of a dick too. Still, I got my comeuppance, didn't I?'

'What do you mean?'

'Well, you're right. It's a ridiculous carbon footprint, having kids. I know that. I've just been choosing to ignore it.'

'Look, Em, don't take it to heart,' said Hazel, furious with herself. 'I was just lashing out. It's PMS. I didn't mean any of it.' But this seemed to offer no comfort; Emily continued staring out at the water, frowning.

Eventually she looked behind her and said, 'We'd better get back. The food'll be arriving soon.'

The steak, it turned out, had already arrived. Hazel stared at it, and thought she sensed everybody else staring at it, and felt as exposed as if she had been served up on a plate herself.

'Start, Hazel, it'll be getting cold,' said Daria, and Alfie said the same, so that she was forced to pick up her steak knife and saw, audibly, at the pink flesh.

When Alfie's meal arrived Hazel felt shame envelop her once again. He had ordered a portobello mushroom burger.

They had talked about veganism once and agreed that they were unlikely ever to attempt it because they simply weren't good enough people. I just wish I could be disgusted by the concept of eating flesh, she had said. It's objectively disgusting, so why does it have to be delicious too? Amen! he had cried, laughing and laughing. Now it appeared he was trying to improve himself after all.

Finally Emily and Daria's food arrived, and attentions were diverted from the cleanliness of Alfie's meal as it faced down the grubbiness of her own. Still, there was a disquietude about everything. There was conversation, but it didn't take flight.

It was Alfie, in his wisdom, who got them out of it. 'So,' he said, 'who's been watching *Fleabag*?' The effect was instantaneous. Through mouthfuls of food they clamoured to have their voices heard, as if he had broken – or perhaps cast – a spell.

27

EMILY FRETTED ABOUT the exchange for days afterwards. She knew Hazel had not been aiming for the bullseye. Nevertheless, that was where she had struck.

There was a contradiction between what Emily believed and what she wanted; of this, she had long been aware. But she hadn't thought of it as actual hypocrisy, she explained to Daria, until, in pointing out the hypocrisy of someone else, she had had her own thrown back in her face. I wouldn't worry about it, Daria countered. It's impossible to care about the planet without being a hypocrite. The planet is being damaged by our very existence. The only way to avoid hypocrisy, as an environmentalist, is to kill yourself. Anyway, she said, what about the people who don't care, who eat meat and have children without ever thinking about the consequences? Technically they aren't hypocrites, but it doesn't follow that they're better people.

That didn't mean you shouldn't strive to avoid hypocrisy where possible, Emily argued. We should get rid of the car! she cried one evening, over dinner. Daria put down her fork in exasperation. So how will we ever go to the coast?

she said. How will we get to Holkham, or Blakeney to see the seals? How will we appreciate the world, if we deny ourselves access to it? It's like with flying, she said: travel is doing irreparable damage to the planet, there's no question about that. But if human beings had never travelled, would they ever have understood what the planet really was, or appreciated the importance of saving it? To stop climate change, everyone would have to shut themselves away in their houses and never go anywhere further than walking or cycling distance. And that will never happen, she said, because we love our world too much to make the sacrifices necessary to preserve it. That, she said, was the ironic, brutal truth of the matter.

'So you agree with me, then,' said Emily. 'You agree that it's all downhill from here.' And Daria shrugged, lost for words.

Why were they doing this? Emily now wanted to know. Why were they producing a new human being, who would lay the foundations of its own eventual suffering just by virtue of existing? To this Daria replied that she had always been in favour of adoption.

For a while afterwards it seemed that Emily might be willing to abandon all her hopes of pregnancy. What she wanted was to be a mother, after all, and there were other ways of becoming one. Look at you, she said – you won't be related to our baby at all, but that won't make you any less of a parent. Really I ought to be disgusted by the whole thing. It's objectively weird, what pregnancy does to your body. Why am I so desperate to inflict it on myself?

But, being now a voracious consumer of articles and TED Talks about the moral implications of reproducing in the age of extinction, she eventually found an argument that eased her conscience. This argument stated that since climate change was being driven by corporations and the governments in their thrall, it was neither fair nor realistic to expect individuals to mitigate it, whether through minor lifestyle choices, like recycling, or major ones, like not having children. In fact, encouraging people to forgo having children was a slippery slope that could end in eco-fascism, possibly eco-eugenics. Moreover, it was a distraction from the real problem, which was the plundering of finite natural resources in the pursuit of profit. It was certainly attractive, this idea that one could help fix the mess by opting in to certain behaviours and opting out of others, but ultimately all it did was take the heat off the real culprits.

'Did you know,' Emily asked Daria one evening in bed, 'that it was fossil fuel companies who popularised the concept of the personal carbon footprint?'

'Are you serious?' said Daria, looking up from her book. 'That's a genius bit of spin.'

'I know! And it's worked a dream!'

'Convincing us that it's *our* job to stop climate change, not *theirs*.'

'You see what this means?' said Emily excitedly, and Daria looked at her over her glasses. 'If we accept the idea that we shouldn't have a baby because our carbon footprint will go through the roof, we're actually just dancing to their tune! We're absolving them from responsibility! We're making personal sacrifices when we should be demanding systemic change!'

'Yeah, I see that,' said Daria, putting her book down and lying back thoughtfully with her hands beneath her head.

'I totally agree. It doesn't solve the other problem, though, does it?'

'Which one?'

'Well, the moral quandary of bringing new life into the world when the future looks so bleak.'

'I've been thinking about that too,' said Emily, 'and I think I know what the answer is.'

'Blimey.'

'We've got to get active, Daria. Do our bit to make the government act. We've got to fight.'

'Fight how, exactly?'

Emily turned her phone so that Daria could see the screen. Open in the browser was a website with a green band across the top and a graphic of an hourglass in the corner. Below, in big letters, were the words, 'JOIN US'.

'Extinction Rebellion?' said Daria. 'You fancy getting arrested, do you?'

'Not particularly. But if that's what it takes … I don't know. Maybe.'

'But isn't getting arrested a personal choice too? How's that going to make a difference in the grand scheme of things, any more than us being vegan? You're just one little person.'

'They're two different things, Daria. One's about *opting out* of a system we know to be damaging. The other's about *demanding* the system changes. One's about living by a moral code, the other's … well, it's lying down in the road and saying, We will shut down this whole fucking *city* until you listen to us.' Emily's eyes were wide with fervour, her cheeks pink.

'Yeah,' said Daria uncertainly. She agreed, in theory, but she had been burdened since her early childhood with a deep aversion to getting into trouble, which manifested itself in an almost pathological respect for rules and regulations. She could not envisage a scenario in which she would willingly give herself up for arrest. 'Is it productive, do you think?' she said. 'To make such a nuisance of yourself? Do you not just piss people off, turn them against the cause?'

'The suffragettes pissed people off,' Emily pointed out. 'The civil rights movement pissed people off. Anyway, what choice is there? People have tried being polite. They've tried marches and petitions and writing to their MPs. And has anything improved? Has it fuck!'

Daria said nothing. 'You're not convinced,' said Emily.

'I don't disagree, exactly,' said Daria. 'I just don't much like the thought of either of us getting arrested.'

'We might not have to,' said Emily. 'I'm sure there are other ways we could help. I'll do some research. Actually, I've got an old friend who's a member. I'll drop her a line, scope it out a bit. You know, Hannah? My first ever girlfriend?'

'The one whose brother went on a date with Hazel?'

'That's her. She's really nice. You'd like her.'

Daria took off her glasses and closed her book. She turned onto her side and propped herself up with an elbow, running a finger lightly up Emily's arm. 'So you're going to lie down in the road with your ex-girlfriend and get yourself handcuffed?' she said, eyebrows raised. 'Sounds suspect.'

Emily snorted, putting her phone down on the bedside table. 'Only to a suspicious mind,' she said.

'It's the stuff fantasies are made of,' said Daria.

'I'm not in the market for an extramarital affair, babe.'

Daria made puppy-dog eyes and said, 'Because I'm the love of your life?'

'You know you are,' said Emily, grinning.

'Your one and only?' Daria moved closer.

Emily giggled. 'Of course.'

'Your ...'

'Heart's only desire?' suggested Emily, as Daria kissed her on the shoulder.

'Your inamorata,' said Daria lustily, rolling her R's.

'My ladylove,' said Emily in a silly voice, sliding her hands up inside Daria's T-shirt, and the exchange continued with increasing absurdity until they had shed the last of their clothes.

28

AT THREE FIFTEEN on March 6th the bell rang at Northchurch Road Primary School and Alfie watched his class file out with a mixture of relief and regret. He had not masturbated in three days and was looking forward to a reprieve from the uncomfortable, twitchy heaviness, thoroughly out of place in a primary school. On the other hand, the monumental responsibility that he had brought down about his own shoulders – getting Emily and Daria down here on the basis of his own ability to supply their needs in a very short window of time, during which all manner of things might conspire to prevent him from doing so – was making him nervous.

He had to time it right. If he began too early he and the sperm would have to wait for Emily and Daria to arrive, and then they would have to race against the clock to get it back to their Airbnb before it started to die. Too late and the looming spectre of Parents' Evening would inevitably thwart his efforts.

The door to his classroom opened and a woman stepped in. 'Mr Berghan? Could I collar you for five minutes?'

Alfie's heart sank. It was the mother of Freema Hermann, a parent notorious among the staff. Mrs Hermann regularly 'collared' Alfie, always calling it 'collaring', and always for five of her own very particular minutes, which were much longer than anybody else's.

'Could we save it for Parents' Evening?' said Alfie. 'I'm a bit busy this afternoon.' This might have had the desired effect had he not put the emphasis on 'bit' rather than on 'busy', which gave Mrs Hermann to understand that even if he was busy, he was not so busy that he didn't have five minutes in which to listen to her.

By the time she left it was five past four. She hadn't made it through every item on her agenda, but he hurried her out of his classroom with the promise that they would reprise the discussion later. He checked his phone: he had a message from Daria, sent three minutes previously, saying they'd just set off from their Airbnb and would be at the school in about twenty minutes. Alfie replied that there was a Greggs around the corner where they could wait, or a Subway if they preferred, and told them to message him when they got out of the tube.

He tried to busy himself while he waited for the next message, opening an exercise book and making a pretence of marking it. He checked his phone at thirty-second intervals, even though it would vibrate as soon as there was anything to see. When the message came he leapt to his feet, snatched up his bag and jogged down the corridor towards the disabled toilet.

As he rounded the corner he almost collided with Akin Hassan, an eight-year-old prodigy fully cognisant of his own uniqueness.

'Hi, Mr Berghan,' said Akin.

'Hello, Akin,' said Alfie, sidestepping him and carrying on.

'Mr Berghan, can I show you my circuit board?' Akin called after him. 'I'm working on it at homework club. It's based on the circuit boards we did in class last week, only I've made it do some extra things.'

'I'm in a bit of a rush, Akin,' said Alfie, walking backwards away from him. 'Tomorrow breaktime?'

'Oh,' said Akin, looking disappointed, but Alfie did not have time to feel guilty about it.

He hurried on, looking around furtively on the approach to the disabled toilet. He could still see Akin, dragging his hand along the wall as he reached the far end of the corridor. At the near end, two year-six girls rounded the corner and strode confidently in Alfie's direction. Alfie swerved away from the disabled toilet and carried on walking.

'Hello, girls,' he said as he passed them.

'Hello, Mr Berghan,' they chorused, tossing their hair.

As soon as they were out of sight Alfie started jogging, towards the exit onto the back playground, around the school building, out of the main gate and into the street. What had he been thinking? He couldn't masturbate at *school*. Whenever he'd imagined this moment the building had been conveniently empty, but in reality there were always the odd few children loitering around the place, toing and froing from after-school clubs and sports practice. There was a Starbucks a couple of streets away; he'd be better off going there, although it was in the opposite direction to the Greggs and the Subway. He started to run.

He found the Starbucks toilet unoccupied, but in need of cleaning. There was a takeaway coffee cup on the sink, and someone had unravelled what looked like an entire roll of toilet paper and left it piled in a corner, where it was gradually soaking up the surrounding puddles. The room itself was gloomy and uninviting: white ceramics, dark tiled walls, maroon lino with shiny bits in. It wasn't in the least conducive to amorous thoughts unless you were desperately deprived. This was precisely what he had believed himself to be, only now he was here he felt like a pressure cooker that had been turned off at the source.

There were no hooks anywhere, so he put his bag down by the door, as far away from the puddles as possible. He took a plastic pot out of its packet and put it on the opposite side of the sink to the coffee cup, ready to grab at the crucial moment. Standing next to his bag, he undid his belt and shoelaces. He took off one shoe, stepped the same leg out of his trousers, then slid his foot halfway back into the shoe again. With one hand he held his trousers up, away from the floor; with the other he tried to pull his shoe on properly without falling over. Then he did the same on the other side. When he was free of his trousers he folded them and put them in his rucksack, out of harm's way, and considered how to best proceed.

He had a choice of three positions: standing with his legs apart, crouching against the wall, or sitting on the toilet. He dismissed the latter option immediately, experimented with the other two, and settled on the first. His boxer shorts were a hindrance, he realised, so he commenced the precarious removal procedure all over again and succeeded, eventually, in freeing himself. He looked around for his phone, realised it was folded away in his trouser pocket, rummaged in his bag for it, nudged his boxer shorts out onto the floor as he did so and snatched them up again, swearing. Eventually he stood up, phone in hand, opened the folder of pornographic screengrabs he had created in advance with a view to bypassing the school internet filter, and set to work.

It took time for things to get going. It was difficult to focus. His phone kept locking itself, which meant he had to keep retyping the passcode with his left thumb, and then a message from Daria – *In Greggs! Vegan doughnuts* 👍🏻 – appeared at the top of the screen and partially obscured the naked woman whose nipples he was trying to imagine licking.

Then, just as he was starting to make progress, a man's voice detached itself from the general hubbub outside and made its way closer. The man declared that he had had enough; he was owed 5k; he would not take on any more work until the client set up a proper payment plan. What was the client actually bringing him, in material terms? To what extent was he a drain on everyone's resources? The voice was loud now; the man was just outside the door. Alfie's erection melted away in his hand.

He put down his phone and closed his eyes, trying to suppress the panic rising in his throat. He imagined that the voice was very far away, in the street outside, and that the words meant nothing, that they were in a language he didn't understand. He imagined that he was in a dimly lit room with a bed in it, or a sofa, or at least some cushions. He imagined that he was only standing up because he was so monstrously horny he couldn't even wait the millisecond it would take him to sit down. But it was inescapable, all of it: the man's voice, the griminess of his surroundings, the fact that – with the exception of the marinading toilet paper – his penis was the only soft thing in the room. He picked up his phone again. Parents' Evening began in fifteen minutes.

There was no time to panic. He had to focus. He ran his hands over his hair and crouched down with his back against the wall. He closed his eyes again and took some deep, slow breaths. In his head he ran through a selection of potential fantasies, and after some deliberation selected the memory of Jasmine's breasts: pressing against him as they kissed, then cupped in his hands, then jiggling above him, and from them he moved on to the curve of her hips, the sheen of sweat at the base of her throat, the way she had moaned and held her hand to her forehead ...

This was working. He should never have bothered with the pornographic screengrabs. It was working so well that he maintained his erection even as the man outside told his interlocutor that he'd be on his way soon but he needed a piss first and someone was taking ages in the toilet. Now Alfie was embellishing the remembered version, bringing in another female body to rub its breasts against him from behind, and things were starting to move towards their natural conclusion when the second woman moved into his line of vision, and he saw to his surprise that it was Hazel, Hazel with her hair up on her head, the way it was when she came out of the shower, Hazel with her nipples erect and her hand clamped between her legs, Hazel leaning forward to take Jasmine's right breast in her mouth—

His eyes snapped open in shock, but it was too late now: he felt the familiar shudder through his body and positioned the pot just in time. A single drop slid down the side and plopped onto the lino; he wiped it up with a dampened hand towel. Then he cleaned up and put his trousers and underwear back on, practised now at keeping his balance without letting anything brush against the floor. He sprayed a little deodorant, straightened his tie, and put the sperm pot in his pocket. For a brief moment he stared at himself in the mirror and wondered how inappropriate his fantasy had been, on a scale of one to ten, where one was perfectly normal and ten was highly degrading. As he rushed out past the man waiting with precisely seven minutes to spare until Parents' Evening started, he thought about Emily, who might be about to conceive a baby with this sperm, coaxed out, as it had been, by thoughts of her sister doing unspeakable things. It was fucked up, he thought to himself – practically incest. If she knew, she would want nothing more to do with him. He jogged out of the door and picked up speed outside, feeling sweat patches beginning to form beneath his arms as he ran full pelt towards Greggs.

29

MILES SUGGESTED THAT Hazel meet him after work to try
out a bar that had just opened in Dalston, and Hazel – eager
to avoid her own flat, and thus Alfie, in front of whom she
had twice humiliated herself – agreed. They met outside
the station, where a red-haired man with scabs on his face
and a sleeping bag draped over his shoulders was shuffling
up to passers-by, holding out a battered paper coffee cup.
The odour that emanated from him pushed people away
with an almost physical force. As Hazel and Miles passed
he jangled his cup in their direction and Miles put a pro-
tective arm about her shoulders. She looked at the man
apologetically, shaking her head.

'Fucking crackheads,' muttered Miles.

In the bar Hazel announced that she had something
she wanted to say. Miles raised his eyebrows, mildly
concerned, and she told him that her follower count
had been plateauing ever since she made the switch to
serious political cartoons. Now, as of this week, it had
started to drop. She knew why, she said: it was because
she just wasn't cut out for that kind of subject matter. She

couldn't do it justice. Miles took her hands and said no, he absolutely disagreed.

'I'm serious,' she said, pulling a hand away to pick up her drink. 'I just can't make it work. It comes out so clunky and unnatural.'

'I really don't see that.'

'Well, I think you're the only one. No one else seems to like them.'

At work that day Nish had asked her if everything was all right. Bemused, she told him that it was, and he said, 'Only Ro was worried.'

'*Ro* was worried?' she retorted. 'How does Ro know enough about my life to be worried?'

Nish looked awkward and said it was only that she thought Hazel's recent cartoons were a bit – well, *off*. Hazel was extremely offended, and asked him if by 'off' he meant 'crap'. No, he said, Roisin's concern was not that the cartoons were crap, per se, but that they were just not very Hazel. There was one thing in particular that she had pointed out: the Jeff Bezos shark fin, in the cartoon with all the surfers. It was too laboured, too grandiose, too self-conscious an attempt at making a point. Hazel's work had always been so fluid and effortless—

'She said that?'

'Yes, but that shark fin ... Look, don't take this the wrong way, Hazel. We're being honest because we care about you. Roisin reckoned that shark fin was so pompous, it must have been someone else's idea.' He winced.

Hazel set her jaw. 'And who else's idea would it have been?'

'You tell me.'

There was a long pause. 'You know what I think?' said Hazel. 'I think Roisin has never liked Miles and now she's got it in her head that he's coercively controlling me into drawing cartoons I don't want to.'

Nish nodded slowly. 'Yeah,' he said. 'Pretty much.' Hazel looked at him in disbelief. 'Ro says, if you let a man interfere with your art, you're basically his prisoner,' he went on. 'If you let him influence your creative process, you're basically giving away your soul. That's what she says.'

Hazel rolled her eyes. 'She's so over the top. Anyway, why are you being her messenger? Ro says, Ro says. Why don't you tell me what *you* think?'

'What I think?' said Nish, surprised. 'Well, I didn't think anything that deep, until I talked to her. I just thought they weren't very funny any more.'

'What's so great about funny?' cried Hazel. 'Why does everything have to be funny?'

'It was just making me a bit sad, that's all.'

'Sad? Why?'

'Because it feels like you're losing your sense of humour,' said Nish. 'And that's not the Hazel I know.'

Now Hazel looked at Miles and said: 'I've made a decision. I'm going to go back to the stuff I was doing before. You know, the silly stuff. The gross stuff. It's been good to branch out. But I think I need to stick with what I do best.'

Miles shrugged. 'Okay,' he said. 'Whatever you think. They do say, write what you know. Or draw, in this case.' For a while he said nothing. He rolled his empty glass in his hand, frowning slightly. Then he looked up at her. 'Do you fancy a kebab?'

As they approached the station, kebabs in hand, they saw the red-haired man still shuffling up to people with his coffee cup. 'Have you got a couple of quid so I can get something to eat, sir?' he pleaded, and when Miles ignored him he turned to Hazel. 'Madam, couple of quid so I can get something to eat?' Again Miles tightened his grip on her shoulder; again she looked at the man and shook her head apologetically. 'That's right, walk away!' he cried after them. 'You're all the same. Nobody gives me the time of day! Nobody gives a fuck whether I live or die!'

'It's because you're a dickhead, mate,' said Miles over his shoulder, steering Hazel onto the station concourse.

'Nice cartoon,' said Roisin a few days later. Hazel was on her way to the kitchen, holding a tray of used coffee cups; Roisin was standing in the doorway. 'Ingrown hairs. Classic Phillips.'

Hazel smiled, very slightly, and Roisin stood aside to let her pass. She stacked the cups in the pot wash, then went back out to the café. Roisin was leaning against the counter, waiting for her.

'Nish told me about your conversation,' she said. 'I'm sorry, Hazel. I was going to tell you myself, I swear. I didn't know he was going to take matters into his own hands.'

Hazel shrugged. 'Guess I needed to hear it, one way or another.'

'He probably put it more tactfully than me, anyway.'

'Probably,' said Hazel, and Roisin grinned shyly.

'Look, I'm really sorry about the exhibition,' she said. 'I was out of order.'

'Kinda,' said Hazel. 'I mean, you were right. But also out of order. But also, I overreacted. So.'

'I should have apologised ages ago.'

Hazel waved her hand dismissively. 'You've apologised now. Anyway, you wouldn't have needed to apologise if I hadn't made such a big deal about it.'

'So?' said Roisin. 'Friends?'

'Go on, then,' said Hazel, and Roisin pulled her into a hug.

Later, when they had warmed up to each other, Roisin said, 'You're still with Miles, then?'

'For now,' Hazel replied, catching her eye. 'I'm meeting him later, actually. We're going up that big red tower thing in the Olympic Park.' This had been his suggestion, after the bar. She had pointed at it from his living-room window and asked if he had ever been up it, and he had said, 'Oh, the Anish Kapoor? I haven't, actually. Shall we do it, Hazel?'

'That ugly thing?' said Roisin now. 'The view will be good, I suppose. Isn't there a slide down or something?'

'Yep.'

'You're going down it?'

'Obviously.'

'Rather you than me,' said Roisin. 'Don't get killed.'

The tower-and-slide experience was extortionately priced, but they paid anyway and took the lift up to the viewing platform, where they stood side by side in front of the big glass window, looking out over the darkening skyline as the lights came on across the city. Miles breathed in audibly through his nose and exhaled the word 'wow'. They could see right into the stadium from this angle, and beyond it the skyscrapers of Canary Wharf, even a glint of the river in the furthest distance. They absorbed this in silence for several minutes.

After a while Hazel sensed Miles turning to look at her. 'Hazel,' he said, and she looked around. 'I actually wanted to talk to you about something.'

'Oh,' said Hazel, suddenly nervous. 'Okay.'

Miles sighed deeply and looked back out at the view. 'You're a really amazing person, Hazel. I hope you know that.'

She laughed. 'I think I'm fairly ordinary.'

He turned back to her. 'You see, that,' he said, gesturing at her with an open palm, 'that's what I'm talking about.'

'All right,' she said, embarrassed. She tried to focus on the skyline, but saw only her reflection.

'And it's exactly what makes this so hard,' continued Miles. Her head shot round towards him; he was holding up his hands to stop her from saying anything. 'Just hear me out, Hazel, please.' He took a deep breath, and continued: 'My ex-girlfriend got in touch a couple of days ago. She moved to New York about this time last year. For good, we thought. That's why we broke up. Only it turns out she's miserable there. She's coming back next month.'

'Oh,' said Hazel. 'I see.'

'I wasn't sure what to do,' he said. 'I was in serious turmoil. But I feel like I've got some clarity now. It's this view, man. It's elucidating everything. What I'm realising, Hazel, is that since I got that message, I've had the same kind of perspective on my life, like I'm looking at it from a great height. And what I'm seeing in this sort of landscape of my life, if you like, is that you're this fantastic pond, Hazel – a really cool, deep, refreshing pond – and I've had

238

the most unbelievable swim. But the thing is, you can only swim so far in a pond, can't you?'

He seemed to expect a reply, so Hazel stammered yes.

'You see,' he went on, 'Cassia's more like a river. There's direction, there's a current. And I need that, Hazel. I'm sorry. I need her. I need to be with her. Until we reach the sea.'

Hazel let out the breath she had been holding. 'Right,' she said. 'Okay. Well, fair enough.'

'I'm so sorry.'

'It's okay. I guess Cassia would never have drawn a cartoon about her ingrown leg hairs.'

'What? That's got nothing to do with it. I mean, you're right, she wouldn't, but that literally has nothing to do with it.' Hazel nodded, smiling placidly. 'Shall we go back down and talk about this properly?' said Miles. 'I could use a drink.'

'If you like,' she said. She felt bizarrely unbothered by the whole thing. Perhaps she was in shock, she thought. Perhaps the sadness would come later.

They moved away from the window. Hazel stopped at the back of the queue for the slide; Miles continued in the direction of the lifts.

'Miles,' she called after him.

He turned and came back towards her, eyebrows raised. 'You still want to go down that way?'

'I've paid twenty-five quid to go down this way.'

'True,' he said, visibly bemused.

'You take the lift if you want,' she said, but he joined her in the queue anyway. They waited. Hazel said nothing but Miles talked enough for the two of them, making hyperbolic declarations about what a stellar person she was and how much he had valued their time together. She grew peevish, but he didn't notice. Eventually she was rescued by one of the operators, who called her forward to Velcro her into her safety gear.

'On second thoughts, Miles,' she said as she waited to climb onto the slide, 'I don't think I need to talk about this any more. I think I'll just be going.'

'What?'

She inclined her head towards the hole in the wall and the disappearing chute beyond it. 'I think I'll just go.'

'Okay,' he said uncertainly. 'Well, I'll see you down there.' The expression on her face evidently suggested otherwise, because he looked suddenly angry. 'Hang on,' he said. 'You don't mean …? Don't be ridiculous, Hazel. Let's talk this out properly.'

But the space at the top of the slide was free now, and the operator was beckoning her over. Miles caught her arm as she moved towards it, but she snatched it away and sat down on a mat with a sort of pouch at the bottom for her feet, which was attached to a rope for her hands. 'Lean back and keep your head up,' said the operator.

She looked back at Miles, who was having a helmet fastened under his chin. 'Hazel, come on,' he said. 'Wait for me at the bottom.'

The operator asked if she was ready, and she told him she was. 'Have a nice life,' she said to Miles.

'You seriously don't even want to hug me goodbye!' he said angrily, abandoning all dignity, but the operator pushed her into the metal tube before she could reply and immediately she was in flight, plummeting down sheer drops and twisting round sharp corners, glimpses of the city lights flashing at her through perspex, down and down and down until the slide spat her out at ground level and she set off running towards the stadium, where her bike was waiting for her.

30

EMILY WAS NOW in regular correspondence with Hannah
Fox about Extinction Rebellion. Hannah was delighted
that she wanted to get involved, and took pains to send
her links and sign her up for newsletters. She informed
Emily that there was to be a big demonstration in the
spring – and by big, she said, she meant huge. Extinction
Rebellion had last been heard of blocking bridges over the
Thames, but this was to be on a grander, more disruptive
scale. Swathes of London would be shut down, hundreds
would be arrested. Politicians would have to take notice,
the media would have to take notice. The message would
be heard loud and clear. We won't stand for this any more!!
wrote Hannah. We won't let them fuck up our children's
futures!! Enough is enough!

It was probably best if Emily and Daria joined their
local chapter, Hannah said, because that way they could
help with the preparations for the rebellion. They could
join focus groups, mobilise their skills for the cause. They
wouldn't even have to come to London and demonstrate,
if they didn't want to, because they could contribute in

other ways. But despite what she'd said to Daria, Emily baulked at this idea. She realised that she had never been one for committees or collectives – the after-work meetings in school halls, the splitting off into discussion groups, the commitment to doing your homework and coming back next week. I'd rather skip straight to the point, she wrote to Hannah. They want people to rebel, so we'll rebel. In that case, Hannah replied, you'd better stay with us. We're taking the week off work, we'll be there every day.

Emily told Daria that she planned to go to London to demonstrate. Not for the full week, she said, but a couple of days at least. She deliberately said *I am*, not *we could*, thinking Daria would be more likely to come if she knew Emily was going regardless.

'You want to do it, then?' Daria replied. 'You want to get arrested?'

But this was so predictable a reaction, and so easily countered, that Emily laughed with glee. 'You don't have to get arrested,' she said triumphantly. 'You can designate yourself arrestable or non-arrestable.' She explained that if you were non-arrestable you simply moved when the police told you to. Only arrestables remained where they were and waited to be moved by force. Hannah's wife was arrestable, for example, but Hannah, who was still breast-feeding, was not.

Daria wasn't sure it could be that simple. It was all very well *identifying* as non-arrestable, but if the police decided to arrest you then you were just as arrestable as anyone else.

'Can you imagine,' she sneered, 'you're being carried towards a police van screaming, Put me down! I'm non-arrestable! And the police go, Oh, very sorry for the mistake, madam, off you pop.'

'They can't arrest you if you've done what they've told you,' said Emily. 'They have to give you three warnings to clear the area.'

'Okay, so you clear the area. Then what?'

'You wait until the coast is clear, and then sit back down where you were.'

'I don't know,' said Daria. 'I don't think I like the sound of that. It sounds like ... I dunno, like teasing a bear or something. I'm guessing this was all dreamed up by white people, wasn't it?'

This caught Emily off guard. 'Oh,' she said. 'Well. I suppose it probably was.'

'Thought so,' said Daria. 'No offence. It just sounds like whoever had the idea didn't have a problem trusting the police to behave reasonably.'

'Oh,' said Emily again, looking troubled. 'I didn't think of that. It didn't even occur to me.'

'It's okay. I'm just saying, not everyone has that luxury.'

'Yeah, I get that. I should have thought of it. Well, look, maybe you shouldn't come, then. I don't want you to feel unsafe. Maybe *I* shouldn't go, for that matter.'

'Why shouldn't you go?'

'Well, I wanted to go because it'd be a *noble* thing to do. A way to be on the right side of history, you know? But if it's all just white people sitting around basking in their privilege ...'

'Look, babe,' said Daria, 'if you want to use your white privilege to cause a public nuisance in defence of the planet – well, there are worse ways you could be using it, put it that way. And anyway, I didn't say I definitely wouldn't come. Just … let me think about it, okay?'

Between work and thoughts of the rebellion, Emily almost forgot that her period was due. It was only on the day it should have come that she realised it had not. She reminded herself that it probably meant nothing. Probably it would come tomorrow.

But it didn't; nor did it come the day after. On the day after that Emily allowed herself to buy a pregnancy test, still terrified that this was all a tragic, psychosomatic attempt at wish fulfilment, that she had brought the lateness into being through sheer force of desire. She worked through the afternoon, not yet tempted to find out one way or the other, because as long as the test remained in its packet, the possibility of her being pregnant remained open. Occasionally she opened her bag and peered in at it, lying between her wallet and her phone, the centre of its own throbbing forcefield.

That evening she sat on the side of the bath and waited for the verdict. Daria was sitting on the floor, back against the wall, elbows on her knees. Neither spoke. After what felt like a very long time, the alarm sounded on Daria's phone and Emily picked up the test with a trembling hand. Two red lines showed in the little plastic window.

She felt her mouth fall open. Speechless, she waved the test frantically in the air, and Daria leapt up and snatched it from her.

'Oh my God,' she breathed, and then Emily found her voice again and said, 'It worked! It fucking worked! What did I tell you?'

The night in London had been exactly as she'd hoped. The insemination had gone smoothly, and afterwards she'd had her orgasm, thanks to Daria, and after that she'd lain with her legs up the wall and watched upside-down TV while Daria took a bath. Then she took a bath herself, and then they ordered a takeaway and went to bed. They went back to Norwich at an entirely civilised hour of the morning, and while Daria was at her research seminar Emily had planted a windowsill herb-growing kit and baked a tray of banana muffins.

'I can't believe it worked!' she said now, in a sort of stupor. 'It just goes to show! Don't you think, Daria!'

But she did not articulate precisely what it went to show, because Daria, having stumbled back against the wall, was sliding down into her seated position on the floor, letting the pregnancy test fall, and dropping her head between her legs. Her hands were shaking violently – and it wasn't only her hands, Emily realised in astonishment: a tremor had taken hold of her from head to foot, and in an effort to control it she was breathing rhythmically, in through the nose and out through the mouth, but the breathing was ragged and uneven and at intervals she opened her mouth wide to gasp for air.

'Daria,' said Emily urgently, and Daria looked up at her. Her eyes were full of tears, and the tears were spilling over, but there was joy on her face too; she was smiling, and now gulping and yelping in a strange fashion that was neither sobbing nor laughter, yet also, somehow, the two at once.

'Daria!' said Emily, crouching down beside her. She put her arms around Daria's body and held tight, as if in this way she could still the quaking limbs. She rested her chin on

Daria's head and felt the chattering of teeth reverberating inside her own skull. 'Breathe like this,' she said, inhaling for a count of four and exhaling for a count of five, and Daria copied her, and for several minutes Emily presided over her breathing until eventually the shaking subsided and Daria sobbed, quietly, instead.

'It's okay,' she whispered eventually, 'I'm okay.' Emily loosened her grip and sat down on the floor in front of her. She took Daria's hands and squeezed them.

'There's something I need to tell you,' said Daria, pressing at her swollen face with the heel of her hand.

They sat on the sofa, their hands wrapped around generous mugs of tea, and Daria told Emily everything. When she had finished, Emily said: 'But why didn't you tell me before?'

'I didn't want to worry you,' said Daria, hollow-eyed and exhausted. 'I thought the best-case scenario would be to just get over it on my own, and that way you'd never have to know.'

'But *why*? Why did you think I wouldn't want to know?'

Daria shrugged, as if she was no longer entirely certain. 'I felt ashamed of it, I suppose. Here's you, about to go through one of the most painful and exhausting things of your entire life, and I'm the one losing my shit over it. It's back to front. I'm not the one who needs looking after.'

'We *both* need looking after, you numpty. We look after each *other*.'

'Yeah, but you've been so stressed out about getting pregnant. I thought that was enough to be going on with. I didn't want to burden you with all my problems as well.'

'Sweetie, I'm a big girl. I think I probably could have handled it.' As she said this Emily remembered her own theory about the detrimental effects of stress on fertility and wondered if, in airing it, she had unwittingly discouraged Daria from speaking out.

'I was worried what you'd say,' said Daria. 'I was worried you'd feel betrayed.'

'Why would I feel betrayed?'

'Well ...' Daria's lower lip trembled, 'because I didn't want it to work, that first time. When we went to Kamran's. Not because I didn't want a baby, just because I didn't know how I'd handle a pregnancy. I hadn't had any therapy or anything at that point. But I swear to you, Em,' she added urgently, 'I do want us to have kids, more than anything.'

Emily stroked her hair. 'I won't pretend I didn't wonder,' she said.

'Wonder?' said Daria. 'About what?'

'Remember that argument we had, before Christmas? When I got my period, right in the middle of it?'

'Oh God, yeah.'

'I thought your big secret was that you didn't really want a baby at all. I was worried I'd twisted your arm, and you were wondering what you'd got yourself into.'

Daria's eyes brimmed with tears. 'It breaks my heart that you thought that.'

'It breaks my heart that you've been suffering all by yourself, and I've just been thinking about what *I* want. You mustn't ever keep something like that from me again, Daria.'

Daria reached for her and they curled into each other, pressing together as if the boundaries between them could be dissolved. On the coffee table, Emily's phone buzzed with a message.

'I didn't want to have secrets from you,' said Daria into Emily's neck. 'I just wanted to tell you when the time was right. I always meant to tell you when you got pregnant. I didn't quite envisage the full-on demo, but I would have told you one way or another.'

'But what if I hadn't been pregnant?' said Emily. Her phone buzzed again, twice. 'What if we'd needed IVF? What if it had taken years? Were you planning to keep it to yourself for all that time?'

'I hadn't really thought that far ahead,' said Daria, as Emily's phone buzzed a fourth and fifth time.

'For God's sake,' said Emily, leaning over to pick it up. 'It's just Hannah,' she announced. 'More rebellion stuff. I'll reply later.'

'You still want to go?' said Daria.

'Yes,' said Emily. 'Why wouldn't I?'

'Well, is it sensible, in the first trimester?'

Emily smiled and rubbed Daria's leg. She would need to make a particular effort to be patient, she thought, in the months to come. There would be a lot of unnecessary fear to quell. 'I'll just be sitting on my arse all day, like I do at work,' she said gently. 'The baby will never know the difference.'

31

'YOU'VE BEEN AROUND a lot lately,' said Alfie, in the kitchen one evening. He was washing up; Hazel had just come in to make a cup of tea.

'Sorry,' said Hazel. 'Would you prefer me to make myself scarce?'

'No! It's not a bad thing. I just haven't seen this much of you in ages.'

Hazel sighed. 'Yeah,' she said. 'It's because I broke up with Miles. Or rather, he broke up with me.'

'Shit, really? I'm sorry. That's crap.'

'Naah,' said Hazel. 'It's not.'

Alfie looked around at her. She was leaning against the counter, sipping her tea. She appeared to have meant what she said. He laughed falteringly. 'Okay,' he said.

'Obviously I'm annoyed he got in there first,' Hazel continued, 'but I'm glad it's over. I should have ended it ages ago.'

'I see,' he said. 'I didn't realise you felt that way.'

'Oh, I knew he was a dick,' said Hazel, determined Alfie should remove 'poor judge of character' from his list of reasons to think badly of her. 'I just sort of ... shut it out.'

'You mean you ... you never really liked him?' Alfie stammered.

Hazel looked thoughtful. 'I don't know,' she said. 'It's complicated. I didn't *dislike* him. I'm not a masochist. I fancied him quite a lot. I suppose I was flattered. Because he's hot, right – you can see that?'

'I can see that.'

'And for someone like that to be into me,' she said, 'it felt nice, you know?'

Alfie hadn't known her to be so suggestible. For a person so wholly uninteresting to have flattered her into being with him, simply by deigning to like her! Could *he* have flattered her into being with him, if he'd only been more demonstrative?

Hazel opened her cupboard and took out a packet of chocolate digestives. She offered it to him, and he took one, and they both sat down at the table. Through a mouthful of biscuit, Hazel said, 'You know how sometimes you stay with someone just because you're scared of being lonely?'

Alfie laughed sadly, thinking of Rachel. 'I wasted a whole year of my life doing that,' he replied. 'But you've never struck me as a person who'd worry about that sort of thing.'

'I had this big barney with my friend Roisin back in the autumn. We didn't talk for months. It was really stupid. I suppose I was pretty sad about that, in retrospect.' She'd been sad about Alfie, too, but this she did not share. 'Plus, I'm twenty-nine soon, and I don't have a career, I earn the minimum wage, I can't afford a room big enough to store my own clothes in. And none of my relationships *ever* work out. I suppose there was a little bit of me thinking, If I end it with Miles I'll be back at square one. And I feel like I've basically been at square one my whole fucking life.'

Alfie had never heard her speak so frankly. She wasn't complaining, merely stating what she saw to be facts. He felt a rush of warmth for her. 'It's not going *back* to square one, though, is it?' he said. 'It's going *forward* to square one. It sets you back, being with the wrong person. It's more like square zero.'

Hazel looked at him. 'Interesting,' she said, a smile playing on her lips. 'I never thought of it that way.' And then, with more resolve: 'I think I like it. Thanks.'

They smiled at each other. Alfie leaned over and put a hand on the kettle. It was still warm, so he got up, in search of a mug.

'The other thing with Miles,' said Hazel, hesitantly, 'is that – this is going to sound really awful – but I just … I sort of thought he might be able to help me out. Career-wise, I mean. Because he knows people. I thought maybe he'd be able to hook me up with people needing illustrators. Are you horrified?'

'Why would I be horrified?' said Alfie, genuinely stumped. On the contrary, he was delighted, though he kept it to himself. Her relationship with Miles had been *strategic*! This was excellent news.

'Well, it's not very feminist, is it? Sleeping with someone because you think it'll help you get ahead. That wasn't the *only* reason, but still.'

'It was one of several very legitimate reasons, all bound up together,' said Alfie firmly. 'Don't beat yourself up about it. Did he help you, out of interest?'

'Nope,' said Hazel. 'He said he would, but in the end his idea of helping was more along the lines of telling me what I should and shouldn't draw.' She shook her head, bemused at herself for having put up with him for so long. 'He did inspire a few cartoons, though,' she said. 'So I suppose there's that.'

After this exchange Alfie and Hazel slid seamlessly back into old habits. They never sought each other out, but often found each other in the kitchen or living room and stopped there to talk for minutes that stretched into hours. To prolong these meetings they made casual cups of tea and opened casual bottles of wine. Once, after two glasses, she told him that Miles hadn't been anywhere near as good at sex as he had, which gave him an immediate erection and forced him to hide in the bathroom, where he thought about his Uncle Steve to make it subside. But such openness was now commonplace. They seemed able to discuss all manner of things that they wouldn't have dared to before, with the exception of the indeterminate future in which Alfie would become the father of Hazel's niece or nephew.

One evening, Hazel asked him for advice about the Miles cartoons. Nish and Roisin had been encouraging her to post them, determined that she should never again allow her creative process to be stymied by a man who didn't fully appreciate her. There were many of them now, not just the one about the fart test or the one about cunnilingus, but an entire series of pictorial send-ups of everything he had ever done to annoy her. Some had been drawn while they were together, others after they parted. She had made a great effort to ensure not only that the men in the cartoons looked nothing like Miles, but also, for added security, that they looked nothing like each other. Nevertheless, if he were to see them, he wouldn't need a particularly refined sense of self-awareness to understand who had inspired them.

Hazel showed Alfie her laptop, where the cartoons were prepped and ready for posting, then disappeared to her own room while he read them. After a while he called that he had finished, and she crept back into the living room, terrified.

'These are hilarious, Hazel!' Alfie said. 'They shouldn't be hiding away on your laptop!' Hazel was so relieved, and so buoyed by his approval, that she posted the first of them that same evening.

Almost immediately, the new cartoons began to repair the damage done to her follower count by the foray into political commentary. With each post, the likes and appreciative comments grew in number. The most loyal of her followers messaged to tell her of their delight. Emily messaged to tell her she was 'back on form'. Best of all, a feminist podcast called *Cutlass* messaged to ask for an interview later in the year. And on the day she posted her most candid cartoon yet, in which a man with a mohawk informed a woman with a drawing pad that her art was 'narrow' and that she needed to 'think big', Miles messaged her on WhatsApp to tell her she was a fucking bitch.

She was in the kitchen, talking to Alfie about nothing in particular. When her phone vibrated she only glanced at it; then, seeing Miles's name, picked it up to look at it properly. The message was long, aggressive and such a departure from everything she had believed him capable of that at first she thought it was a joke, that his phone had been stolen or hacked, and that everyone in his contact list was now being subjected to the same merciless tirade. She read it again, and realised that it was personal. It could only have been written by Miles. It could only have been intended for her.

'What's the matter?' said Alfie. Wordlessly, she handed him her phone. As he read the message a cloud seemed to pass across his face. A muscle throbbed slowly in his jaw. He looked at her, frowning. 'This is unbelievable,' he said.

But as he said it he remembered that he was partly responsible. He had encouraged her to post the cartoons in the first place, because he was in awe of her talent, and delighted by the indictment of a person he had never liked. He should have known better. Men who were harmless when they got their own way could transform in an instant when they were denied it, and with a viciousness that increased in direct proportion to their humiliation. Even placid men could turn, as he himself knew, having once punched a man at a party and then wrestled him out into the street. In retrospect he believed he had been justified – the man had said terrible things, *racist* things, insulting Rachel as well as himself – but it had been a shock to feel himself propelled by a force hitherto unseen, to know himself capable of mutating into something monstrous. Hazel, untroubled by extremities of testosterone, would not have realised the danger she was in.

'Hazel—' he began, but her shoulders were heaving, her head bowed in an effort to conceal what she could of her tears. 'Hey, come here,' he said, and she got up and stumbled into his arms. He could smell her shampoo, she his washing powder. She gripped her own wrist behind his back and let her tears seep into his T-shirt, and did not move away for a very long time.

They sat in the living room to discuss her next move. They agreed that she should reply with something so cool, so bitingly sarcastic and yet so glassily polite that he would crawl away in shame, if he did not first combust with rage. They tried on several such responses for size and settled on, 'Thanks, always a pleasure to receive such nuanced feedback.'

'Are you sure?' she said. 'It's very short.'

'It's perfect, Hazel,' he assured her. 'You're showing him he can't hurt you. You're so unbothered you're actually laughing at him. You think he's an idiot, but you have too much dignity to spell it out.'

'If you say so,' she said, and sent it.

Alfie asked if she had any more cartoons lined up that might provoke Miles's ire, and she said she had pretty much posted them all now, barring a couple, plus the one she would inevitably draw about this evening's episode.

'You're still planning to post them, then?'

Hazel hesitated, wondering: What would Roisin do? 'Fuck it,' she said. 'I'm going to post them. He doesn't get to dictate what I can and can't put on my own Instagram. I'm not doing anything wrong. I haven't identified him.'

Alfie, though he admired her gumption, was uneasy. He wanted to ask her if she featured in any compromising material that Miles might be able to use against her, but he couldn't quite find the words.

'Make sure you block his account, then,' he said instead. 'Men are bastards. Don't ever forget that.'

'Are you speaking from experience?' she said. Her head was lolling back against the sofa cushions; she turned it now, to look at him, smiling.

'Oh, yeah, I'm a total bastard,' he said, mirroring her. She grinned, and turned her body so that it was in line with her head, and he was just doing the same when her phone rang. She groaned and considered ignoring it, but pulled herself forward at the last minute to pick it up. It was Emily.

'Hi! Happy Friday!' Emily cried, and Hazel blinked with the bewilderment of a person who has been woken suddenly from a dream.

'Oh, right,' she said. 'I mean, I'm working all day tomorrow, but yeah, happy Friday.' *Emily*, she mouthed at Alfie.

'Are you with Alfie?' said Emily.

'How did you know?'

'You do live together, it's not unheard of. Is he there now? Can you put me on speakerphone?'

'Okay,' said Hazel, and put the phone on the coffee table.

'Hi, Alfie!' called Emily, her voice tinny, and then Daria's voice joined hers and a chorus of well wishes ensued.

'What's this all about, then?' said Alfie.

'We've got some news,' said Emily. Hazel and Alfie glanced at each other nervously.

'Go on.'

'Well, it turns out we won't be needing you next month, Alfie,' said Emily, and Alfie thought for a moment that Daria's brother had come back from wherever he was, then realised that if that were the case Emily would at least have made a show of remorse.

'Why's that?' he said, half excited, half afraid.

'It worked! I'm pregnant!'

'*What?*' screeched Hazel. '*Already?*'

Emily had had the confirmation from the doctor that week, they learned. It was very early, so it was to remain strictly between them and their parents. They must all be realistic about the possibility of miscarriage, and should try hard not to get too excited before the first three months were up. But still, said Emily. She shrieked with joy.

When the conversation was concluded Hazel and Alfie stared at each other.

'Well then,' said Hazel.

'Yeah,' said Alfie.

'Fucking hell, you've fathered a child! How does it feel?'

'I'm not really sure,' he said. 'I can't quite get my head around it. Actually, I might ... do you mind if I ...?' He indicated the door.

'Oh, sure, of course.'

'I think I need a moment to process it.'

'Me too, quite frankly,' said Hazel. Alfie got up, touched her briefly on the shoulder, and left. His bedroom was opposite the living room, and as he closed the door he snatched a glance at her. She was still on the sofa, staring straight ahead. She didn't look particularly happy, he wouldn't have said. In fact, if he'd been asked, he might have answered that she looked rather sad.

32

HANNAH FOX AND her wife Becky welcomed Emily and Daria to London like old friends. Daria warmed to them immediately. There was no ceremony or pretence about them, and they fed her and Emily handsomely, telling them to make themselves at home. The flat was full of books and pictures and the friendly sort of mess that evidenced a child in residence.

Hannah and Becky spotted Emily's Baby On Board badge, and were delighted. They had much to say on this topic, and asked a lot of thoughtful questions. In the course of the conversation, Emily said delicately that Daria had some 'issues' with pregnancy, and Daria found that, with them as her audience, she was able to talk with candour about her anxiety. Becky confessed that she had a lesser version of the same phobia. The thought of being pregnant had given her nightmares; the difference was that it hadn't bothered her to witness Hannah going through it. Everybody laughed, and Becky reached for Hannah's hand. She thought there was something rather special about Daria's fear, she said, because it was bound up with compassion, and love, and evinced a rare kind of oneness that caused her to feel Emily's pain as her own. Daria had never thought of it this way before, and found herself moved almost to tears.

The next day they went to the rebellion on Waterloo Bridge, Daria having been reassured that they would move at the first sign of trouble. She had never imagined that breaking the law could feel so peaceful. 'Obstruction of a public highway' sounded violent and dangerous, and yet here she was, lying on a blanket, gazing up at the sky through the leaves of actual trees, which had been dragged into place along the crash barrier that morning, their roots wrapped in sacking. She could hear flags fluttering in the breeze and the lap of the Thames below them. To her left, Hannah was breastfeeding and Becky was leaning back on her elbows, surveying the scene with satisfaction. Their placards, which read 'FOSSIL FUELS = EXTINCTION' and 'OUR HOUSE IS ON FIRE', had been propped against the nearest tree. To her right, Emily was engaged in animated discussion about vertical farming with a man called Nathan, a friend of Becky and Hannah's to whom they had been introduced as 'first-time rebels from Norwich'. They had been introduced to a lot of people in this way, and welcomed with great warmth and excitement.

When it was time to leave, because she was to return alone for teaching the next day, she found she wanted to stay. At least five people, excluding those she had arrived with, stood up to hug her goodbye. Will we see you tomorrow? they asked, and she was genuinely aggrieved to tell them that they would not.

*

Emily had taken three days off work, and so was back on the bridge the following day with Hannah and Becky and baby Noah. Hazel had let it slip that she was off that day too, and Emily was determined that she should join them. Hazel messaged that she didn't want to get arrested, and Emily replied that no one was getting arrested, there were only a few policemen here and there and they seemed fairly friendly, and that even when the arrests began there would be plenty of warning. *Plus*, she wrote, *Hannah wants to see you.*

This seemed to do the trick, and Hazel appeared at around lunchtime. 'If I'd known there was going to be yoga I'd have worn something comfier,' she said, by way of a hello, indicating the collective sun salutation taking place on sheets of corrugated cardboard further down the bridge.

'Hazel!' cried Hannah, leaping up for a hug. 'How the hell are you?' They always had got on well, Emily remembered as she watched them catching up. Silly, really, that they had had no contact for ten years. Ridiculous, that when relationships ended the attendant friendships got snuffed out too.

'Did I tell you Hazel went on a date with your brother?' said Emily, and Hannah said she hadn't, that was hilarious, how had it been?

'He still seems to hold a bit of a candle for Emily,' said Hazel, 'so it was … a little awkward.' Hannah rolled her eyes and said he was incorrigible, she gave up, and Hazel, quite frankly, had had a lucky escape.

A few strains of mournful harmonica music floated over on the breeze and Hazel looked behind her to see where they were coming from. Almost immediately she turned back around and ducked her head, pulling up her scarf to cover her hair.

'What's the matter?' said Emily.

'Have you seen who's over there?' said Hazel. She jerked her head backwards, and Emily craned her neck in the same direction.

'Back to us,' said Hazel in a low voice. 'With the harmonica.'

'Oh!' cried Emily, her eyes finally landing on the dark bun, the camera slung across the back. 'What's he doing here?'

'Same as you, apparently,' said Hazel. 'Saving the world.'

Emily leaned into the circle and hissed, 'Hazel's ex-boyfriend is sitting over there.' Hannah and Becky gasped and gaped and grinned. 'Who's that with him?' said Emily.

'His girlfriend, I guess,' said Hazel. She looked at Becky and Hannah and explained: 'The one he dumped me for.'

They gasped again. 'That fucker,' said Becky.

'He looks like a twat,' said Hannah.

'She showed him, though,' said Emily. 'Didn't you, Hazel? Can I tell them?' Hazel, still hunching forward to make herself smaller, said she supposed so, and Emily launched into the story of the tower and the slide with great jubilation.

'That's awesome,' said Becky, when it was concluded.

'You legend, Hazel,' said Hannah.

'Right?' said Emily. 'I didn't know she had it in her!' Hazel smiled, affecting modesty.

'So, those cartoons you drew,' said Hannah. 'Recently. The ones about straight men being pricks—'

'You follow my cartoons?' interjected Hazel, grinning broadly.

'Of course! You wouldn't have noticed. My Instagram handle doesn't have anything to do with my actual name.'

'Oh, Hannah!' Hazel sat up straight again and put a hand to her heart. 'That's so sweet! No really, I'm touched!'

'But those cartoons, though—'

'Oh yeah. They were all about Miles, yeah.'

Emily looked shocked. '*All* of them?' she said. 'They were *all* about him?'

Hazel turned to face her. 'Who did you think they were about?'

'I don't know, I thought maybe someone else. I thought maybe you just made them up.'

'Nope,' said Hazel.

'Jesus,' said Emily. 'What if he'd seen them?'

'He did see them.'

'He saw them? Actually? What did he say?'

Sighing, Hazel reached into her back pocket for her phone, and handed it to Emily with Miles's message open on the screen.

As Emily read it her face darkened. 'What the fuck!' she cried. 'This is unbelievable! These are *threats*!'

Hazel shrugged. 'Yeah, well. It's fine, I'm over it.'

'Fine? It's not *fine*, Hazel. He can't be allowed to get away with this!'

'Well, what do you want me to do about it?'

'*You* shouldn't be expected to do anything,' said Emily, handing back Hazel's phone and standing up.

'Em,' said Hazel, 'what are you doing? Sit down.' But Emily was already picking her way through the crowd of sprawling demonstrators towards Miles and his friends. Hazel watched in anguish.

'Hi, Miles!' Emily trilled, but then she crouched down next to him and her voice became inaudible. Miles was

263

visibly surprised. He seemed to be introducing her to his girlfriend. But soon he was gesticulating angrily, and so was Emily. Several times, Emily jerked her thumb behind her, in Hazel's direction, possibly on purpose, but probably without realising. Eventually Miles looked at where she was pointing. His eyes found Hazel's, and Hazel, for all that she wished Emily would stop and come away, found herself staring back at him defiantly.

'Guys,' said Becky. She was looking in the other direction, towards the South Bank. Hazel followed her gaze and saw a gathering of police officers heading slowly for the centre of the bridge. 'Looks like they might be about to start clearing the area,' she said. 'You'd better go.'

'Right,' said Hannah. She was strapping Noah into his sling. 'We won't be far away,' she told Becky. 'We'll stay as close as we can.'

Hazel looked for Emily and saw that she was heading back towards them. Miles and his girlfriend were standing up, moving towards the pavement.

'I don't know what the hell you said to him,' Hazel said as Emily reached them, 'but we need to go.'

'I told him he was lucky we didn't call the police on him. I said if he ever threatens you again, we will.'

'My knight in shining armour,' said Hazel, her voice steeped in sarcasm. 'Come on, hurry up.'

But Emily was sitting back down in the road. 'I'm staying here,' she said, linking arms with Becky.

'If you stay there you'll get arrested,' said Hazel.

'I know,' said Emily. 'It's fine, Hazel. Don't tell Daria. I'll call her when it's over.' She pointed at her. 'You watch out for Miles. If he messages you again I'll kick his arse.'

Hannah caught Hazel's arm and they stepped out of the road and onto the pavement, where a crowd of non-arrestables was moving slowly away from the danger zone. Emily made a phone sign with her hand and mouthed, *See you soon.*

'Are you serious?' Hazel called, raising her arms in a gesture of defeated despair. 'Did you know she was planning to get arrested?' she asked Hannah.

'I knew she was thinking about it,' said Hannah.

They watched as the line of police officers encircled the area where Emily and Becky were sitting. One of them read something out; then there was a pause, and then the arrests began. The first of the protesters were peeled from the pavement and carried away, a police officer to each limb. For every arrest, a cheer went up from the crowd.

It happened so slowly and methodically that Hazel began to wonder if they would get to Emily and Becky at all, or if they might tire and let them go. She leaned against the parapet with her chin on her arms, watching the water below as it rolled, glinting, in the sun; beside her, Hannah bounced Noah, grizzling in his sling.

Then Hannah touched her arm. 'I think it's them,' she said, and Hazel stood up and peered into the crowd. 'That's Nathan,' said Hannah, as a man was carried towards the police van further down the bridge, floppy as a sack of compost. 'Becky'll be next, I reckon.' And sure enough, first Becky and then Emily were carried away in the same manner as the others, amid cheers and claps from the crowd.

Hazel cheered so loudly she felt something cracking in her throat. 'WE LOVE YOU, EMILY!' she screamed. To her surprise, she found that she was crying. She looked at Hannah, whose eyes were red, and they both laughed.

'What are we like?' said Hannah, putting an arm around her shoulders.

'What's going to happen now?' said Hazel. 'Are they going to throw her in jail?'

'Just a police cell,' said Hannah. 'She'll be all right. She'll be out by tomorrow morning at the latest. If they pursue it they'll set a court date for the summer, I should think. She'll get a fine, or community service. But they might just dismiss it.'

'What if they mistreat her?'

'Hazel,' said Hannah, 'she's white, she's middle class, and she's wearing a Baby On Board badge. They'll treat her fine.'

Hannah promised that she would take great care of both Becky and Emily as soon as they were released, and then Hazel, who had had her fill of protesting, announced that she would be going, if that was okay. They parted with hugs and kisses and promises to meet up again soon, and Hazel walked north towards the Strand, wondering what to do with the rest of the afternoon. As she went she caught sight of a familiar figure standing across the road from her. He seemed to be alone. Possibly he was waiting for someone, staring back towards the melee as if his girlfriend might be about to emerge from it. He was wearing aviators, cut-off jean shorts and Converse, a plaid shirt over a white T-shirt. Still hot, Hazel caught herself thinking, and immediately reprimanded herself.

Part III

33

EMILY LOOKED BACK on the moment she had been carried away by the police with a mixture of pride and disbelief. The reaction of the crowd had made her feel like a hero, such that she barely noticed her back scraping the tarmac, or the dead weight dragging on her shoulder joints, or the friction of police hands on her forearms. She was released later that evening, and woke up the next day on Hannah's sofa-bed, wondering if any of it was real. She was almost grateful for the aches in her shoulders and the wounds on her back, because they proved that it was.

Daria had also had difficulty believing it. 'I thought you were going to be non-arrestable!' she cried, on hearing the news, and Emily had pointed out that she hadn't actually said *she* was going to be non-arrestable, only that one *could*. Daria had bombarded her with questions, and seemed so to dread the consequences of Emily's rule-flouting that Emily feared she would always blame her for it. But eventually Daria had come around – had been put to shame, she said, by a colleague who had mistaken her surprise for disappointment, and told her she ought to be proud. She *was* proud, she said, intensely so.

At work Emily was one of three arrestees, now treated like celebrities. Somebody started a crowdfunder for their legal fees, which raised a considerable sum in a matter of days. A new clause was written into the company handbook, confirming that 'arrest in defence of the planet' was not in itself grounds for disciplinary action, contract termination or dismissal. There would be some who disapproved of these developments, Emily suspected, but if there were, they kept their opinions to themselves.

She didn't yet know if she would be charged, but if she was she expected her pregnancy to work in her favour. She had made much of it at the police station, reading out a statement that she had prepared in advance. The law says I have a duty of care to my child, she had said. It is my responsibility to ensure that my child is fed, that my child is safe, that my child has a home. But because of the climate crisis, my ability to provide those things will sooner or later be compromised. Therefore, it falls to me to do everything in my power, including risking my own liberty, to ensure that such a bleak future is averted. This forms part of my duty of care.

She thought over these words a great deal in the days that followed. It had been a good speech. She was extremely pleased with herself, and grew more so as hindsight augmented her skill as an orator. Her voice had trembled; she had never been far from tears; and yet she had so clearly and eloquently laid out the absurdity of a law that would condemn her, on the one hand, for neglecting the needs of her child, and condemn her, on the other, for protesting a government and a system that were neglecting the needs of all children. In the remembered version of the speech her confidence grew under the eyes of the police, because she knew that they were slaves to the law, compelled to enforce it whether it was morally defensible or not. If they had any backbone, they would envy her freedom to break it. In fact, if she wasn't greatly mistaken, the eyes of at least one police officer had been shining.

She was in a meeting on a perfectly ordinary Wednesday afternoon, a fortnight or so after the arrest, when she started bleeding. She remained where she was for as long as she could, then made an excuse and stumbled to the toilets, cramping and sticky.

There was too much blood to be in any doubt as to what was happening. Her trousers were light grey; she had made it just in time, and wouldn't be able to go anywhere now without a sanitary towel. But she didn't have any. She began to cry. She had visions of herself at the end of the working day and long into the night, sleeping with her head against the wall, stuck for ever on this toilet seat, cold and stiff and sad.

Bewildered, she thought again about her words to the police. It dawned on her that they had been hollow and foolish. She had gone too far, spoken too zealously. It seemed now as though the fervour of her address had radiated out through her body, its shockwaves reaching the womb. The womb had sensed danger, and panicked. Perhaps it had known how hopeless everything was. This knowledge had been physical, after all; it was there in her thumping heart, her wavering voice and her trembling hands. Perhaps her body had concluded that the whole project should be abandoned – not because the foetus wasn't viable for the world, but because the world wasn't viable for the foetus.

Emily had been in the habit of shielding Daria from the details of her pregnancy, in case she heard more than she could handle and was reduced to a quivering heap on the floor. She had only revealed the things Daria needed to know, like which foods she was now required to avoid, or the things that were impossible to conceal, like her unremitting flatulence. It was from Hazel that she had sought sympathy for her morning sickness, which she had borne with as much discretion as possible; to Hazel that she complained about her constipation, her tender breasts, and the reduced capacity of her bladder. It was to Hazel that she turned now.

'What's the matter?' said Hazel, picking up after Emily's third attempt at ringing her. 'Are you okay?'

'No. I'm bleeding.'

'Oh, fuck. Bleeding how? Spotting?'

'No.'

'Like a period, then?'

'Heavier. And it hurts!' She had composed herself before the phone call, but now she began to cry again.

'Oh, Em. Where are you?'

'At work.'

'You need to go to a hospital,' said Hazel.

'I can't! I haven't got any sanitary towels! I'm stuck on the loo, Hazel! I don't know what to do!'

'Okay,' said Hazel with resolve, and was about to instruct Emily in one way or another, only Emily cut her off.

'Someone's coming,' she hissed. The outer door to the toilets was squeaking open. 'I'll call you back.' She hung up as the inner door opened and planted her chin in her hands, trying her best to be quiet. It wasn't a great success. There was evidently a quality to her snuffling and nose-blowing that suggested tears, not a cold, because when the newcomer had finished washing her hands she stood outside Emily's cubicle and said, 'Are you okay in there? Do you need anything?'

'Oh, that's kind. I could really use a sanitary towel, if you've got one.'

'I've got tampons?'

'No,' said Emily, her face crumpling again. 'No, I think it's got to be a towel.'

'Okay,' said the woman. 'I'll find some. You wait here.'

Her footsteps retreated and Emily waited. After five minutes the woman came back and a bouquet of sanitary towels appeared beneath the cubicle door. It was a gesture of such kindness and simplicity that Emily dissolved once more into tears.

'Thank you,' she said.

The woman was still standing outside the door. 'Is it a miscarriage?' she said softly, and when Emily did not reply in words, but only in quiet sobs, continued: 'You poor thing. I've been there. We need to get you to a hospital.'

'I can't go to A&E,' Emily wailed. 'You're not supposed to, are you? Not unless it's life-threatening.'

'There's a walk-in centre,' said the woman. 'You sort yourself out, and I'll call you a taxi.'

In the taxi Emily messaged Hazel. *On my way to walk-in centre. Nice woman helped me.* Hazel replied that she could come and meet her there, if Emily wanted. Emily wanted this so much that a fresh procession of tears set off down her cheeks, but it was really too much to ask of anyone, even her sister. *Don't be daft,* she replied. *It's too far.* Hazel said that if she left work now she could probably make the 14.25 train from King's Cross. From there it was only fifty minutes to Cambridge, and then, what, fifteen in a taxi to the hospital? She thought she could make it in two hours. Probably Emily would still be waiting to be seen, but if she wasn't they could go back to Norwich together. Hazel was off work the next day. *You might have to lend me some pants,* she wrote.

Emily thought this might be the kindest thing anyone had ever done for her. She sent Hazel a string of heart emojis. *If you really think it's doable,* she wrote, and Hazel replied, *See you soon.*

34

WHEN HAZEL ARRIVED Emily was in the waiting room, gaunt and slightly gray in the fluorescent light. She stood up at the sight of her sister and stumbled into her open arms, curling her head into Hazel's shoulder and holding her weakly around the waist. Hazel was slightly taller, and felt now like a giant. Emily seemed diminished in both stature and character. Her voice was small, and so were her gestures. Hazel asked if she wanted anything from the vending machine, and she shook her head rapidly, bewildered by the question.

She hadn't yet been seen, she said. She'd been told she was high priority, but that meant waiting times of two hours, rather than four. It had been two and a half, so she could be called at any minute. She chewed her bottom lip and gripped Hazel's hand in her own clammy one. At intervals she lifted her other hand towards her face and then replaced it on her lap, as if she was fighting an urge to suck her thumb. Hazel watched her with a throb of grief. Emily had always been more of a grown-up than her, ticking off half of the conventional markers of maturity when she was younger than Hazel was now, but this most grown-up of all her projects, now ebbing quietly away, seemed to be taking with it her very adulthood itself.

Eventually Emily was called. Hazel squeezed her hand and watched her disappear down a corridor with a woman wearing a lanyard. When she was out of sight Hazel flicked aimlessly through a magazine without reading it. Then her phone rang in her pocket and made her jump. It was Roisin.

'Hey,' said Hazel, glad of the distraction. 'How's it going there?'

'Fine, thanks,' said Roisin. Her voice was oddly strained. 'How's your sister?'

'Not good. She's just being seen now.'

'Poor thing. It's so rough. Look, I'm really sorry to have to call you at a time like this—'

'It's fine. I'm just sitting here twiddling my thumbs.'

'Oh, Hazel,' said Roisin, and there was a quality to her voice that made Hazel afraid. 'Something's happened. I'm guessing you haven't seen.'

'No? What?' said Hazel, feeling a chill spreading outwards from her heart. A succession of faces flashed into her mind: her parents, then Alfie, then Nish. Roisin was hesitating, evidently uncertain how to continue.

'What is it? You're scaring me.'

'Okay, so I was just on Instagram,' began Roisin, and Hazel relaxed a little. This wasn't how people learned of untimely deaths. 'I saw your cartoon, the one you just posted. I was in the comments. I was going to write something. But just before I did, this other comment got posted. It said, "The artist at work." And there was a link.'

She stopped speaking. She seemed to be steeling herself for the punchline. 'Well?' cried Hazel. 'What was it?'

'It was a video, Hazel.'

'What sort of video?'

'A *video* video. An *intimate* video.' Roisin paused, waiting to see if Hazel had picked up her meaning, but Hazel was still one step behind. 'Of you,' finished Roisin.

'Of me?' cried Hazel. 'What? How? I've never been in—' She stopped, remembering that she was in public. 'I've never been in an intimate video,' she whispered.

'Well, maybe it was filmed without your knowledge, then, or maybe it was Photoshopped, but it's you, Hazel. Or your face, at least. I didn't watch it, obviously,' Roisin added hastily. 'I turned it off as soon as I realised what it was.'

'Maybe you were mistaken, then. Maybe if you'd watched it a bit longer, you'd have seen that it wasn't me.'

'I'd love it if that were the case, Hazel, but ... Look, I'm sorry, I hate so much that I have to be telling you this, but there's really no way around it. Someone's put a porno-graphic video of you on the internet, and the link's all over Instagram and who the fuck knows where else.'

Hazel found the comment, not only on the post Roisin had mentioned, but on numerous others as well. There was one at least on each of the cartoons she had posted in the wake of the break-up with Miles. The commenter was called 00_xXx_00, and when she looked at the account she found there was nothing on it at all, except for the link in the bio. She didn't dare tap on it in the middle of the waiting room, so she took herself to the toilets and did it there.

Roisin was right. The video was of her. It was her face, contorted with pleasure. It was her naked body, lying in a tangle of white cotton sheets, and although there was nothing incriminating in the frame, no bedside table, no lamps, no pictures on the wall, nothing to indicate that the sheets belonged to anybody in particular, she knew, instantly, that they belonged to Miles.

The quality of the video was good. It was well framed and well lit. Clearly it had been shot on a proper camera, and Hazel remembered with a wave of nausea that Miles's bedroom doubled as a photography studio. Yet how could she have spent so much time in his bed without noticing one of his cameras trained on her? He surely didn't have a system of hidden devices, rigged up behind pot plants and bookcases? But then the image glinted in a strange way, as if the light was bouncing off it, and it dawned on her, all of a sudden, that the camera had never been trained on her at all, but on the mirror opposite the bed.

She groaned involuntarily. A cold sweat had broken out on her temples and on the back of her neck. The *mirror*. He must have taken his time angling the camera, so as to conceal the telltale flicker of its red light. It was ingenious, in its way. How proud he must have been, to have devised such a creative system by which to violate a person. The satisfaction it must have given him, to see her so thoroughly taken in. What fun he had had! Acting out a part, feigning concern for her sexual well-being, posturing like some sort of maverick because he believed the female orgasm to be no less important than the male. It was obvious now that he had been mocking her. And all along she had basked in the glow of his admiration, too vain and too naive to see him for who he really was.

The video was still playing. Somewhere in the depths

of her anguish she found the wherewithal to be grateful that it only showed her from the waist up. She supposed Miles was just outside the frame with his head between her legs. At least he had cropped himself out, and spared her further indignities. And yet it was odd, she thought, observing herself almost dispassionately, that on this particular occasion she had gone to such extremes to imitate pleasure, even down to the twitching of the muscles in her cheeks. It was entirely convincing, uncannily so. She did not recall Miles's technique ever producing such results as she now saw, written across her own face.

The truth of it struck her in a dizzying rush, and was confirmed almost immediately by the video, which now zoomed languidly out until her entire body was in view. *Plot twist!* the image seemed to say, as it became apparent that Miles was not there, that nobody was involved but herself, and that the only thing between her legs was her own hand.

She sat down heavily on the toilet seat. He had been in the habit of showering after sex. On countless occasions she had used this reprieve as an opportunity to bring herself to the climax he believed she had already reached. It was quickly and furtively done, under the covers more often than not. Apparently she had been bolder this time, and he had seized on this boldness, singled it out as the most shaming episode in all the humiliating footage he must have of her, and made it public precisely because she had felt so secure in her solitude.

Why had he filmed her? Was it for his own private gratification, or had he been gathering evidence to use to his advantage, in case of need? Could she have prevented his eventual betrayal, if she hadn't posted the cartoons, or run away from him at the bottom of the slide, or if she'd stopped Emily from confronting him on Waterloo Bridge? Or perhaps if she had never masturbated in his bed, and he had never found out that she'd been faking her orgasms, he wouldn't have felt sufficiently humiliated to seek revenge. But she couldn't be certain he had registered his own failure to satisfy her. Perhaps he simply thought she was insatiable, and deserved to be shamed for it.

These questions consumed her until her phone rang. At the sound of it she began to tremble, but it was only Emily, wondering where she was. She went to the sink and tried to lessen the impact of her red face and panda eyes, but when she returned to the waiting room Emily still looked shocked.

'Hazel?' she said. 'What's the matter?'

'Nothing,' said Hazel. 'How was it?'

Emily shrugged. 'Got some leaflets,' she said. 'I've got to buy sanitary towels. And a pregnancy test, for when it's over. I just have to wait it out. The doctor wasn't worried. Just your regular miscarriage.' She laughed bitterly, and Hazel tried to make a noise of sympathy, but it came out rasping and phlegmy. Emily frowned. 'Hazel, seriously,' she said, 'what's going on? Why are you crying?'

Hazel sniffed and shook her head. 'I can't say.'

'What? Why not? Has something happened?'

'Don't worry, everyone's fine, Mum and Dad are fine—'

'You clearly aren't fine!'

'Please don't ask me to tell you,' said Hazel. She could not begin to contemplate communicating what had happened. There would be so many words to find, so many sentences to formulate. And Emily's righteous anger would not help. It would make things worse, because it would make them real.

'Okay,' said Emily. She squeezed Hazel's hand, her face lined with concern.

Outside the hospital Hazel waited while Emily made a tearful phone call to Daria, and then they took a taxi back to the station. 'Do you mind if I don't come to Norwich with you?' said Hazel on the way.

'No, of course not,' said Emily. 'Although if you came back we could look after you.'

'Don't be daft. You've got enough to worry about.'

'But—'

'I don't want to leave you when you're ... you know,' said Hazel. 'But I really need to go home.'

'I wish you'd tell me what's going on,' said Emily, but Hazel shook her head, her insides constricting with shame.

35

DARIA RANG ALFIE to inform him he was no longer an expectant godfuncle.

'Oh my God,' he said, stupefied. 'I'm so sorry.'

'Yeah,' she replied. 'So are we.'

He was on his lunch break, marking exercise books in his empty classroom. He went over to the door and locked it, then stood by the window, watching the children in the playground as if seeing them for the first time. To think that *he* had so nearly produced one. A miniature human, with arms and legs and thoughts of its own. It seemed miraculous, now that it was no longer happening.

'How are you both?' he said.

'Emily's in a state. She's been on the sofa all morning. Hugging cushions, crying a lot. Chewing hangnails practically down to her knuckles. And I can't do anything. All I can do is make the fucking tea.'

'What about you? How are you feeling?'

'Oh, you know,' said Daria. She was at the bottom of the garden, looking back at the house. A lump was forming in her throat. Since holding Emily's fragile frame in her arms

282

the day before, on the concourse at Norwich station, she had been struggling beneath the full weight of their loss. 'I'm not great,' she said. 'Turns out there's only one thing worse than knowing there's a tiny little lifeform leeching off Emily, and that's knowing that it's gone.'

'Oh, Daria.'

'And the irony is, that's progress for me! I actually, actively *want* Emily to be pregnant! Thank you very much, therapy!' She laughed bitterly and sat down on an old tree stump, plucking at the grass near her feet. 'I was always glad on some level, when I made progress before. Like, Emily would get her period, and I'd be disappointed, but I'd be glad I was disappointed. Or I'd resent the nurse at the clinic, being the one to do the insemination, but I'd be glad I was resentful. I can't find anything to be glad about this time. It's just really fucking sad.' There was silence; then she said, 'How are *you* feeling? It's your loss too.'

Alfie sighed deeply and said, 'I don't know, really.' He had spent much of the last few weeks bewildered by the magnitude of what he had started. At home, he and Hazel no longer sought each other out, and this sense of an unspoken agreement, of a silent understanding that things were different now, that they must keep away from each other, was the surest sign he had ever received that she felt for him what he did for her. If it was nothing but a simple friendship, after all, there would have been no need to put a stop to it.

He had considered confronting her. Would it be so terrible, he wanted to ask her, for them to start a relationship even as he fathered her sister's child? It was only ill-advised because something might go wrong. What if nothing went wrong? What if it was all just lovely, for ever?

But if it wasn't. If it did. He thought of Rachel's cheer-leaders at school – all people he had been friendly with once. The potential losses would be greater this time. He could damage his relationship with the child, if he and Hazel broke up acrimoniously and forced Emily and Daria to pick a side. If he lost Hazel, he might lose all of them. If they thought he had wronged her they might elbow him out, or exclude him organically, without really meaning to. Even if they remained neutral they would still be caught up in a drama not of their making. It was like Daria said, life threw you curveballs sometimes. He did not believe they would have asked him to be their donor if they knew there was a risk of such discord.

He wished it hadn't taken him so long to see things clearly. It had been reckless to make his decision in the shadow of the genetic test: he had allowed it to cloud his judgement, to eclipse all other considerations. He wished, too, that there had been no Miles to muddy the waters. Above all, he wished he had spoken frankly to her in the living room that evening, when they had discussed Emily and Daria's proposal, and told her: It's complicated, Hazel, because I'm in love with you.

Daria was waiting for him to elaborate. 'I'm feeling lots of things,' he said. 'I don't know if I can fully articulate them at the moment.' He caught sight of the clock and realised that the children would be back within minutes. 'I'm sorry,' he said. 'I need to go. Let's talk again soon?'

They said their goodbyes, and were about to hang up, when Daria said, 'Oh, sorry, one more thing. Did you see Hazel last night?'

'Hazel? No.'

'Would you mind checking on her this evening? Emily's a bit worried about her.'

'Really?'

'Yeah, she went all the way to Cambridge so she could go with Emily to the walk-in centre, and she was going to come back to Norwich too, but in the end she had to leave. Quite abruptly, Emily said. She was upset about something, but she wouldn't say what.'

'That's weird,' said Alfie. 'I'll check on her, for sure.'

'Let us know, would you? She's not responding to any of Emily's messages, and her phone's going straight to voicemail.'

Daria's request unnerved him, so he left school as soon as the bell rang that afternoon. Back at the flat, Hazel's door was closed, which usually meant she was in. He tapped on it lightly. 'Hazel?' he said. 'Are you in there?' There was a groan from the other side. 'Hazel?' he said again, alarmed.

He heard her clearing her throat. 'Don't come in,' she said.

'I'm not going to come in. I just want to know you're all right.'

'I've got flu,' she said. 'I think it's pretty contagious.'

'Oh, no. Do you need anything? Tea? Ibuprofen?'

'No, thanks.'

'I spoke to Daria earlier,' he ventured. 'She told me what happened.'

'What?' said Hazel sharply.

'About the miscarriage.'

'Oh. Yeah, it's really sad.'

Alfie hesitated, wondering whether to say any more. 'I think you should message your sister,' he said tentatively. 'She's worried about you. She's been trying to get in touch.'

Hazel groaned again. 'Do you mind doing it?' she said. 'Tell her I'm sick. My head hurts. I can't deal with screens right now.'

'Of course,' he said, and retreated to his own room. He tapped out a message to Emily, then lay back and stared at the ceiling. He had brought home his laptop and a stack of marking, but he was in no mood to concentrate on work. He thought of Emily's child. *His* child. It had been growing inside her only yesterday, and now it simply did not exist. The ceiling blurred beneath his gaze; a tear trickled down the side of his face and plopped into his ear. There was no relief at having been freed from his obligation – not even a tiny, guilty glimmer of it.

It was clear to him now: he wanted things that were mutually exclusive. He had put himself in a bind, whereby whatever he now gained would be matched by an equivalent loss. He had started something with Hazel and he had started something with Emily and Daria, and these two things could neither co-exist nor be undone. He was properly crying now, sobbing messily into his pillow. It was a long while before he could stop.

He was in the kitchen later, staring vacantly at a bag of pasta and wondering whether to make extra for Hazel, when the intercom buzzed. He went out to the hall and picked up the phone. 'Hello?'

'Hello,' said a woman's voice. 'This is Hazel's flat, right?'

'That's right.'

'I'm a friend of hers. My name's Roisin. Can I come up and see her?'

'She's actually got flu.'

'Like fuck she has. Please, would you let me up? It's urgent.'

Bemused, Alfie buzzed her in and opened the door, and a minute later a tall blonde woman appeared. 'Thanks,' she said, then marched straight past him and tapped on Hazel's bedroom door. 'Hazel? It's Ro,' she said. 'I'm coming in, okay?'

Alfie ate his pasta alone at the kitchen table, the sound of voices rising and falling in the room next door. He caught himself trying to listen, and felt guilty, so he propped up his phone in front of him and distracted himself with YouTube videos.

Tony came in and poked about in cupboards and the fridge, then began heating soup in the microwave. He evidently felt more comfortable than before about using the common spaces when Alfie was in them, because these days they saw quite a lot of each other. Alfie paused his video, and for a minute or so they made conversation – friendly, but unilluminating, because Alfie's mental bandwidth was low and Tony did not venture beyond small talk unless Alfie did so first. Soon they were both nodding in lieu of saying words, and then Tony was taking his soup, and leaving.

Alfie resumed watching his video. A LinkedIn notification appeared as he watched, obscuring the picture; irritated, he swiped it away. Out in the hall, Hazel's bedroom door opened. There was a mumble of voices, and then someone went out of the front door.

When the video ended, he got up and took his plate to the sink. Instead of washing it, he stared out of the window. A crowd of vaping teenagers had gathered on the strip of grass that separated the flats from the street. A man and his dog were ambling along the pavement, the man pausing to wait as the dog busied itself with sniffing and pissing. People stood at the bus shelter and the buses pulled in and away again, their interiors glowing in the fading light. Everything outside, in short, was proceeding exactly as it always did. But inside, something was wrong. He felt uneasy in the pit of his stomach. What was the matter with Hazel? Why didn't Roisin believe she had flu?

Absentmindedly, he took out his phone, as if it might hold some kind of clue. The LinkedIn icon was cluttering up the notifications bar at the top of the screen, so he swiped down to look at it. It was a message. To his astonishment he saw Hazel's name in the subject line, although he didn't recognise the sender. He opened it, and almost cried out. There were no words, just three photographs. They had been taken from above, and showed Hazel in a state of such intimacy and indignity that Alfie burned with shame just to have seen them. He closed the message like it was infected.

He left his plate unwashed in the sink and went back to his bedroom, his heart thumping. What was he supposed to do? What was expected of people, in situations such as these? Before he could decide, his phone rang. It was Emily.

'Alfie,' she said urgently, 'I need you to talk to Hazel. We've both had these emails—'

'Oh, Jesus. You too?'

'What? You mean you've had one? With the photos?'

'Yeah.'

'Oh my God. Oh my God. Where is she? Have you seen her? Her phone's off, I can't—'

'She's in her room,' he said in a low voice. 'Her friend Roisin's been here with her. I don't know if she'll talk to anyone else.'

Emily exhaled loudly. 'So she hasn't done anything stupid?'

'Not that I'm aware,' said Alfie, stunned at the turn things had taken.

'You know, my mum rang?' said Emily. 'My dad got sent one. My *dad*. The subject line was "Important information about your daughter Hazel Phillips", and then a link to a video—'

'Jesus Christ.'

'It's vile!' said Emily, wild with distress. 'It's just horrific!'

Alfie heard the front door opening, and looked out into the hall. It was Roisin, balancing two pizza boxes in one hand. He beckoned to her frantically and she stepped into his room, looking wary.

'Emily, listen, I've got to go,' said Alfie, shutting the door behind her. 'Hazel's friend just came back. I'll get her to call you later, okay?' He hung up.

'What the fuck's happened now?' said Roisin.

He steeled himself. 'There've been – messages. Emails. I've had one. That was Hazel's sister. She's had one too. And her dad—'

'Her *dad*?' said Roisin. She closed her eyes. 'What was in these emails, exactly?'

'Photos. Of Hazel.'

Roisin nodded. 'Explicit ones.'

'Yeah.'

Roisin pursed her lips and set her jaw. The pizza boxes were starting to bend beneath her grip. She put them on Alfie's desk and sank down into the chair. 'I am just. So. Fucking. *Angry*,' she said through clenched teeth. 'That pathetic, lying *cunt*. I am going to fucking *murder him*.'

'This is Miles we're talking about?'

'Don't even say his fucking *name* to me,' she spat. She paused to compose herself, then snapped her head round to look at him. 'You haven't deleted the message?'

He shook his head guiltily, wishing he had. But Roisin seemed satisfied. 'Good,' she said. 'We'll need it, for evidence.'

'Oh, right. Of course,' he said. 'Look, how did this …? I don't … like, what even—'

'He was taking secret videos of her,' Roisin explained. 'He's a photographer, right? Lots of cameras in his bedroom. Yeah,' she said, as Alfie's mouth dropped open. 'He's that fucking sick. He put one on a revenge porn site yesterday and posted links all over Instagram.'

'*What?*' said Alfie, feeling heat rising up his neck.

'Yeah,' said Roisin again, her voice shaking with rage. She stood up. 'Look, I'm going to need you to call her sister back. Tell her not to delete anything. Tell her to tell her parents not to delete anything. The more we have on him, the better.'

'Okay.'

'We're going to bring him down,' she said, and Alfie nodded, with resolve.

36

EMILY WAS FULL of remorse, and would not be reasoned with. Everything bad that had happened, she felt, could be traced back to her decision to go to the protest in London. For the miscarriage she blamed not only her impassioned speech to the police officers, which she still believed might have sent an unconscious command to her uterus, but also the bumps and bruises that she had sustained while being carried across the tarmac. For the crime committed against her sister she blamed her own insistence on confronting Miles, exposing him in front of his girlfriend and no doubt igniting a wildfire of latent rage.

Daria said it would all have happened regardless. She read the leaflets from the hospital and declared that first-trimester miscarriages were usually caused by problems with the foetus or placenta, not by the odd bump or bruise. As for Miles, he was responsible for his own actions. By blaming herself, Emily was effectively letting him off the hook. Daria did not stoop to commenting on the speech to the police officers.

Still Emily wrung her hands and wept that if it hadn't been for her hubris everything might have been different.

What if one of her bumps or bruises had been the *origin* of a problem with the foetus or placenta? What if her intervention with Miles had pushed him over the edge? Daria placated and reassured to no avail, until eventually she lost patience and snapped, 'Do you know what I think? I think you *want* to blame yourself.'

'What?'

'I do! I think the idea that you were responsible for the miscarriage is much easier to accept than the idea that it was a random act of nature. If you were responsible this time, that means you can prevent it happening again next time. But that's not true, Em.'

Emily opened her mouth to argue, but words failed her.

'And it's the same with Miles,' Daria continued. 'It's a lot less scary to think that you might have pushed him over the edge than to admit that your sister was dating a malicious lunatic who fooled everyone into thinking he was harmless.'

There was silence; then Emily began, quietly, to cry. Sometimes Daria had a way of getting straight to the heart of things.

'Oh, babe,' said Daria, wishing she had spoken less bluntly. She reached for a tissue and dabbed away Emily's tears. 'I just mean, it can be hard to accept when things are out of your control. I'm sorry, I didn't mean to upset you.'

'I don't know what to do!' cried Emily. 'I don't know how to help! She won't pick up the phone!'

Daria suggested research, so Emily read everything she could about revenge porn, about its legal ramifications and effects on its victims. She encountered the word 'suicidal' so many times that she rang Alfie to tell him she was coming to London. She needed to see Hazel in person.

Alfie warned her that Hazel seemed not to have got out of bed for three days straight, except to go to the toilet. He had been leaving food and cups of tea outside her door, but Roisin was the only person who had seen her face to face. Apparently Hazel was staying away from the internet because she didn't want to know the extent of the damage Miles had wrought, and it might be a while yet before she could be persuaded to turn on her phone.

The air in Hazel's room was stale and there was a faintly putrid smell, probably from the dregs of an old mug of tea. The curtains were half-closed; the floor was littered with dirty crockery and balled-up tissues. Hazel herself was cocooned in the bed, swollen eyes peeping over the top of her duvet.

Emily picked her way over to her, and Hazel hoisted herself up, allowing Emily to gather her into her arms.

'I'm sorry about the photos,' she whispered. 'You didn't need to see that.'

'Don't you apologise,' warned Emily. 'None of this is your fault.'

'That's what Ro says,' said Hazel, staring at her lap. 'But I don't know.'

'You couldn't have done anything differently,' Emily insisted. 'This is a man who took secret videos of you, Hazel! Do you think it was in your power to make him behave like a decent human being?'

Hazel was silent. Then she said: 'He warned me I'd regret it if I posted any more cartoons. And I thought, What are you going to do? Murder me? If I'd *believed* him—'

'*I* confronted him on Waterloo Bridge,' interjected Emily. '*I* humiliated him in front of his girlfriend. I've been beating myself up too, thinking maybe it's my fault, maybe I was the one who pushed him over the edge.'

Hazel looked up at her.

'But do you honestly believe either of us could have stopped him?' Emily continued, channelling Daria. 'He didn't need a reason. This isn't about you or me and what we may or may not have done. It's about him being a vile person. It isn't up to us to take responsibility for his decisions, Hazel. It's up to us to make sure he gets punished for them.'

Later, Emily bought non-vegan food for the first time in seven years, hoping it would entice Hazel out of her room and into the kitchen.

'Are those steaks?' said Alfie, emerging from his own room to cook dinner. Emily, surrounded by packets and jars, was chopping tomatoes for a salad. In the bathroom, the hum of the electric shower signalled Hazel's first step out of hiding.

'They are,' said Emily. 'Quite a departure from my usual repertoire.'

'Are *you* having one?'

'Oh God, no. Actually, one's for you, if you'd like. Because you've been so kind.'

'Really? That's very nice. I won't say no.' He sat sideways on a chair and leaned against the wall. 'I'm so sorry about the baby,' he said.

'Thanks.' She carried on chopping, her back to him.

'How are you doing?' he ventured, then added hastily: 'It's fine if you'd rather not talk about it.'

The chopping slowed, then stopped. 'I'll be okay,' she said. She turned around and leaned against the worktop, gesturing vaguely at the air with the knife still in her hand. 'It's nothing to all this business, is it?'

'I don't think it's a competition.'

'No,' she said, 'but it's not like anybody *tried* to do me harm. It's not like anybody deliberately set out to ruin my life.'

'So?' said Alfie. 'It's still shit. Still stinks.'

She made a brave attempt at a grin. 'Still stinks, yeah,' she said. Her grin fell away and she blinked, then blinked again, and again. Alfie looked at his hands.

'There's just this sort of … emptiness now,' she said, almost whispering. She swallowed audibly, and he waited, unsure if she was going to elaborate or start crying. 'There are pregnant women *everywhere*,' she said. 'Have you noticed?'

'I do get a bit of a pang when I see one,' said Alfie, which was true, although he couldn't agree that there were significantly more of them in the world than there had been before.

'Do you?' she said. 'Really?' She put a hand on her forehead. 'I'm so sorry, I never even thought to ask how you were feeling about it.' She shook her head, angry with herself.

'It's okay,' he said. 'You've got enough to contend with. I mean, yeah, I do feel pretty sad, but it's nothing like what you must be going through.'

To his surprise, Emily laughed. 'There's some very British suffering going on in this room, isn't there?' she said. She assumed a plummy accent. 'No no, ignore me, I'm fine, my pain's nothing to *your* pain. I never held much truck with all that stiff-upper-lip stuff,' she went on, in her normal voice. 'But look at us.'

Hazel appeared then, her hair wrapped in a towel. Emily stood up straighter, visibly mustering her strength. She put out an arm and draped it around Hazel's shoulders.

It was the first time Alfie had seen her since the video was posted, and he could tell she was uncomfortable. She made eye contact, but only fleetingly. He felt awkward and ashamed of himself, as if he had read her diary, and she had found out. Fortunately the dinner menu provided an instant distraction.

'Emily!' cried Hazel, with more animation than had been heard from her in days. 'What are those?'

'Steaks,' said Emily, turning back to the half-prepared meal. 'What do they look like?'

'But you're vegan!'

'Extreme times, extreme measures.'

Hazel, rendered momentarily speechless, hugged Emily from behind as she lit the cooker and poured oil into a frying pan. 'Thank you,' she said. Then she turned to Alfie and thanked him too. 'For those dinners,' she said. 'I really appreciate it.'

'I'm sorry it was all just variations on pasta and sauce,' said Alfie. He did not admit how worried he had been that she would let herself waste away into oblivion, or how relieved he was that she had accepted his offerings.

The kitchen filled with the smell of frying meat. Emily served the meal, and as Alfie picked up his knife the others noticed that his hand was bandaged.

'What happened there?' said Hazel. He grimaced, and instinctively hid the hand under the table.

'You have to tell us now,' said Emily.

'Well,' he began, casting around for words that would

infuse the truth with a flavour of dignity, and realising there were none. 'I sort of punched a tree.'

'A *tree*?' said Hazel.

'Ouch,' said Emily.

'It was ouch, actually. It was really fucking ouch.'

'Why did you do that?' asked Hazel.

'I wanted to punch Miles,' he said. 'But he wasn't around, so I had to settle for what was available.'

Hazel grinned, and Alfie felt immediately that it had been worth it, that he would punch another tree in an instant, with the same hand, even, if he thought it would coax another smile out of her.

37

THE POLICE OFFICER looked at Hazel over the table, her expression unreadable. 'So he had one camera that was filming your reflection in the mirror,' she said, 'and you think maybe another one on the wardrobe or the bookcase?'

'Yeah,' said Hazel, looking down at her lap. The police officer's gaze was penetrating. It exhausted her. 'There were photos, too,' she explained quietly, 'and they were taken from an elevated angle. I think maybe he had a little GoPro up there, something small.'

The police officer nodded. 'Did you have any idea you were being filmed?'

'No.'

'Can you remember ever discussing the idea of making an intimate film with him?'

'No.'

'Not at all? Not even briefly?'

'No.'

There was a slight pause, as if she was being given the opportunity to change her mind. Eventually the police officer sighed and said, 'Okay. And how did you find out that this film was online?'

Hazel explained about the phone call from Roisin, the comments posted on her Instagram. She recounted how Roisin, sitting on the side of her bed, had informed her that there was more, that there were photos, too, that they had been sent to Hazel's family and friends. The police officer asked for names, so Hazel listed them: Alfie Berghan, Roisin McIver, Anish Chowdhary. Emily Phillips and Daria Ghasemi. Jim Phillips, and by extension Diane Phillips. The generic enquiries email for The Robin's Nest café in Bow.

'Thank you, Hazel,' said the police officer. 'Do you by any chance have copies of these messages?'

'No,' said Hazel, 'but my friend Roisin asked people not to delete them.'

'That's good. Could you collate them and send them to us, do you think?'

'Me?'

'Yes.'

'Oh.' She tried to imagine how she would do this without actually looking at the emails themselves. 'I ... I suppose so.'

'Great. Now, is it okay if you show me this film?'

'Sorry?'

'I'll need to get the URL and the date.'

'Oh,' Hazel said again. She reached in her pocket for her phone. She didn't know how to access the site except via the link on Instagram. But she could not find Instagram. She fumbled, confused. 'I'm sorry,' she said, 'I don't know what's happened.'

Then she remembered that Emily had taken her phone yesterday and gone through the backlog of messages that she couldn't face reading. She had deleted the Instagram app so that Hazel wouldn't be tempted to look at it, which probably meant it was full of insults and solicitations.

She explained this to the police officer, and the police officer said it was okay, they ought to be able to find the link on the computer sitting on the desk between them. She offered Hazel the keyboard. Obediently, Hazel opened Google and typed in her own name.

When the results appeared her heart began pounding in her ears. Her Instagram account was among them, but it was preceded in the list by three porn sites.

'Ah,' said the police officer, looking at the screen. 'Is it one of these?'

Hazel shook her head. Her throat was constricted, her face burning. 'It didn't have my name on it, originally,' she said. 'It must have been reposted.'

'Oh dear,' said the police officer, looking genuinely sympathetic for the first time since the interview began. 'Yes. This is something that can happen. The material can spread, a bit like a virus.'

Hazel stared. The full impact of what Miles had done now dawned on her. He had set something in motion that had taken on a life of its own. It was out of everyone's control, even his. The realisation made her sweat, first in her armpits, then all over. Her heart hammered so violently that she feared it would wear itself out, and stop altogether. Her chest began to feel tight. Her lungs would not do their job. She looked at the police officer and whispered, 'I can't breathe.'

She was vaguely aware of the police officer picking up the phone, of a glass of water appearing, and then of Emily, rushing across the room and crouching down in front of her. Hazel looked at her through blurred eyes. 'I think I'm going to die,' she said.

'It's a panic attack, Hazel,' said Emily, and at these words Hazel felt her heart beating even faster.

'No it isn't!' she said, crying in frustration. Were they going to just sit here, waiting for her to keel over?

'Try and breathe,' said Emily, which was all very well for her to say. Still, she did as she was told, making a frenzied effort to breathe in and out on her sister's instruction, and to her eventual surprise, she felt her heart beginning to slow. As it returned to its normal pace she felt herself overcome by a profound weariness, the like of which she had never felt before. She wanted to cry, but she didn't have the energy.

She returned to the waiting room and let Emily talk to the police officer. On the bus home she hunched in a window seat, trying to make herself as small as possible. She felt sure people were looking at her. Any one of them might have seen the video. Any one of them might have masturbated over the video, or saved a copy to their hard drive, or shared it on another website. All strangers, she realised, were now tainted.

When they got home she went straight to bed, resigned to the impossibility of ever getting up again.

Part IV

38

TO EVERYBODY'S SURPRISE, Kamran announced that he was coming home for a visit. He would be in the country for three weeks. He was very sorry for the short notice, but he hoped he wouldn't miss anybody because he was bringing someone with him and he was anxious for them all to meet her.

There was little room for doubt about the role this someone played in Kamran's life, but the announcement still sparked off a clamour of excited speculation. Leila wanted them all to be there when he arrived, so Emily and Daria took the train to Heathrow and met Daria's parents in the Terminal 5 arrivals hall. When Kamran appeared he was accompanied by a tall woman with strands of bouncy red hair escaping from her ponytail.

Kamran hugged everyone and then stood back, looking nervous. 'Okay,' he said, exchanging complicit smiles with the woman. 'Everybody, this is Jude. She's my wife.'

There was a stunned silence, then an eruption of euphoria. 'Your *wife?*' cried Leila, fanning her face and blinking back tears. 'Oh my goodness! Oh my goodness!' She drew Jude into a tight hug and rocked her from side to side.

Jude was an MSF doctor from Canada, and they had met in the refugee camp in Bangladesh. The reason for the whirl-wind wedding, it was explained, was to increase their chance of being posted to the same places in future. At the news that there were to be future postings Leila's face fell, although not to the extent that anyone other than Daria or Ramin noticed. Nevertheless, she was delighted that Kamran would have a partner accompanying him on his adventures into the unknown. 'I know you'll keep him out of trouble,' she said more than once to Jude. 'Just don't let him go to Iran.'

Emily and Daria joined the rest of the family at Daria's parents' house for a weekend of languid lunches and National Trust visits. Kamran and Jude stayed there for a week, then spent the second leg of their trip visiting friends in Manchester and London. For their final few days they stayed with Emily and Daria in Norwich. It was warm, so they had picnics and sat in beer gardens and walked along the river. Emily and Daria found Jude delightful. She was sharp, sensitive and funny. She wasn't at all intimidating, even though she spoke four languages and was a graduate of Harvard Medical School.

When the visit was over they drove Jude and Kamran to the airport and gave them a tearful send-off at the security gate. On the way home they agreed that this had all been an excellent decision on Kamran's part, that they were grateful to him for having gifted the family such a superla-tive person, entirely out of the blue.

'I mean, Lily was good,' said Emily, wondering if it was too soon to have shifted loyalties so unambiguously. 'Lily was great.'

'But Jude's better,' said Daria, and Emily laughed guiltily.

Later in the journey it was remarked upon that no one had mentioned parenthood, or miscarriages, or Alfie. 'I feel like we had an unspoken agreement not to bring it up,' said Daria.

'I mean, it was kind of their honeymoon, right?' said Emily. 'Wouldn't have been appropriate.'

'True. Although I could have taken him to one side for a private chat, if we'd wanted. Just to see where he stood.'

'Mm,' said Emily doubtfully. For a while they sat in a pensive silence, the only sound the hum of tyres on tarmac.

'What about if he'd come home on his own?' wondered Daria. 'Would we have discussed it with him then?'

'I don't think there would have been much point in just *discussing* it, given that we have no idea when he'll next be in the country.'

'Okay, would we have asked him to do a donation, then? Just a one-off, like last time?'

'Well, leaving aside the fact that I had a miscarriage last month, what about the sexual health check thing? Seems riskier than last time. Who knows what he's been getting up to in Bangladesh?'

'So we wouldn't.'

'I just don't think circumstances were in our favour.'

'Say they had been, though—'

'What's with you? You're like a dog with a bone,' said Emily, but Daria pressed on.

'Say you'd never been pregnant, you'd never had a miscarriage, and he just so happened to have had a sexual health check before he arrived. Would we have asked him?'

'I've no idea how I'd feel if I'd never been pregnant. Why all this hypothesising?'

'Why the refusal to answer a simple question?'

'It's actually a complex and highly speculative question, Daria!'

'I know how I'd answer it.'

'How?'

'I want to hear your answer first.'

Emily tutted, smiled, shook her head. 'You're infuriating, do you know that?' she said, her eyes on the road.

'Sorry,' said Daria.

Emily was quiet for a while. 'I just feel like Alfie's invested in this now, you know?' she said eventually. 'And we're invested in him. After everything that's happened, for us to turn round and say, "Oh, actually, we don't want you after all …" I don't think I could do it. Could you?'

'Honestly? No.'

'So you wouldn't have asked Kamran to donate.'

'Nope.'

'Even if there was no Jude?'

'If there was no Jude, if there'd been no miscarriage – even if he announced he was moving back here permanently – I still don't think I'd want to ask him, unless Alfie backed out of his own accord.'

'Seriously?'

'It's quite simple, the way I see it. Alfie's our guy.'

Emily grinned, then laughed in surprise. 'Yeah,' she said, 'I suppose he is.'

Having reached this conclusion, they were impatient to share it with Alfie. They called him on WhatsApp when they got home that evening, provoking a flurry of nerves on his part.

'So my brother came to visit,' Daria began, and Alfie thought: Right, there we are. That's it, then. He made an effort to keep his face neutral. He had promised that there would be no hard feelings if this happened; still, he felt the sting of rejection.

'Okay!' he said brightly.

'We didn't ask him to donate for us,' said Daria.

'Oh! Wait – what? You *didn't* ask him?'

'No. Partly because he brought his new wife with him, so, you know, it might have been a bit awkward. Partly because he's clearly with MSF for the long haul, which means he'd probably end up seeing the kid, what, once a year? If that.'

'But mainly because we're invested in doing this with you,' said Emily. 'We've come this far. We want to see it through.'

Alfie's heart was thumping hard. 'Really?' he said. 'Wow. Okay. I … wow.'

'If you want to carry on, that is,' said Daria. 'Obviously, there's no obligation.'

'I do!' cried Alfie, surer than he had ever been that this was indeed what he wanted.

Emily and Daria grinned. 'In that case,' said Emily, 'how would you feel about trying again next month?'

'I'd feel very good about it,' he said, smiling, and Emily and Daria whooped and cheered. They got their diaries out and agreed on a new date, and then there was quiet, and then, unable to think of another outlet for their exhilaration, they all burst out laughing. After that there was nothing left to do but drink wine and talk in sweeping platitudes about how grateful they all were and how much they all appreciated each other. When they'd said goodbye Alfie lay on his bed for a long time, thinking about things. Eventually he sat up with resolve, and reached for his phone. There was a call he needed to make.

39

HAZEL RETURNED TO work in mid-June, over a month after Miles's betrayal. Nish and Roisin acted as go-betweens with the café manager, and arranged it so that she would always be rostered with one or both of them. It wasn't so bad, really. She was pleased to be kept busy, and it was excellent to be in the company of Nish and Roisin after so long at home. They made her laugh, which was an unfamiliar feeling, and there were times when everything felt almost normal.

Then, one day, she saw Miles. She'd just come back from her break. She was walking back out into the café, tying her apron around her waist, and there he was: a man, sitting at one of the tables with his back to her, his dark hair tied in a bun. She stopped abruptly, as if by freezing she could make herself disappear. She couldn't move, not even to return to the staffroom. After a matter of seconds the man turned his head, and immediately she saw that he was not Miles, he was someone else entirely, a complete stranger – and really it should have been obvious, because he was too thickset, and he had a Windows laptop, and his trainers were all wrong. But by then the damage was done. Her heart was pounding, her hands trembling. Her throat had constricted, and there were tears in her eyes. She recovered her power of movement and stumbled back to the staffroom, where Nish was eating a sandwich and scrolling on his phone.

'Hazel!' he cried in alarm, leaping up and coming towards her. He sat her down and ran her a glass of water and rubbed her back until she calmed down. Then he sent her home in an Uber, and cut his own break short to cover for her.

After that he and Roisin spoke to the manager again and arranged it so that Hazel could be kept on the quietest shifts possible. This meant she now worked Mondays to Fridays, and had whole weekends free for the first time since starting at the café. A consequence of this was that she saw more of Alfie, who spent large chunks of each weekend working on his laptop in the living room. Hazel took to sitting in there with him, knitting. This had been recommended by her new therapist as a way to keep herself calm, and now she knitted religiously in spite of the warm weather, producing scarves so long they could be wrapped several times around the neck and still trail on the floor. When she knitted she sank into a state of focus in which nothing existed but the click and rub of the needles, the circular motion of the hand as it drew the yarn back and around, and the soft heat of the scarf, piling slowly in her lap. Her emotional scale now ranged from violent anger to paralysing anxiety, but when she knitted she could keep the balance hovering somewhere in the neutral centre.

On these occasions Alfie often observed her, surreptitiously, over his laptop screen. Her gaze was always fixed, her face rigid with concentration. She seemed to show no interest in the end result of her endeavours, only in the process, which had such a hypnotic hold over her that he suspected she was becoming addicted to it.

She had certainly changed. Her conversation was more stilted; her ready humour was gone. Sometimes when they talked he caught a sudden flash of animalistic terror in her eyes, and wondered if it had come upon her out of the blue, or if he had done something to provoke it. Once he found her leaning against the kitchen counter with her fists clenched and her jaw tight, exuding rage like an odour.

Alfie learned from Emily that there was a helpline Hazel had called, and that the people she had spoken to had managed to have the video removed from all the sites on which it had been tracked down. As far as anyone knew the photos had only been emailed around, not posted anywhere public, but there was nothing to say they might not eventually be discovered on some website. Emily said *she* had nightmares about this possibility, so she dreaded to think how Hazel felt about it.

Hazel did not talk much about how she felt, or about Miles, or what he had done – except, presumably, to her therapist. In company she was often happiest saying nothing at all. Alfie had never known her so quiet, but he made no attempt to elicit conversation from her. They spent hours together without saying a word, him reading when he wasn't working, listening to the gentle rhythm of her knitting, glad only that she was there.

One Saturday afternoon she broke their comfortable silence. 'Can I talk to you about something?' she said, her voice croaky with lack of use.

'Of course,' he said.

She cleared her throat. 'I've had a bit of a dilemma,' she said. 'I've been really torn. It's been keeping me awake at night. But I think I've made a decision.'

'Okay.'

'I've decided to withdraw my statement against Miles.'

He thought he had misheard, or else misunderstood. But she was looking at him evenly. 'Oh,' he said in surprise. 'Why?'

'I don't know how much Emily's told you about this. But basically, I'm not entitled to anonymity. If it goes to trial, I mean.'

'What? Why not?'

'Because revenge porn isn't classified as a sex crime. It's classified as a communications crime.'

'So that means – what? You could be written about?'

'Yep. Any media coverage could use my real name.'

'That's ridiculous! That's fucked up!'

'It's the way it is. The thing is, I would do it, if I thought it would be worth it. I'd make the sacrifice, if I thought he'd be properly punished. But the maximum sentence for revenge porn is two years, did you know that?'

'Is that it?'

'Yep. Two years. And it's unlikely he'd even get that. He could get community service, or a suspended sentence, or he might not even be convicted. The thought of sitting in court while people rake over all those pictures and watch that fucking video, and being written about in the paper, and all that happens is Miles gets ordered to sweep up a few leaves, or paint a few fences … I mean, what would be the point? They wouldn't even put him on the sex offenders' register.'

Alfie was dumbfounded, partly by the fact that she had opened up to him so suddenly, and in such detail, and partly by what she had said. The injustice of it was so flagrant.

'What does your therapist say?'

'She says I need to do what's best for me. She says there's no point seeking justice if I get punished worse than him.'

'Too right!'

'But I keep thinking about all the other women he might do this to,' she said. 'Even if he got some pathetic punishment, at least it'd be on his record. People could google him and find out he's a creep.'

'Hmm.'

'But then I also keep wondering if they can even pin anything on him at all. All those accounts he used to send the pictures and post the links, they were all anonymous. He'll have deleted them by now. He probably used some dark web wizardry to set them up in the first place. How can they prove it was him? It'll be my word against his. And I'll go through some massive ordeal, and I won't have *anything* to show for it. I won't even have helped anyone.' She picked up her scarf and knitted some frantic stitches, frowning.

'I'm sure there are ways you can help people without putting yourself through all that,' Alfie said. 'In fact, there are probably things you could do that might even be more useful, in the long run.'

'Like what?'

'You could campaign for the law to change.'

She snorted. 'Me?'

'Why not?'

She looked intently at her knitting, saying nothing.

'You could volunteer for that helpline you called. Or some other kind of support system for people this has happened to.'

'Mm. Maybe.'

'You could write a graphic novel.'

She looked up at him. 'Ro said that.'

'You should!' he said. It was perfect, he realised. He could see the book in his head, page after page of Hazel's funny little drawings, all the more powerful for their humour. 'You could take back the narrative that way, Hazel! Oh, please write a graphic novel. It'd be *brilliant*.'

She shrugged, more interested in her knitting. 'I just don't feel much like drawing at the moment,' she said.

The day Emily and Daria came to London to pick up their next dose of semen, stopping by the flat with a delivery of iced coffee and giving out sticky hugs before rushing off to their Airbnb, was also the day Hazel stopped knitting scarves and started knitting a hat. This felt momentous. For the first time since her life had changed she was taking a long view, envisaging an end goal. She could see beyond the process to the product. The task so engrossed her that she finished it by the end of the weekend. It was only when she held the hat up to admire it that she realised how ridiculous she must have looked, knitting winter woollens in shorts and a vest top with all the windows open and a fan blasting cool air in her face.

This realisation sparked a small glimmer of excitement in the pit of her stomach. It was a familiar feeling, but also strange, like a long-lost friend. There had been a time when she felt it regularly. It meant she had an idea for a cartoon.

She retrieved her drawing pad from the space under the bed to which it had been banished for weeks. She was nervous to open it, knowing what she would see. The last thing she had drawn was one of the cartoons about Miles.

But with the pad open before her, she could almost have laughed. The cartoon was so very benign. So were the ones that preceded it. In her head she had built them into heinous slurs, for which sexual humiliation was a fitting retribution. But they were so gentle in their mockery – almost fond, in a way. Miles wasn't even identifiable as the target. To have been so angered by them must have taken an ego of staggering fragility.

Further back she found the cartoons she had drawn on the basis of his advice. They were po-faced and lacklustre. They had no spirit or vitality. She tore them all out, ripped up the pages, and threw them away.

The cartoon she drew then was only a tentative beginning – just a picture of a woman knitting, oblivious to the baking heat while everyone else sweltered and sweated around her. There was no caption, no second panel, no storyline. Nevertheless, it was something.

40

ROISIN AND NISH threw a party at their flat for Nish's thirtieth birthday, and although they insisted she was under no obligation, Hazel was determined to go. She asked Alfie if he would go with her, and he said yes, of course.

Nish and Roisin were occupied with entertaining, so she sat with Alfie in the corner and used him as a shield against all the people she did not want to speak to. They shared a bottle of wine and sat turned in towards each other, so that even people who waved in their direction recognised that they were not invited to sit down.

Alfie asked Hazel if she had any more knitting projects on the go, and she shook her head.

'I've actually started drawing again,' she said.

He looked genuinely delighted. 'That's great, Hazel!' he said. 'It makes me really happy to hear you say that.'

'Thanks! It's good to get back to it. I've missed it.'

'What sort of thing have you been drawing?'

She hugged her knees and squeezed her shoulders up by her ears. 'I don't want to say,' she said coyly.

'Go on, just tell me the general ballpark.'

She made a noise like he was prising something from her, then said, 'Okay. I guess it's a graphic novel sort of ballpark. Or maybe a graphic memoir. I don't know yet.'

He grinned and nodded. He looked at her, then out at the room, then back at her, nodding and grinning all the while. 'That's really fucking cool, Hazel,' he said. 'I won't ask any more.'

They moved on to discussing Emily's court appearance, which was next month. 'She'll get off lightly,' said Hazel. 'It's a minor charge and she's a first-time offender. It's just a shame she has to go to court at all. Most of the arrests get dismissed, apparently. She was unlucky.'

The injustice of this situation – of Emily going to court, while Miles carried on with an unblemished record – was not lost on them. They ruminated on it silently, disinclined to acknowledge it out loud for fear of spoiling a pleasant evening.

Then Hazel said: 'I missed you last weekend. I've got so used to sitting in the living room with you all day.'

'Same,' said Alfie. 'It's a bit of a thing now, isn't it? We should probably both be getting out more.'

'Well, *you* just left London for two whole days,' she said, smiling. 'How was it, anyway? You didn't really tell me properly.'

Alfie breathed in, inflated his cheeks, and let the air out slowly. 'It's a long story, that's why,' he said. 'It's not like I just went and visited my grandparents. I mean, I did. But not in the normal way. There's a backstory.'

'I love a backstory,' said Hazel.

'Well then,' Alfie replied. The short version, he said, was that he had not seen his grandfather in over ten years – not because they'd fallen out, per se, but because everything was complicated, and everyone had been very hurt, and no one knew how to talk about it. Hazel made a noise of sympathetic dismay and said she was sorry, she had no idea. Then he asked her if she wanted the long version, and she said she did, of course. So he told her about the dramatic history of his family: his grandmother's death when he was seven, his grandfather's remarriage and his mother's anger; then her death, when he was sixteen, and the feud between his father and grandfather. Finally he told her about the fateful Christmas which, unbeknownst to any of them at the time, had marked the end of his relationship with his grandfather as he knew it.

'Jesus Christ, Alfie,' said Hazel when he had finished. 'I never knew any of this. I mean, I knew your mum died, and your grandma. That already seemed like a lot.'

'There's just never really been a good moment to bring it up. It's all a bit heavy.'

'You're telling me. So why did you suddenly decide to go and see them now? Because of the baby thing?'

'Pretty much,' he said. 'But I'd kind of been wanting to for a while. Since I got that test result, really. It made me sort of ... less fatalistic, I suppose. I felt very *alive*, all of a sudden. And I sort of thought, well, carpe diem, go and see the old man before it's too late. Only then I was so nervous I didn't do anything about it for a few weeks. But when we decided to start trying again after the miscarriage, that's when I was like, just *do* it, for fuck's sake, he's going to have a biological great-grandchild, and he's eighty-whatever, what if he dies before I get a chance to tell him? So I rang them up.'

'And what did they say?'

'Well, it was Doreen, on the phone. I thought she might be angry. I thought, maybe from her perspective it looks like they tried to be welcoming and hospitable, and I was just a dick to everyone, and then I fucked off and never came back. But she was actually lovely. She started crying. She said she's always regretted that they let me get away. She said they should have made it clearer that I'd always be welcome back, when I was ready. She said my grandpa gets really quiet sometimes and doesn't want anyone to disturb him, and she knows it's because he's thinking about me and Mum, even though he never says so.

'And then when I got there he was so pleased to see me. He just hugged me for a really long time, and so did Doreen, and we all cried. And we had this amazing meal, and Doreen left us alone together for a bit, and we talked a lot, and it was just really, really good.'

'That's amazing,' said Hazel, smiling broadly. 'That's so cool.'

'I told them about me being a donor for Emily and Daria,' said Alfie. 'I was a bit worried about that. I didn't know what they'd think. And yeah, granted, they were quite surprised, and it took a bit of explaining for them to understand how it's all going to work, that I'm not going to be a dad as such, all that stuff. But by the end they were super excited. They're definitely going to want to meet the baby. My grandpa cried again, and so did Doreen, and then he just held my hand for ages and ages. And then we had a beer.'

Alfie stopped. Hazel was still smiling. 'Wow,' she said. 'I don't really know what to say. I … yeah. That's brilliant. Wow. You must be so pleased.'

'I am,' said Alfie, nodding firmly. 'It's a bit like there was a little stone in my shoe all this time, and I'd got so used to it I almost didn't notice it any more. But now I've taken it out and it's like, yeah! That feels good!'

Hazel laughed. 'Well, cheers to that,' she said. She lifted her glass, and Alfie lifted his, their eyes meeting as they clinked them together.

'I suppose what really struck me was that I wasn't angry,' said Alfie ponderously, after a swig of wine. 'It isn't that I expected to be or anything. It was just that the feeling of *not* being angry kind of made me realise I'd *been* angry all this time without being fully aware of it. I think it's because there was a little part of me that felt like he'd replaced us because ... well, because we were *faulty*. As in, we were programmed to get sick. And so there I was, doing all the grieving for my mum and waiting around to get sick myself because I thought I was probably carrying all her cancery genetics, and in the meantime he'd just ridden off into the sunset with his lovely, healthy new family.'

Alfie stared down into his glass, then tipped the remaining wine back into his mouth and reached for the bottle. Hazel didn't know what to say.

'Obviously that's completely ridiculous,' he continued, 'and maybe if I'd actually been able to articulate it to myself before now, I would have seen that it was ridiculous. Because he *didn't* replace us, and *clearly* he was grieving. He still *is*. He lost his only child. And he's been worrying about me all this time as well. I told him about the test result, and he was so happy. I just wish I'd taken it sooner, because maybe then I would have got in touch with him sooner.'

'Don't think like that,' said Hazel. 'You're in touch with him now.'

'Yeah,' said Alfie, on a sigh. 'Yeah, you're right.'

There was quiet then, or what felt like quiet. Somewhere far away, the party carried on.

'I feel like I've learned more about your life in the last ten minutes than at any point in the last year,' said Hazel. 'Or however long it's been.'

'And? Are you terrified?'

'No,' she said. 'Very much not. Although I was wondering ...' She deliberated for a moment over whether to continue, and Alfie cocked his head in curiosity. 'I was wondering if you'd ever thought about having therapy.'

To her surprise, Alfie burst out laughing. 'Daria asked me that exact question a while back. I guess maybe I should take a hint. But do you know what, Hazel? I reckon this is all the therapy I need. Just sitting here, talking to you.'

She laughed then, a little sadly, and her eyes shone. 'You're making me cry,' she said. She sniffed and took a breath to compose herself. 'Well, I think you've done a really great thing, making it up with your grandpa. For the pair of you, but for the baby too. There are going to be so many people who love it.'

'That's the idea.'

'And you could be a dad next year! Isn't that crazy? How does it feel?'

'Don't speak too soon,' he said. 'Emily's not pregnant yet. You'll tempt fate.'

'Sorry.'

'Anyway, I'm not going to be a *dad*.'

'Whatever,' she said, waving her hand dismissively.

'It's exciting, though,' he said. 'It'll be something new. I mean, I'm terrified. But I won't have to do any of the actual work, so I don't know why I'm terrified, exactly.'

'Of course you're terrified,' she said. 'You're making yourself vulnerable. You expose yourself to all this potential pain when you have a baby. That's why I'm never going to have one.'

He smiled at her. Neither of them said anything for a while, though each was acutely aware of the other's presence. Then Alfie, made braver by the wine and by having just bared his own soul, decided to ask Hazel a personal question.

'How does it feel to be at a party?' he said gently. 'With all these people?'

'It's nice,' she said. 'So long as I can just sit here with you.'

'Would you have come without me?'

'I'd like to think so,' she said. 'I think I'd have forced myself. It would have been harder, though, having to talk to everyone. I'd have felt ... exposed.'

'Because you'd be worried they might have seen the video?'

'Yeah, or the photos. I know quite a lot of these people. He could have found them on my social media and sent them anything he felt like. It's the thought that somebody might have been sent something and not mentioned it to me.' She shuddered. 'Just looked at it, and not said anything. It gives me the creeps.' She paused, fiddling with her shoelaces. 'It makes me want to get away.'

'Get away?' said Alfie, with a prickle of alarm. 'How do you mean?'

She shrugged. 'Just go somewhere that isn't here. It's not just the idea that someone might have seen the video. It's that I could run into Miles. I thought I saw him the other week, I don't think I said. It wasn't him, in the end, but it was horrible.'

'Ah, shit.'

'And there are so many men like him. They're everywhere. They come into the café with their MacBooks and their man buns, just like Miles used to do, and I just – I sort of hate them. Through no fault of their own. They're probably all perfectly nice men who'd never do anything to hurt anyone. But I see one and I think, What kind of horrible, sadistic bastard are you really? Half the time they get vegan cakes and plant milk in their coffee, and I'm thinking, You fucking hypocrite, acting like you wouldn't harm a living soul. It's not healthy, Alfie. I can't go on like that. I need a break from it.'

'Right,' he said. 'Yeah, I can see that. So, what, you want to move away, or …?'

'I was thinking maybe I could go on some sort of trip. Not that far. Maybe Italy or Spain or somewhere. Or Eastern Europe. I don't mean for ever. Just for a bit. A few months, maybe.'

'Okay, cool,' he said, partially relieved. Still – a few months! He hadn't gone longer than a week without seeing her in all the time they had known each other.

'Did you know there are all these places you can volunteer in exchange for bed and board?' Hazel went on. 'Farms, smallholdings, that sort of thing? I was thinking maybe I could do that. Then I might actually be able to afford it. I'd still have to move in with my parents for a while, obviously. Work in a pub or something, so I've got some savings.'

Alfie looked at her. 'You're really serious about this, aren't you?'

She shrugged. 'It's only an idea. But I think it'd be good for me. It would have been good for me before all of this, but especially now. Just to see something new. Do something different. After all, it's not like I've got a career or a – a relationship or anything.' She looked up and met his eyes. 'What is there to keep me here?'

Me, Alfie thought. *There's me.* He thought it loudly, holding her gaze for a second longer than usual, willing her to understand. But he couldn't say it. He couldn't stop her. It wouldn't be fair. Instead he said, 'What about Emily and Daria? Don't you want to be around for the birth and stuff?'

She chewed her lip. 'Yeah,' she said. 'Of course. It's about timing, I guess. I don't know. I'll think about that later.'

'I'd miss you.'

'I'd miss you too.'

'But I'd *really* miss you,' he said, the words coming out of him before he'd thought them through.

Their eyes met and held. 'I would too,' said Hazel. 'But I'd come back. And maybe when I came back, I'd be better.' Then she turned her attention to the carpet, poking at it with the end of her lace.

Later there was birthday cake, and then someone turned up the playlist and people started dancing. Alfie asked Hazel if she wanted to join them, and she smiled, and said, 'Why not?'

They danced awkwardly at first, but soon found their rhythm, moving towards and around and away from each other with a giddiness that sat somewhere in the grey zone between friendship and flirting.

'Hazel!' cried a voice at some point during the second or third song. 'I've barely seen you!' It was Nish, bouncing drunkenly towards her. He pulled her into a hug. 'Thanks for coming,' he whispered. 'I'm really proud of you.' He took her by the shoulders and planted a kiss on her cheek. Then he caught sight of Alfie over her shoulder.

'Oh my God, I'm so sorry to disturb,' he said pointedly, loud enough for Alfie to hear. 'I love you!' he called, as he bounced away again.

She shook her head apologetically at Alfie, and he held out his hand in answer. She took it, and he twirled her round and round until she stumbled into him, dizzy. When the first slow song came on he pulled her in towards him, and she threaded her arms around his waist and put her head on his chest.

'Shall we go?' she said when the song finished. It was unclear to Alfie whether she was trying to accelerate the course the evening seemed to be taking, or put an end to it.

On the bus nothing was said. Out in the cool of the evening they made stilted conversation, suddenly shy with each other. But as they approached the flat Alfie slowed to a halt, emboldened by the fear that whatever was hovering in the air between them would dissipate as soon as they got inside.

'Hazel,' he said, tugging gently on her arm, and she turned around without hesitating, and kissed him.

41

IT WAS STRANGE being back in his bedroom, now that everything was different. There was nothing daring about this encounter, not like last time. There was no kneeling, no use of hands, no textured wallpaper beneath her forehead. No laughter either, or jokes whispered in ears, or drunken, flailing limbs. She lay on her back and held him tight, her eyes fixed on his. The intensity of his gaze made her happy and sad all at once. They smiled at each other, but there was a weight behind her smile, a growing warmth in her chest, a fullness that threatened to spill over.

He went slowly at first. Even as things accelerated there was a gentleness about the way he held and looked at her. The feeling in her chest expanded into her throat and abdomen. She didn't trust herself to maintain eye contact, so she lifted her forehead and fitted it into the curve where his neck became his shoulder. She breathed in the scent of him, the humidity of the space between their bodies. She kissed his collarbone, twisted her legs around his.

There seemed to be no space left in her for the happy-sad feeling filling her up. It felt like love, but also a little like pain;

desire, but also distress. Then, as things built towards their natural conclusion, it broke through the confines of whatever had been holding it in. First one tear, then another, slid from the corner of her eye and dropped downwards onto the pillow, and then she began to sob, open-mouthed and hiccuping, her torso contracting as if it was being wrung out.

'Hazel!' Alfie cried, pulling out of her. He sat with a knee raised to hide the inelegance of his shrinking penis, encased in wrinkled latex. He was mortified. To the best of his knowledge, no other woman he had slept with had been reduced to tears by the experience.

Hazel turned onto her side so that he wouldn't see her face, and he lay down behind her and wrapped her in his arms.

'I'm sorry,' she wept, and he whispered that it didn't matter, and they repeated this sequence over and over until eventually the sobbing died away. They lay in silence for what seemed like an age, and then Hazel turned around and looked at him. Her face was red, streaked with rivulets of black.

'It wasn't you,' she said. 'You didn't upset me.'

'I know,' he said. 'It was everything else.'

She nodded. 'Everything's fucked up now,' she said. '*I'm* fucked up now.'

'You just need time,' said Alfie, stroking her hair. 'It's still early days.'

'I don't know. Feels like a lot of this might be here to stay.'

He let her fall asleep with her head on his shoulder, rolling her gently back onto the pillow when he started getting pins and needles. He lay awake into the small hours, thinking, and the same thoughts woke him up well before her. He got up, went to the kitchen and made a pot of coffee.

'Oh, you're sweet,' she said, when she blinked awake and saw him sitting on the side of the bed, waiting to give her a mug. He got back into bed next to her and they leaned against the pillows, sipping.

'Look, Alfie,' she said after a while. 'The crying thing. I feel like it might have been the universe reminding me that sleeping with my sister's sperm donor is a bad idea.'

'Actually, I've been thinking about that,' he said, turning towards her. 'Listen, I'm going to tell them I can't be their donor any more.'

'What? Why?'

'Because I really, *really* like you, Hazel,' he said. 'I want us to be able to give this a shot.'

'I thought you wanted to be their donor.'

'I do. But I want you more.'

'But you just told your grandparents!'

He bit his lip. 'I know. They'll be disappointed, obviously, but they'll understand. We're back in touch now anyway, that's the main thing. The baby was sort of a bonus.'

'Oh, Alfie. I love it that you'd do that for me,' she said, and he sensed the 'but' coming well before it was out of her mouth. 'But,' she began, and he looked back down at the duvet, his eyes blurring over. 'It's too late for that now. Emily might be pregnant already.'

'I know,' he said. 'But if she isn't.'

'I still think it's too late.'

'Why?'

'Because she wants this more than *anything*. And she's been through so much already, with the miscarriage and everything, *and* she's got this stupid court appearance to think about. We can't dump this on her as well. I don't want to be the reason all her plans get derailed. Not when she's been bending over backwards to try and help me.'

Alfie stared into his cup, unable to argue. Emily and Daria had offered him the chance to back out last month, he recalled. That would have been the moment to change course.

'You're going to have a baby, Alfie,' Hazel went on. 'That's huge. It's *for ever*. Do you really think you wouldn't regret passing that up? Like, say it didn't work out between us, for whatever reason, but by that time Emily and Daria'd had a baby with someone else. Can you genuinely say you'd have no regrets?'

Alfie couldn't say that, so he said nothing.

'And the thing is,' she continued, 'I don't even know if I can be in a relationship at the moment. I'm in a state. I'm unpredictable now. I don't really know myself any more. Quite honestly, I can't trust myself not to screw you over.'

'I'd take the chance,' he said, looking at her, but she shook her head.

'If it wasn't for all this other baggage I'd say what the hell, let's give it a go,' she said. 'But there's too much at stake now. If I mess this up, I'm messing up a whole family. I can't deal with that kind of pressure.'

He sighed, and nodded. 'Yeah,' he said emptily. 'Yeah, I see that.'

Hazel burrowed down under the covers. She was reluctant to leave his bed, knowing that she would not be getting back into it. Alfie did likewise, and they curled around each other.

'The irony is, I was trying not to like you at the beginning,' said Hazel, 'because I thought there was too much at stake then. Because of living together. If only I'd known! That was nothing!'

Alfie frowned. 'What do you mean, trying not to like me?'

'Well, I always *liked* you,' she said, as if it was obvious. 'Right from when you moved in.'

'Seriously? The whole time?'

'The whole time.'

'So how did you end up with Miles?'

She shrugged. 'I thought you didn't like me back.'

'Whatever gave you that impression?'

'Well, I heard you having sex with someone else a couple of times, and you kept mentioning your ex, so I put two and two together and—'

'Made five fucking hundred!' he cried, jerking upright. 'Are you serious? Is that the reason?' He slapped a hand to his forehead. 'Oh my God,' he said. His eyes were pricking; he pressed them with the heels of his hands until he saw stars. The tears came anyway.

'Alfie?' said Hazel, as his shoulders shook. 'Oh, Alfie!' She sat up and lay her head on his shoulder, threading her fingers through his.

'It's so frustrating!' he cried. 'If we'd just *communicated*! If we'd just been straight with each other! Everything could have been so different!'

'I know,' she said. 'But I can't think like that. It's dangerous. If I think like that it means I could have avoided meeting Miles.'

Alfie sniffed and wiped his eyes. 'That way madness lies,' he said shakily.

'Exactly. Anyway, when you've got a kid, you'll be glad it all happened the way it did.'

Eventually Hazel prised herself away and went to the supermarket to buy pastries. She realised she didn't know what kind Alfie would most enjoy, so she took one of each. They were still warm. As she waited to pay she looked out of the window at the trees lining the opposite pavement, wondering if the tree he had punched was among them.

He was in the living room when she got back, dressed in a T-shirt and pyjama bottoms. A fresh pot of coffee was waiting on the table, the plunger still raised. She fetched a plate from the kitchen and laid out the pastries on it. Alfie took one for himself and put another one back in the bag.

'Let's save this for Tony,' he said.

She sat down on the sofa beside him, then realised she should have sat in the armchair instead. The sofa sagged in the middle and they had to lean outwards to keep from tumbling in towards each other.

It all felt different, now that they were out of bed. Truths that had been clearly visible that morning seemed to have been covered over again, as though the sun had come out, and then retreated behind a cloud. Hazel steeled herself, and spoke anyway. 'I had an idea,' she said, with a rush of nerves.

'Oh yeah?'

'It's unconventional,' she warned.

'That sounds about right for us.'

'I was just thinking, maybe we could sort of compromise?' She winced. It sounded ridiculous, now that she was saying it. 'Maybe,' she continued feebly, 'we could sort of … put things on hold?'

'How do you mean?'

'I mean revisit. In, say, two years. Get on with our lives for a bit, and then sort of … check in, I suppose.'

'To see if we still like each other?'

There was a smile in his voice; she felt certain that he was laughing at her. It sounded so juvenile, put like that.

'We don't have to,' she said. 'I just thought of it in the queue at Tesco. It's probably a stupid idea.'

'It's not a stupid idea,' he replied. 'It's a good idea.'

'Really?' she said, turning to meet his eye. His expression showed him to be in earnest, and she sagged with relief. She let herself fall in towards him, and he put an arm around her. She wondered, fleetingly, how things might have turned out if she had always been this brave.

'It just occurred to me,' she continued, 'that if we still feel the same by then, we're probably safe to take a punt on it, aren't we?'

'I'd say we probably are, yeah,' said Alfie. 'I've just got one condition.'

'What's that?'

'We have to promise to actually talk about it,' he said. 'Whatever else might have happened. Even if you're working on a farm in Bulgaria. Even if one of us is with someone else. No more of this assuming we know what the other one's thinking.'

She smiled. 'I'm all for that. We can set a date. What's the date today?'

'The fourteenth.'

'Okay, so on the fourteenth of July 2021, we'll go for a coffee or a walk or something, or we'll Skype, if we have to, and ... Well, we'll see.'

They moved apart, and looked at each other. There was an anticipation in the room now, an eagerness.

'Let's shake on it,' said Alfie. So they did.

Epilogue

IT'S A WARM evening. In the garden, Hazel lays out cutlery and lights a pair of citronella candles, then sits down and looks up at the sky. They're far enough outside the city that she can see the stars appearing; it's one of many things she likes about the new house. Children, she thinks, should grow up knowing what stars look like. She ought to brush up on her constellations, so she can teach them one day. Species of tree, too. And birds. For a person who spends hours of her life poring over social media, her views on childhood are surprisingly bucolic.

Jim, Diane, Leila and Ramin are sitting on the benches at the bottom of the garden, drinking wine and laughing and generally disturbing the peace. Emily and Daria are upstairs, putting Mina and Roxie to bed. Mina and Roxie turned six months old this week, and no one can quite believe it. They are celebrating because they are allowed to celebrate, and because there has been so little cause for celebration lately, and because no one can be sure what the world will look like by the time the twins turn one.

Alfie appears at the kitchen door, pushes it open with his foot, and crosses the patio towards Hazel, a dish of something in both hands.

'Don't touch this, it's hot,' he says, putting it down on the table next to the dishes Leila and Diane have already laid out, and setting off again towards the kitchen. He goes back and forth a few more times, until the table is so laden with food that there's barely any room for the plates.

'This is amazing,' says Hazel, surveying the spread. She points at Alfie's contributions. 'Is this all stuff you've learned from Doreen?'

'Pretty much,' he said. 'Or else I learned from the internet, and then she taught me all her little tricks and modifications.'

Doreen has been teaching him to cook over Zoom. He wants the twins to have sensory memories of him like the ones he has of his mother and grandmother, and Doreen says it is her privilege and honour to teach him the things they cannot. He would have liked her to be here this weekend, but it's a long way for her to come. She's had a terrible time of it recently, and it's starting to show in her gait and her demeanour. She's exhausted from worrying about her son, who in the last few years has been wrongly threatened with deportation, prevented from working, almost made homeless, embroiled in a Kafkaesque battle with the Home Office to try and prove his right to be in the country, and eventually diagnosed with PTSD. Thanks to the pandemic, Doreen has also endured months of separation from everyone she cares about – her children, her grandchildren, her church. Now Sam is gone too. He died in January, a week before he was due to be vaccinated. The funeral, with its regulation fifteen guests, was held the week before Mina and Roxie were born. The unfairness of it, Alfie knows, will smart for a long time.

*

The moon is out now. The house is mostly dark, except for the landing window and the glow from the night light in the twins' room. From neighbouring gardens comes the sound of conversation, cutlery clinking against china. Alfie sits down next to Hazel and fans himself with the tea towel.

'God, it's nice here,' he says.

It's starting to feel like a home from home. Since the last lockdown lifted he's been coming here three weekends out of four. The agreement they all signed said he would come once a month, but the world in which they signed it belongs to a different age. They could never have imagined a life reshaped by masks and social distancing and the constant threat of illness: Daria ushered from the maternity ward when the twins were half an hour old, Emily left alone with them, struggling to breastfeed, Alfie stuck in London for the first few weeks of their lives. They've learned not to take their freedoms for granted. Anyway, Emily and Daria are worn out, even with Hazel's help. Emily cries a lot, and Daria's hair has gone full salt and pepper. Alfie makes himself useful, when he's here: he's learned to change nappies and defrost breastmilk and burp one over his shoulder while someone else burps the other. That old saying about it taking a village to raise a child – well, this is their village.

Hazel has been here since September. She's been waiting for her life to start back up again, and there are signs that the wait is coming to an end. She is now the author of a graphic novel called *Revenge*, which her Instagram followers seem to be turning into something of a cult hit. The

339

first print run was small, but it's already reprinting. The helpline she phoned all those months ago now lists it in their brochures under 'recommended further reading', and she was mentioned in an article in *Vice* last week. Requests for illustration work are coming in with increasing frequency. She might even be able to afford to move out soon, so long as she can find a part-time job somewhere to plug the gaps in her income.

She wrote the book for cathartic reasons, not career-building ones, and its success has come as a surprise. It began as a way to come to terms with what Miles had done, and evolved into a way of keeping herself sane during the first lockdown, which she spent at her parents' house, furloughed indefinitely from the pub she'd been working in and mourning the cancellation of her trip. The date of her flight to Italy sailed by as Italy itself groaned under the strain of the virus, its hospitals overrun. Whether or not to go there next year, or give the whole thing up as a path not taken, has been preoccupying her for some time.

'Can I ask you something?' she says now, to Alfie.

'Of course,' he replies.

'So I've been thinking about the future, and what I'm doing with my life and all that stuff,' she says.

'Okay.'

'And I reckon if I'm serious about art, and I want to make a proper living from it, it might be good to broaden my skill set a bit. So that people could hire me to do design and lettering and things like that, as well as just the drawing part. I mean, I can do a bit of that already, but it's not really my thing. I could do with knowing a lot more about Photoshop and InDesign and stuff.'

'Right,' says Alfie. 'Sounds sensible.'

'Well, it just so happens that there's a diploma in graphic design at Norwich University of the Arts.'

'Really? That's perfect! Are you going to apply?'

'Well, maybe. I could. I can afford it. I've got that money saved now, haven't I?'

'Oh,' says Alfie. 'Right. I see. You mean the money you saved for your trip?'

'Yeah.'

'So you're thinking you won't go on the trip after all?'

'Well, this is the question. I can't do both. The diploma feels like a really good idea. But I was *so* disappointed when I couldn't go on the trip. I really thought I'd do it one day, when things go back to normal. So now I'm just going round in circles. I don't know what to do.'

'Well,' says Alfie ponderously, 'maybe don't decide right away? Maybe just apply to this course, and then make a decision if you get a place. I reckon if you get a place, and you know for sure you can do it, your gut will tell you what you really want. If you get a place and you're disappointed, well, maybe that's a sign you need to go on the trip instead. You see?'

'Yeah, I see.'

'It's easier to figure out what you need in life when you know what's actually possible,' he says, and Hazel smiles.

'You're so wise,' she says fondly.

Alfie is about to respond, but there's a sound of voices inside, and then Emily and Daria emerge through the kitchen door. They both look pleasantly tousled. Daria's hair is piled messily on top of her head; Emily has a pixie cut now. She booked herself in as soon as the hairdressers reopened, in need of respite from the twins and their tiny, sticky fists. Daria puts the baby monitor on the end of the table and Emily calls to their parents, who get up and make their way languidly to the table.

'Asleep?' says Leila.

'Yes, finally,' says Emily. 'Sorry to keep you waiting. Look at all this *food*!' There are salads and grilled vegetables, gheymeh bademjan and rice and peas, a loaf of Hazel's homemade sourdough and an excessive quantity of Diane's vegan chilli, which everyone but Diane herself expects to be the blandest thing on offer. There isn't space for them all to sit around the table, so they serve themselves, buffet style, then sit in a rough circle with their plates on their laps. Alfie opens a new bottle of wine and tops them all up. Emily holds her glass aloft, and everyone else does likewise.

'To reunions,' she says.

'And Mina and Roxie,' says Leila.

'And the end of lockdown,' says Daria.

'And vaccines,' says Ramin. After that none of them know what they're supposed to be toasting, so they just say 'cheers'.

'Can we also just take a moment,' says Daria, 'to say thank you to Alfie and Hazel?'

'Yes,' agrees Emily. 'We don't say it enough. But I honestly don't know what we'd have done without you both. A newborn would have been hard enough, but two newborns, and in the middle of a pandemic ...'

'And with me back at work now too,' says Daria. 'It's been intense, but if we'd been on our own ... I can't even fathom it. We'd be zombies, basically.'

Alfie's face is warm with wine and gratitude. 'You're welcome,' he says. 'Thanks for letting me get so involved. It's been an absolute pleasure.'

'I'm just glad there's a way for me to earn my keep,' says Hazel. 'Otherwise you'd be thoroughly sick of me by now.'

'Don't ever move out,' says Emily. 'I'll pay you to stay. I'm not even joking. And Alfie, if you fancy moving to Norwich – I mean, it's *lovely*, isn't it? Much nicer than London.'

He smiles and shrugs in a way that says: Well, maybe. He knows she's joking, but he's been thinking about it more and more lately. Could he leave London? His own domestic set-up is vastly improved. The new flat is clean and modern; there's a south-facing balcony for his tomato plants, and Clara has proven herself an excellent flatmate, only grating on him a little during lockdown, and that was more because of his frazzled nerves than anything she actually did. But if he moved here, he could have a place of his own. Maybe he could even buy somewhere. He'd be able to see the twins without travelling for two hours on buses and trains. And Hazel is here now, too. Whatever unprecedented complications they have brought into their lives, one simple fact remains: he is yet to meet anyone whose company he enjoys as much as hers.

The baby monitor emits a burbling noise, which turns into a yowl. Emily and Daria exchange tired glances.

'Right then,' says Daria, getting up and going indoors. On the screen, Emily watches Mina stretching her tiny arms over her head, her face a picture of sadness, and it's like a hand has closed over her heart. She'll have to go upstairs in a minute too, because when one twin cries, the other one soon joins in. But even when they cry, it still feels miraculous. They are hers and Daria's, tangible and alive.

They won't try for any more, they're agreed. They have no desire to relive these early, colicky months. And they got two for the price of one, in the end – or two for the price of four, depending on how you want to look at it. There are three young trees at the bottom of the garden now, one for each of the babies they lost. A mini-orchard: plum, apple and pear. By the time it starts producing fruit, the twins will be old enough to help pick it.

As predicted, Roxie's cries begin to chime discordantly with Mina's, and Emily gets heavily to her feet and makes for the stairs. The others eat until they can eat no more, and then, all of a sudden, the evening is coming to an end. Jim collects the plates; Diane spoons leftovers into Tupperware; Leila stations herself at the dishwasher. Ramin goes down the garden for a quiet cigarette. Hazel and Alfie pour more wine and stretch and sprawl. Their feet brush against each other and they adjust themselves in their chairs, neither knowing quite how to respond.

'What time's your train tomorrow?' says Hazel.

'Early afternoon sometime,' says Alfie. 'One thirty, maybe? I'll have to check.'

'Do you still want to walk there?' she ventures, her heart starting to thud. She's been thinking about the walk all week, wondering what they'll say, how they'll begin.

'We said we would, didn't we?' he replies, an equivalent thud starting up in his own chest.

'Yep.'

'You're still up for it?'

'Yep. Yeah. Absolutely.'

'Well then,' says Alfie. 'That's what we'll do.'

He leans back, his hands behind his head. Hazel yawns deeply as the adrenalin subsides. She bats at a mosquito, whining next to her ear. There is bustling inside the house: the parents going upstairs, cooing over the twins, giving hugs and kisses. They are all fully vaccinated now and no longer take any social distancing precautions whatsoever. They come back out and bid noisy goodbyes, say they will be back for brunch tomorrow, and then leave for their Airbnbs. Hazel and Alfie listen to their voices getting further away, then to the sound of cars starting up and driving off. They stay sitting where they are for a moment, enjoying the quiet. Then Hazel slaps at a mosquito on her arm and they agree that it's time to go in.

In the kitchen Hazel puts the kettle on and Alfie gets out mugs.

'Do you fancy a game of Scrabble?' he says, leaning against the worktop.

'That'd be nice,' says Hazel. She looks up towards the ceiling. 'Those two will probably fall asleep. But that's okay, isn't it?'

'Fine. We can divvy up their points.'

The kettle boils and clicks itself off. Alfie pours the water. He and Hazel take a mug each, leaving two steaming on the worktop. Upstairs the crying has stopped. They hear the door to the twins' room open and close, and then there is creaking on the floorboards as Emily and Daria make their way down to join them.

ACKNOWLEDGEMENTS

Turning an idea into a real-life book is a collective endeavour, and I am hugely indebted to the many people who have helped this one on its journey. Endless thanks are due to my editors, Sarah Hodgson and Lindsey Rose, and agent, Philippa Sitters, for bringing their creativity and clear-sightedness to bear on the manuscript and helping to sculpt it into the best version of itself (and for the small matter of making my childhood dream a reality).

Equally endless thanks are due to my friends and fellow writers Katie Greening, Claire Lowdon and Georgie Hildick-Smith, without whose feedback and encouragement I might never have written all the way to the end.

I am very grateful to everyone who gave their time and energy to read the manuscript: Ashley Hickson-Lovence, Lola Boglio, Ellen Dobbs, Shauneen Magorrian, Emily Frisella and Nikki Ikani. Thanks, also, to all at Corvus, Dutton, DGA and the Independent Alliance, whose tireless work helps keep the world of books spinning on its axis. And thank you Eloise Daria, for unwittingly lending me your name.

As in any work of fiction, many of the ideas for this book were pilfered, magpie-like, from the world around me. One particularly direct influence deserves credit: Meehan Crist's article 'Is it OK to have a child?' (*London Review of Books*, 5 March 2020), which shaped Emily's thinking in Chapter 27.

Last but not least, particular thanks are due to my mum, Margaret Brook, and my partner, Roberto De Spirito, for the deep wells of love and support. And finally, to my much-missed dad Tim Brook, who never got to read this book, but who instilled in me a love of reading and writing, and thus laid the foundations for its existence.